TUCK and NIP

TUCK and NIP

A Novel

Barend Van Kimball

SANTA FE

Sunstone books may be purchased for educational, business, or sales promotional use.
For information please write: Special Markets Department, Sunstone Press,
P.O. Box 2321, Santa Fe, New Mexico 87504-2321.

Book and Cover design › Vicki Ahl
Body typeface › Basketville Old Face
Printed on acid-free paper
∞
eBook 978-1-61139-267-8

Library of Congress Cataloging-in-Publication Data

Kimball, Barend Van, 1932-
Tuck and nip : a novel / by Barend Van Kimball.
     pages cm
ISBN 978-0-86534-989-6 (softcover : alk. paper)
I. Title.
PS3611.I45723T83 2014
813'.6--dc23

                                   2014011375

WWW.SUNSTONEPRESS.COM
SUNSTONE PRESS / POST OFFICE BOX 2321 / SANTA FE, NM 87504-2321 /USA
(505) 988-4418 / ORDERS ONLY (800) 243-5644 / FAX (505) 988-1025

PROLOGUE

During a fierce Texas Blue Northern two nearly frozen travelers dressed in bear and buffalo hides staggered into Ben Lilly's mountain campsite. Ben Lilly, a wolf, bear and mountain lion bounty hunter, had six considerable lion hounds that would have attacked the scruffy looking strangers if Ben hadn't called them off. His loaded rifle lying across his lap, he cautiously invited them to share his campfire and grub.

One of the men was Jim Bridger, a famed mountain man. His companion was a tall, muscular, gray-eyed Ute Indian named Koot. Even with a gallon jug of Pecos Lightening between them, it was too freezing cold to sleep. The storm lasted a full week. So the three of them, snow blown up to their ears and nearly sitting in the campfire, swapped tall tales, one after another until their breath commenced to freeze on their teeth. The year was 1869, the winter of the big blizzard.

During the winter of 1892, Ben rescued a young and recently orphaned Charlie Bennett from certain death. Charlie became Ben's eager apprentice and favored listening to Ben's tale of life as a mountain man. History said little about old Ben. He died in 1912 when Charlie was thirty-two years old. Like father and son, Ben and Charlie had hunted together for over twenty years. In the early 1970s Charlie was past ninety years old and nicknamed Mountain Lion Charlie by those few who knew him. He'd spent the better part of the last sixty years living alone in the western wilderness.

I met Mountain Lion Charlie at the Bar-B Ranch just north of Bishop, California. Rare for Charlie, we hit it right off, and I spent as much time with him as possible. Our last chat at his campfire he told me about his writings, journals telling of his and Ben's travels and adventures. Keeping an old vow, he'd mailed one journal each year to an old friend in Fort Stockton, Texas.

We'd just finished sharing a bowl of venison chili as a full moon was cresting the White Mountains. Charlie's unsteady hand reached out and handed me a silver dollar and he asked if I would mind mailing his most recent journal for him.

I waved off the coin and said, "Be happy to, Charlie," placing the journal in my pack. Later I bid him, "Adios." Charlie grinned, lifted his head, looked at the rising moon and shaped his mouth like he was about to commence howling. I left him sitting there by the dying coals of our campfire. Nobody ever saw Charlie again.

Curious about the Old West and a bit of a writer myself, I sought out the address written on the brown paper sack wrappings of Charlie's journal. I was fortunate enough to locate the family and all sixty of Charlie's journals. The first story I read in those journals was an astonishing tale Jim Bridger told Ben during that fierce snowstorm. Bridger and Koot agreed they knew the facts personally. Koot the Ute claimed he was a shirt tail relative of the main character of who Bridger spoke. So there is likelihood the legend is true.

As sometimes happens, certain stories are good enough to be worth telling time and time again. Bridger and Koot told Ben, who subsequently told young Charlie, who eventually wrote the tale in one of his journals.

Eighty years later I am about to let you in on this same story—a tale about a fellow named Tuck and the wolf he called Nip. There was nothing in the West those two didn't hunt, including man.

1

"SOMETHING SPECIAL"

Nevada Territory, Moon of Falling Leaves, 1840s

"*You* best heed *my* words, boy!" Otto pounded his fists and shouted, "You go get me a big fat buck, *damn* quick, by *gott*. Three days, you be back, *das it*."

Tuck knew nothing was worth the risk of his father, Otto, beating him. He'd learned never to come up short when it came to Otto's commands, so there was little doubt in his mind—he *would* make the kill.

He was doing a man's job now and he detested the feelings of fear Otto provoked. Just yesterday, he'd made up his mind it was *not* going to be like this much longer. He'd bide his time. For now, he'd do what he must and not only because of Otto's threats.

When he left the cabin, all he could hear ringing in his was Otto's raging about his wounds and his god-awful thirst. Tuck set himself to some mighty swift trekking.

Thus far, he'd spent many unfruitful hours on this hunt. Now it was late afternoon of the third day and he anxiously glanced at the sky. Dusk was quickly spreading darkening fingers across the hills. Lowering gray skies rolled and rumbled, cold mountain breezes slid down from distant white tipped peaks. If this hunt weren't successful there'd be a heap of trouble back at the cabin.

They'd run out of gunpowder a month ago, but that was fine with Tuck. He actually preferred hunting with his bow. Being this far from the cabin, free from Otto's raging, gave him some quiet solitude and time alone with his thoughts. Although he always worried about the safety of his mother, Spring Willow, back at the cabin alone with Otto. He knew whenever Otto got the opportunity he'd trade their pelts for corn liquor—his drunken rages were to be avoided at *all* cost.

Sometimes, when Otto got crazy, bind drunk and passed out, Tuck and his mother would sneak off from the cabin, her taking that time to teach him Indian talk and the sacred ways of her people, the Ute.

Since he'd been big enough, Tuck helped Otto run a short line of beaver traps in the big valley to the west. Less than two months ago, the drunken Otto got caught in one of his own traps. Tick heard it snap shut on Otto's calf, cutting him nearly to the bone and almost severing an artery. Even with Spring Willow's attentive doctoring the wound soon became infected. Otto blamed her and swore, as soon as he could walk, he'd get even.

Tuck reckoned that was threat enough, but even more so, without provisions and winter almost on them, *all* their lives were in big trouble. And at present, there was darn little food left. Way last spring, even before Otto's injury, Tuck realized he had become the family's only hunter. Just the thought of that responsibility made him stand tall and feel proud. Otto's threats didn't matter when he was on the hunt.

Now, with a soft wind at his back he remembered the image of his mother smiling. Or the nearest thing to a smile he'd seen in a long while. He'd figured, she's thinking about something that's making her plenty happy. She was. Spring Willow would no longer call him Tuck. With his thirteenth winter upon them, she gave him the Ute name, *Dotseno*, meaning, Something Special—as Tuck was the only child that hadn't died at birth, or Otto, on one of his murderous rages, hadn't killed outright.

That day, when Spring Willow spoke his name, her dark, usually downcast eyes glowed and her moth turned up. It sounded good hearing his Indian name—made him feel more like a man than a boy.

As long as he could remember, he'd watched his lean and sinewy mother quietly do Otto's every bidding. With her working, waiting hand and foot on Otto most of the time, there was little time for him. Around the cabin she was always so quiet, often, during Otto's rampages she moved even more cautiously, making every effort to keep to herself. To Tuck she seemed like that solitary bobcat that lived in the canyon up above the cabin. She was there, and then suddenly it was like she wasn't. Those times he sometimes wondered if anyone cared about him.

Today, with only the soft sounds of his footfalls in the wilderness silence, Tuck considered those things Spring Willow had told him recently. She'd gazed east, pointed toward the rising sun, and said, "Far away, over there, I was born a Ute. When just a child, and first captured by the Comanche, I carried a sharp knife hidden in my knee-high moccasins and I *still* carry it." She slipped it out and showed it to him. Her eyes narrowed and light flashed in them when she said, "I know *how* to use it."

She had said, "Two winters, and the Comanche, who treated me as a dog, sold me to the Cheyenne. Those many years, before Otto bought me, the Cheyenne also taught me to accept my low place as a slave. You see, I will do as he says, unless he dies or I...or *we* escape."

He'd listened carefully, but when she said the words, 'Far away, over there,' he could hardly wait to speak. "Mother, we *can*, I have a plan. We can escape...I think?"

She held up her open hand and shook her head, no, "I do not think so. Perhaps you, but—"

"*Never*, Mother."

"My son, you are young, strong and...almost white. You could make your way. But me, an old, tired and ugly squaw...no, nobody..." Her voice trailed off.

Tuck wanted to argue, but he saw a distressingly pained expression suddenly furrow here face.

She swallowed hard, held up her hand again and continued, "My son, have you ever wondered *why* I bathe so little? Sometimes smell like a *dog*? Do you know *why* I chopped off all my hair?"

"Mother, it is not for me to question."

"You think me ugly?"

"*No*, Mother. I think you are," he paused, "a fine and beautiful mother."

Desperation filled her face and she cried, "If it would help, as the Comanche sometimes do, I would *cut off my own nose*."

Not sure of her meaning, all Tuck knew was, like a trapped antelope, tears were in her eyes and words seemed to choke back in her throat.

Heaving a deep sigh and looking away as if ashamed, she had said, "Listen, I will tell you."

It was several moments before she spoke. When she did speak her voice trembled, "After you lived several winters, *Spirit* told me you would grow to be a *strong* man." A bitter smile formed and words burst forth, "To dishonor Otto, I made myself ugly, hoping Otto would keep his filthy hands off of me." Again, she hung her head, "You know it has not always worked."

Tuck's face blushed. He'd seen Otto take her and mount her like a dog.

Otto roaring, "*Anytime* I damn well please"

At those times, Tuck thought, Otto, you are the *real* dog.

Later that day, Tuck seemed to be hearing a voice on the wind telling him to be strong. *Spirit* spoke, "You are a man now, protect your People." What people? Surely not Otto?, Or was it, Mother's people?, He wanted to know more.

That same day Spring Willow told him, "When you were but a skinny brown baby, I hid you down by the spring. Sober, Otto, sneaked up behind me. He saw you were still alive. He growled, 'You still got that bastard pup? That youngin's sure got *tuck.*' And Tuck, became your name."

Contritely, she patted Tuck's hand, "If I'd protested, he would have killed you like all my others. Anyway, that is how you got named Tuck."

"It is not a bad name, is it Mother?"

"No." she sighed. "Now, it's not important. Son, you are the only baby Spirit that stayed more than two moons. And now that my womanly moon cycles are over, you are to be my last child. At first I schemed like a cunning coyote to keep you fed and hid away. Even now I would fight *anyone* or *anything* that tries to harm you."

Recalling those words, Tuck spit and cursed Otto's name, whispering an oath, "Mother, I'm tall now, I *too* will fight for you." Fight Otto? Would he, could he? When alone hunting, he felt *Power* living in those thoughts. But face to face? To *fight,* with Otto?

The lower hills of the eastern Sierra were his favorite place to hunt and for Mother's sake he'd never go back empty handed. He believed he knew the best locations. He daydreamed—the mountain, the sky, the waters, they belong to me and I belong to them. Those thoughts gave him Power during the hunt.

Crouching low he moved deliberately, yet cautiously, eyes searching hill top ridges on both sides of the arroyo. As the sun dropped beyond the Sierras, Tuck knew in the darkening shadows, those he hunted, instinctively felt safer and grew less cautious. He silently continued his stalk upward.

There it was, a dusty trail, heavy with yesterday's hoof prints. Several pointed tip hoof prints, side by side, the tracks led uphill. A heavy buck's tracks, large six inch prints, were pressed deep into the trail. Lesser ones trailed after. Dusk, the herd should begin moving back down. Twilight turned everything to shadowy gray, creating perfect tones, a ghostly blending of fur, antlers and hooves, sage, earth and sky, they'd become nearly invisible. His buckskins gave him a similar advantage. Down wind, his scent would not give him away. His lips moved without sound, "Keep looking."

Spring Willow had said, and he proudly believed, blue or black eyes, his eyes were as keen as any hawk. Yet it troubled him. What-who, was he mostly Indian? Cheyenne raised, Mother was full-blooded Ute and except for his blue eyes, his own coloring was dark like hers. Otto, from Germany, with his milky-white skin, often bragged of being "White American."

Many times Otto boasted to Tuck; he was once a member of a famous expedition—the first trappers into the Rocky Mountains. Then one day for no apparent reason, stumbling drunk, a crazed look in his eyes, he said, "Tuck, I once *killed* two very stupid trapper fellows. *Stupid*, just like you." And he's slammed Tuck to the ground.

He wasn't hurt. He knew of the dead babies, but hearing that murder confession sure put the goose bumps up his neck. The only reason Tuck killed anything was for hides and meat.

Ironically, except for his own instincts, Tuck's hunting and trapping skills had been honed razor sharp from Otto's abusive words and fist. As far as Tuck was concerned, those lessons were neither good nor bad, just a fact of life. When he thought of *manly* responsibilities, it set his heart to pounding. Neither threat no chore, his *duty* was to bring *big* meat back to the cabin. Not rabbits or squirrels, but enough to last until his father's leg healed and they might hunt together. Something to which Tuck cared less and less.

His stomach growled. He hadn't eaten, but hungry he was as better hunter. Then, halfway up the arroyo, his thoughts again went back to the cabin. He figured he knew why Otto avoided other white men and why he usually only traded with the Northern Paiute. No doubt his father kept to himself because of the murders.

During the recent, Yellow Grass Moon, the Paiute traders had *not* come. Now, even Spring Willow was worried about food supplies. All the more reason he must make a deer kill. Spring willow said it was an honor for him to be such a good hunter and last summer she'd made him thick elk-hide moccasins and clothes of bleached, nearly white doeskin so he'd not easily be seen during winter's snow hunts. Being the *best* hunter was the most important thing to him.

Otto taught him, movement was one thing upon which both the hunter and the hunted depended. Once in a while Tuck heard the deer, but rarely. Most often, seemingly without looking, he sensed the twitch of long ears or the switching of short black-fringed tails. Occasionally, when the winds are just right and there were enough of them, he could smell their sweet-sour musky aroma.

Wolves, he'd heard wolves the past two nights, but he'd seen no tracks.

Maybe the deer herd is heading toward me at this very moment? Where are they? "*Great Spirit* please help me." Wind swirled, blew dust in his face. A sneeze welled up threatening to fill the silence with his presence. Clamping his hand tightly over his nose he breathed deeply...*smell*...there it was...close...unmistakable fresh deer scent. "Thank you, *Great Spirit*."

Instantly, in his veins, something hot, strong and exciting surged. Like a puma ready to pounce, nothing of him moved except his silver-blue eyes and the silent pounding in his chest, though he hadn't yet seen the deer.

Staying low, he stepped silently sideways alongside a large boulder next to the trail, and retreated fully behind it. In one easy soundless movement he removed an arrow from the quiver slung across his left shoulder. He set the arrow-shaft to the taught bowstring—drawn to half pull he waited. It always amazed him how such large, hard hoofed animals could move so silently. As a hunter he prayed for such stealth.

And came the big buck plodding slowly past. A few strides and it was upwind. His heavy antlered head snapped up. He smelled *man. Alarm*! Powerful muscles bunched and the old buck leaped several feet down the trail. That was fine with Tuck; he did not want the tough and stringy flesh of this old buck. Let him live to enjoy many does. A plump, forked horn or slightly younger spike buck—*that* was prime. Tuck would wait. The herd rapidly crowded past, not sure of their leader's reactions.

There was no time to measure or think only react. Instantly the worthy target was there right in front of him. Plump and round from a summer of feeding. A big forked horn. The bow fully flexed he released the arrow powerfully driving the steel blade and wooden shaft into its place.

A perfect shot, but perhaps *too* perfect? The steel blade and shaft ripped through the chest exiting the young buck's far side. Still, it looked like a kill shot. Bounding off the trail to the right the young buck sped. Legs pounding, it raced to the bottom of the arroyo.

Tuck expected a downward flight but the mortally wounded buck turned and headed back up toward the top of the arroyo into the shadowy safety of tall pines and dense sage. In an instant, it disappeared over the crest.

He believed the trail of blood shouldn't be hard to follow. Where he saw the buck leave the arroyo, as expected, there were crimson splotches every several feet. Enough to track it, in spite of the diminishing twilight, he hoped. But once up under the pines, where rusty red pine needles carpeted the forest, signs were difficult to see. The fleeing buck's tracks slowed to a walk and appeared to be staggering. Tuck's eyes watered from the intensity of tracking in the windy chill of the darkening forest.

Kneeling, he touched a dark spot and lifted his finger close to his eyes. Yes, it was wet and crimson. He had never lost any target hit so cleanly. Then, before he had a chance to stand fully upright, Tuck heard a low thundering growl. He lifted his face toward the sound. Perfectly blended with the forest floor, nearly impossible to see, the mound was not more than a few feet in front of him. His deer kill.

Yet something else thought the kill belonged to it. Barely discernible on the opposite side of the dying deer, silver and gray fur, massive head, yellow fangs, a twitching muzzle soaked in blood.

In the last throws of death, the buck's legs still quivered, though his throat was ripped open. Tuck's eyes froze locked onto what he considered a would-be thief. The wolf assuming the same glared back with glowing red, hate filled eyes.

He knew the wolf's nature would claim and protect its kill. Tuck's instincts flared, demanding the same. Smooth as a swooping hawk, he and his weapon were instantly at the ready.

The wolf lunged straight toward his face, yet strangely sluggish. Faltering...stumbling.

Tuck's arrow struck the wolf square in the front of its rumbling throat, buried up to the feathers deep into its chest and right through its fierce heart. Twisting and flailing in the air, it dropped at Tuck's feet like a sack of stones.

2

"WITH HONOR"

Spring Willow taught Tuck, "Always honor the Spirits. Do not doubt."

Again Tuck gave thanks to *Great Spirit*. The deer's severed head he set facing toward the east where tomorrow's dawn would welcome its spirit. With each kill a small tobacco offering was made to Everywhere Spirit. After the skinning he cut the carcass into quarters all the while singing the Spirit song his mother taught him:

"My Cousin, I thank you for your life. Go over now, purpose is fulfilled. Run with your Brothers, your purpose is fulfilled."

He dressed the meat carefully as he'd done so many times before. His favorite meal, the thought of it made his mouth water, heart and liver sliced thin and roasted right on the coals. It would be his reward as soon as he got home.

Those parts he wrapped carefully in his linen 'innards cloth.' Then he tied the hind leg portions together and made a sling to carry the quartered carcass. All that remained, head, hocks, hooves and entrails he offered to Mother Earth. "Might as well not let this wolf pelt go to waste." A thought flashed in his mind, maybe Otto would be pleased. "*Humph*!" he grunted, "Why trouble myself on his account." He then decided, winter wolf fur is special for keeping out the cold and Mother would be happy. That thought set him to whistling.

Rolling the wolf on its back he'd remove its pelt in about the same way—except for its ears, muzzle and paws; they'd remained attached. He noticed something odd about the wolf's front legs and at the same time her teats. To his surprise all the toes of both front paws were completely severed, more than likely from someone's steel trap. Her two hairless milk filled teats told him, "She's nursing one maybe two pups, but my Lord she's skinny as a beanpole." On close inspection the pelt lacked the luster and density of well-fed wolves. Picking up the wolf's head he looked into her lifeless eyes, saying, "Mama, you were pure starved, no wonder you leaped at the chance to down my wounded buck. Likely you were crazy hungry with needing to feed your pups." Crazy or not Tuck admired her courage. "Had you even one good front leg you might have been quick enough to take me down."

Hands on his hips he stood looking down, "Should I bother?" Was the wolf pelt worth taking? Again came that thought, could he ever please his Father?

Knowing the vexing truth, exasperated he kicked at the dead carcass. "To hell with Otto, I'll bring the pelt for Mother."

He set to his task repeating similar ceremony.

A swift and skilled skinner he was, but in the time it took to prepare both kills, night's full darkness fell. Temperatures dropped suddenly and under the pines light from the starry mountain sky didn't help much. So he finished butchering by chilled touch. Blood caked and stiffened crumbling in-between his fingers, but it was no use trying to clean them without water. That would have to wait.

No room in the meat bundle for the wolf pelt. He tied the skin of its front legs around his neck leaving the flesh side out—a crimson, fur-trimmed cape, he thought. The pelt hung down his back almost to his ankles. The wolf's bushy tail dragged the ground but the pelt covered his entire back. No need being cold he figured. On his left shoulder hung his bow, quiver and nine arrows. The arrow that went through the deer was lost. Otto wouldn't be happy. But hanging there on his right shoulder was the all-important venison and nobody could complain about that.

Looking around he checked the butchering sight. Did I forget anything? Patting himself he made sure he'd returned his skinning knife to its sheath. He checked his load to see if was balanced and comfortable. It had to stay put while he covered the twenty miles back to the cabin. Breathing a deep sigh, he whispered, "Okay," and set his pace back toward home.

Within a hundred yards the darkened forest opened into sage covered hill country. And he was just in time to greet the rising golden arch of the moon peeking over the White Mountains. "Good now I can see the trails. In about six hours I should be home."

Dampness seeped down the backs of his legs and into his moccasins. The wolf's pelt was still dripping a bit of blood and droplets of milk from the knife cuts through her teats. He would have to live with that until Spring Willow cleaned his buckskins tomorrow. His load was heavy and that was good. His pace remained strong and steady. Spirit's winds were at his back.

In front of him a glistening moonlight lit the trail. The hunt was successful. His heart swelled with pride.

The down trail swung toward the spring. At first he thought his moccasin snagged on a cola cactus. Whatever it was that stuck him was now tugging at his right heel. Irritated he gave a spontaneous yank, *"Ouch,"* swinging his leg forward to free himself. It was something heavier than a cola. Whipping past his left leg out of his own shadow into full moon brightness it released its prickly hold, tumbling end over end and plopping in the middle of the dusty trail.

Scrawny and potbellied it yelped as the wind was knocked from its tiny undernourished body.

Tuck cried, "By *dang,* a mangy little wolf pup." His first reaction was, stomp it dead. But before he could move the pup sat up, a cloud of dust puffing up from its behind. "I'll be, the stupid thing is wagging its tail." It tilted its head, lifted its nose and let out the most pitiful little howl he'd ever heard.

Tuck figured the pup was barely two months old.

It stood up, shook off the dust and trotted over to Tuck's blood and milk splattered moccasins.

The pup did the unexpected, sniffing Tuck's moccasins, licking the milk drops and bloodstains crying like a baby while its fuzzy tail beat a frantic flagging.

Tuck hadn't seen much of what could be called compassion. According to Otto's ways there wasn't any need. Mostly back at the cabin they lived on the ragged edge of survival. Still Spring Willow did teach him respect for his 'Cousins': Great Bear, Puma and Wolf.

"Brother Wolf," she said, "was sometimes a messenger sent from Everywhere Spirit." He squatted looking closely at the little wolf. "Okay. So what is it ya got to tell me?"

The pup tilted its head in the direction of the voice, ears at attention and nose twitching as it sniffed at the unfamiliar sound and scent of human breath.

It was then Tuck noticed the pup's eyes were closed matted and puss filled.

"Your nose and ears are working, but dang you're near blind aren't ya."

Confused, the pup's nose sniffed the scent of its mother's fur, blood and milk were there and the scent of food. But this new smell, where were the familiar sounds of mother's panting and her soft growl and warm licks? And why was he making strange noises?

It plopped again on its rear lifted its runny nose, a piteous whine turned into another forlorn howl.

Tuck smiled. It had been a long while since he had reason to really laugh and laugh he did. "You're about the *sorriest* looking thing I ever did see."

The pup, its mouth still open, and hearing the mocking laughter stopped in mid-howl and took a blind nip in the direction of the annoying sound.

"Ha, you missed but by dang you do have a little 'tuck' in ya too, don't ya." He laughed again reached out and gingerly picked up the wolf pup by the scruff of its neck.

The pup responded. Now, that's more like it. Being familiar with that sort of carrying, its mouth pulled back into a strained smile, the pup wagged its tail again.

"*Phew,* what a stinker. Your sickly mama couldn't keep either end clean. Pitiful pup, the least I can do for you is give your eyes a good washing." He lifted its tail, "Oh, a little bastard pup, with dingle berries, too." Tuck headed for the spring.

Ten minutes later, side by side on all fours, both were lapping spring water. When they had their fill Tuck took out his skinning knife, "Bet you're hungry," and sliced off a strip of venison. The pup sniffed it but didn't seem too sure what to do. Tuck understood, "It's not up-chuck like your mama fed you." So he rubbed it across the pup's needle like teeth.

That's all it took. He grabbed the meat, one end hanging from its jaws, one paw holding the other end against the ground, snarling and tugging and the venison soon disappeared down his throat. A whining snarl and a near feeding frenzy, blindly he lunged toward Tuck and nipped at his buckskins, demanding more.

"Go easy there little pup or you'll bust a gut." He cut one more strip off the deer's tough flank. "Give you something more to chew on."

Butt turned toward Tuck and its tail between its hind legs, between chews and snarls, it glanced anxiously back over its shoulder.

"Reckon me an Indian giver, do ya?" Tuck crooned softly. He lay back resting on the deer-hide bundle arms behind his head waited and watched. Soon the frantic hungry noises stopped and its tail curled into a satisfied tick-tocking fuzzy loop over its back. Following his nose he trotted to his side and laid his bloody muzzle on the wolf pelt next to Tuck's head and in seconds was sound asleep.

Tuck didn't move, just looked sideways keeping an eye on his new needle-toothed guest. "I ought to get a move on," he muttered, frowning but not moving.

Warm and asleep its quick puffing puppy breath tickled Tucks ear. He smiled, relaxed and found his own eyes drooping. After all it had been a long hard hunt. He got his deer and he was tired. Another few minutes won't make any difference.

A lick on his chin, his eyes popped open. Was the sky getting light? How long had he slept? Last seen the moon was pulling loose from the eastern mountains. Full moon bright it was now directly overhead. "Five-six hours I've been sleeping. I better get moving."

He sat up sharply sending the pup tumbling. "Oops," he reached over, again taking it by the scruff of the neck and set him on his lap. Scooting on his rump to the pond's edge he tore off a piece of the clean 'innards' cloth. Dipping it in water he began to sponge the caked on muck from around its eyes and then its behind.

The pup drew back with a start. Wondering why his Mother's tongue so cold...but still it feels good. At last she is going to open my eyes. Now I can see what Mother looks like. Patiently without any resistance he allowed Tuck to cleanse his bottom, too. Once his eyes were cleaned Tuck expected to find the dull white eyes of blindness. But he was wrong. His eyes, still puppy eyes, were gray-blue and clear.

Then, for a just a fleeting instant, Tuck imagined the wolf pup in full, waist-high maturity. Its eyes a piercing golden/yellow and his teeth, long white with bone crushing strength. In that same moment Tuck saw himself and the wolf standing side by side in some far off place. The Spirit picture was clear and vivid. Was that the vision message brought to him? He set the pup down, stepped back and stared. Could that be? He should consider that carefully.

The pup had never seen man, so accepting Tuck as a caregiver happened quickly. Through its newly cleaned eyes the first living thing he saw was a tall gangly, two legged, familiar smelling food source. Mother?

The wolf pup's attachment to Tuck and lack of inborn caution came as a complete surprise. Nevertheless, after he cleaned its eyes and filled its belly, he planned to leave him at the spring where he would at least have a chance. He knew not much of a chance. But then there was the Vision? Yet he should hotfoot it for home or face a raging Otto. Otto was an altogether different vision.

Tuck looked down at the pup and wondered. A few times he'd watched Spring Willow nurse an injured bird or animal back to health almost like they were people. He could feel the pup's tiny body trembling between his knees as it peered out into this strange new world of moonlit darkness.

He thought, "Heck I got what I came for so what's my hurry? As long as I'm back by sunup." He saw the pup was still shivering, "Why not make a small campfire?"

Stripping dry paper like bark from dead sagebrush—flint and striker in hand—in just moments he produced a twisted wisp of smoke, blowing softly in short puffs the crackle of flame and aroma of burning 'sweet sage' filled the air.

He wondered if what he was feeling was *manly*? Babying a dang wolf pup? Otto more than likely will stomp its butt. But this little critter sure seems to like me. He smiled.

Peeking out from behind Tuck's back the he-pup didn't quite know what to make of fire and chose to stay where he sensed it safe.

Forgotten during his two day hunting fast Tuck now remembered the small hard corn cakes Spring Willow sneaked into the beaded bag that hung from his waistband. Soften up, heated on a hot rock, they'd taste mighty pleasant. Soon warmed he offered the pup a small piece but it seemed not to its liking. So he cut a thumb-size hunk of fatty venison and seared it juicy brown on a hot rock. Hardly without chewing, hot or not, the pup swallowed it whole. Tuck said, "You've had *enough*; the rest of this meat is for home." So resting on his pack, crumb-by-crumb Tuck allowed each piece of corn cake to dissolve slowly on his tongue, savoring his mother's cooking.

Again for just a moment he and the pup dozed off. Waking with a start this time for sure it was time and he must hurry. At the moment his mind was captive to but one image: Otto's fists clenched and coming at him. Anyway, he had his doubts about the wolf pup vision.

Hoisting his bundles moving swiftly he paused and quickly glanced back at the pup. No time for other visions now and he shook his head, no. Heading down the trail he tried to ignore the tiny blue/gray eyes watching him leave.

The wolf pup had other ideas. With its belly round and full he couldn't move fast, but his short legs double-timed it, not letting him out of his sight.

"Go on!" he shouted without looking back. Of course the pup didn't understand and anyway it was used to Mother being grouchy. "Git, dang you." But nothing dissuaded his little tag-along.

Tuck shrugged, like Otto's, sometimes he knew his own words could be mean and sharp. He asked himself, but isn't that like it is? Isn't that the way *men* really speak? Especially to something so no account as this mangy wolf pup? But the truth was, he liked the little newcomer. He didn't yell at it again.

Within a half mile the pup was lagging behind. Its tongue lolled out the side of his mouth but he never whined, just kept quickstepping it as best he could.

Tuck slowed then stopped, turned on the trail and waited.

The pup loped the last few feet and plopped down exhausted on top of his moccasins.

Tuck squatted and patted its head, "Oh man, what am I going to do with the likes of you?" A few silent seconds passed.

"*Okaaay*," and he removed the arrows from his quiver and slid them into the deer meat sling then picked up the pup and slipped him into the buckskin quiver. "There." Satisfied, Tuck resumed his pace.

High on his shoulders it rode head and paws bobbing to the rhythm of Mother's pace.

"Stop it."

It kept licking Tuck's ear.

He cuffed him lightly.

It nipped Tuck's ear.

He smiled, shrugged and let it have its way.

Deep inside he felt something different. Maybe just maybe bringing the pup back to the cabin would be all right?

The last several miles he pushed his pace. The sun was a few degrees above the canyon's ridge when he finally caught sight of the cabin. He was late but only a little. Pride and excitement filled him. He'd accomplished what he'd set out to do, and a bit more. He stopped abruptly, exclaiming, "Where are all our beaver pelts?" When he'd left they were bundled and stacked under the lean-to on the north side. Now they were gone.

But foot and hoof prints were everywhere!

He shoved open the rough-hewn cabin door. Had traders been there? On the floor sacks of cornflower, tubs of sugar molasses and a few parcels of things he couldn't yet make out. But there was no doubt about what he could smell—corn whisky—and Otto was passed out cold on the pallet.

Mother was nowhere to be seen.

3

"TELL ME"

Back outside he raced, paying little attention to the many horse and mule hoof prints. He searched just the human tracks hoping to locate his mother's small moccasin prints. There were several shoe sets and sizes especially where the traders loaded the pelts on mules. Not Otto's.

Kneeling he looked closely. Among the deeper man size moccasin tracks was one odd shaped set, side by side a large boot and a round plughole. Must be a peg legged man he reasoned.

Yes, at last. There were Mother's but something seemed amiss. Her prints were smeared. A scuffle? None of her prints led back to, or away from the cabin. I best calm down. Maybe her footprints are just hidden under the horse tracks?

There, close to one of his own footprints—how had he missed it— why, he had almost stepped right on Mother's knife. Its slender blade was snapped in two and its daintily beaded handgrip buried in the dirt under the weight of mules hooves.

Holding its pieces in his hand the broken blade showed signs of blood! Whose blood? Don't panic. Maybe a horse cuts itself?

He lifted his head skyward and called, "Mother...Mother." His only answer echoes from off the canyon walls. All the stranger's tracks led southeast up the canyon.

Tuck knew beyond the canyon's rim the land stretched east and north for hundreds of miles. All barren and little or no timber, just brush covered mountains. To the south were valleys and most of them desert. Mother might be anywhere.

Their canyon was steep-sided, rocky and treeless except for the few willows around the seep-spring close to the cabin that dripped just enough to supply their needs. Rain when rarely did fall it came as roaring desert cloudbursts turning the canyon bottom into a raging flood. And that's why Otto had built the cabin on high ground.

Except for the one time he and Otto went beaver trapping, spring, summer and most of early fall they'd been trapping closer to home. Wolf, mountain lion, bobcat, badger and coyote were pelts they took almost everywhere. Few if any white men lived or hunted anywhere near their cabin in this isolated wilderness.

That was the way Otto wanted it. No, needed it to be. In the isolated canyon Otto felt safe from his past. He traded only with Indians and an occasional settler's wagon train heading west. Maybe she'd been captured by some of them?

Though Tuck had never seen any, according to Spring Willow, a few bad men came this way. Both Indian and white who dealt stolen horses and human slaves kidnapped from tribes to the west. Most of those tribes Tuck and his father were on friendly terms with. The Paiute and Mojave were the ones who usually came near their cabin to trade. Now he stood staring down at the tracks. Who were these men and why had they come?

And where was Spring Willow? Tuck hoped she was just hiding somewhere up the canyon.

Suddenly, as in times past, the hated retching sounds and cursing came from inside the cabin. He knew without seeing. He silently reentered the cabin. The stench of fresh vomit hit him. Otto was sitting up, his naked hairy chest covered and dripping with the sour contents of his stomach. The wolf pup still slung over Tuck's shoulder almost forgotten let out a panicky cry and squirmed to the bottom of the quiver.

Trying to contain himself, Tuck asked calmly, "Where's Spring Willow?"

"That squaw bitch tried to kill me," Otto slurred holding up his right hand. The blood had congealed but his palm was laid open from middle finger to wrist. Otto looked at the wound. "If I hadn't grabbed for her knife she'd have nailed me plumb through the heart. That's the thanks I get for keeping her all these years."

Tuck's eyes narrowed, his jaw set firm, lips thin and tight, he snarled, "Where is my mother?"

"Your mother huh?" He waved his slashed hand at Tuck and whined, "What about me? She may have dropped ya but you were just one of her sickly half-breed litter. T'was me who be your sire and took pity to even let ya keep breathing."

Tuck glared at him, his eyes full of hatred and fear. "Tell me, Damn you," he yelled. For the first time, cursing his father.

With Otto's hand and leg both injured, recognizing he might be at a disadvantage, he just glared back, and growled, "Youngin, if you know what's good for ya, ya best pull in your horns." Otto made a threatening move to rise. Still numb from the liquor, he tried to push himself up with the injured hand. He grimaced and tumbled back on his haunches. "None of your account anyway," he sneered, "But I traded her back to her own kind."

Tuck expected a beating. When it didn't come his rage leaped beyond good judgment. Years of fear and abuse erupted. "You bastard. You did what with my mother?"

"Traded the bitch, I said."

Tuck's eyes swept the cabin. Only one thought possessed him—punish this man. On the mantel above the stone fireplace hung Otto's treasured rifles, a Hawkin .30 and a larger Hawkin .50. Tuck clutched the .50, turned and in one swoop laid it hard upside Otto's head. The rifle ricocheted off Otto's skull slamming into the cabin wall breaking the stock in half. Otto was out cold. Tuck believed he'd killed him.

A moment of remorse clutched Tuck but fear dominated. In a panicked flurry Tuck thought only of escape. Bounding through the front door, he ran. Skidding around the cabin corner, he charged up the canyon. In his haste the wolf pup was jarred loose from the quiver and slammed to the ground yelping with pain and surprise.

Tears streaming from Tuck's eyes, he stopped and cried out in frustration, "I ain't got time to mother you. I got to find my own." But he did stop. The moment was pause enough for him to regain some composure. He cried, "What am I doing?" realizing he had no food or weapons to be traipsing after that gang with. Even his bow and arrows he'd left lying on the cabin floor. He reasoned, if I killed Otto he's not gonna be needing nothing anyway.

Wiping his tears with his sleeve, he sat down, picked up the pup, and cradled it in his arms. Speaking to the pup he said, "No need to go looking for mother empty handed. There's fixin's and trail-goods enough to see us for some time." With the pup under his arm, he ventured back toward the cabin.

Spitting distance from the cabin he heard a familiar sound, Otto's snoring. Mixed feelings but what a relief he hadn't murdered him after all. He ran to the open door. Sure enough, on Otto's head glistened a big goose egg and a trickle of blood. But flat on his back arms and legs splayed mouth agape, in-between rasping snores he breathed deep and regular.

Working as fast as he could, before Otto woke up, he divided the supplies down the middle. Even at that there was too much for him to carry. What should he do? More than once over the years Otto had outfitted him with a shoulder travois to haul their green pelts back from the Sierras. That would have to do. He learned at an early age to lean into the travois and haul like a mule.

Axe in hand down by the spring, he chopped two stout long willow branches, slung a tarp between the two poles, tying it firm with strips of rawhide. I won't be hauling that big a load. Reckon I'll keep my arms free and tie the travois off around my middle, he thought. He gathered up all the arrows he could find, loaded half the food, covered it with a black bear pelt and looked around. At the last minute—figuring he earned it—he helped himself to the Hawkin .30 and all the leads shot of that caliber and enough wadding and powder.

Otto's moans stirred him to action. Stuffing the pup back into his quiver, he took one more glance around the cabin. Without looking back he walked out the door. Securing the travois to his waist and following the stranger's tracks he began his trek.

Two-day-old tracks were easy to follow but he hadn't given much thought to what might happen if he came upon those who made them. And if the tracks were any indication, there were at least seven or eight on horseback not counting the pack mules whose hoof prints were longer and narrower than the unshod riding horses. Three pack mules maybe four—of one thing he was sure—on one of them rode his mother.

Noonday sun was directly overhead and the canyon's bottom sandy but easy walking. The two poles from his travois left clear lines in the earth behind him. A gradual slope up the canyon, it would take maybe two hours to crest the upper end. He knew, once on top and looking east, the terrain appeared deceptively flat. But it was otherwise just wastelands stretching for miles and miles. The last green and, as far as he knew the last water he would see for days, was at the big springs at the upper end of this trail he now climbed. There he would fill his canteen.

The pup's chin rested on Tuck's shoulder next to his ear. Seemingly without cause, up jerked its head giving out a short yip both ears pointing up the trail. Instinctively Tuck stopped and listened.

Through the willows three riders loped toward the cabin, two Indians and one white. Tuck froze seeing them before they saw him. The white man wore a great bear claw necklace and the garb of a mountain man similar to what Otto wore.

The Indians were dressed like none he's ever seen with gaudy glass trade beads. Their saddles were decorated with silver and pieces of mirror that sparkled and flashed in the sunlight as they rode. They rode, not on Indian ponies but high stepping long legged horses with full manes and tails. The horses had silver bits in their mouths instead of the usual Indian thong and their polished leather bridles and saddles were also encrusted with silver.

Spellbound by their showy display, Tuck didn't even blink

Then they saw him. Shouting what Tuck figured was a war cry, instantly they spurred their mounts and charged but at the last instant pulled to a stiff legged halt inches in front him. The two poles on his travois were the only thing that kept Tuck from falling over backwards. With a yip the pup ducked its head down into the quiver.

Looking down the barrels of two huge pistols, Tuck in complete surrender threw both arms in the air and blurted, "I'm Tuck...it's me... Tuck."

"Wait that's not the old man...that's her youngin," shouted the white man.

"Tall youngin almost dead youngin," grinned the nearest Indian.

Looking down from his saddle the white one ordered Tuck, "Keep movin in the direction you were." He jabbed up the trail with his thumb. The three strangers started to ride off. "We'll be right back," said the white one.

It was then Tuck noticed the man's peg leg. Immediately his fists clenched. It was him. The one who took his mother. Again anger overruled discretion. "Wait damn you, where's my mother?" he demanded.

Lucky for him, he'd packed his rifle on the travois. Mistakenly he might have tried to use it.

"What?" Peg Leg reined up turned in the saddle a look of surprise on his face. "Damn who?" Peg Leg had the kind of face when you looked up at him all you could see was big hairy nostrils and beady little eyes. Swallowing what he had a mind to say he just sniffed and growled, "Stop frettin' your maw's in good hands."

Tuck tried to read the mountain man's bearded face. Friend or foe he couldn't tell.

"Like I said, just keep walkin the way you were goin." Again Peg Leg pointed up the trail. "We'll take you to her when we finish our business." Off they trotted down the trail.

Fortunately Tuck followed instructions. Actually there was no choice in such steep sided canyons with him dragging such a load.

So he kept walking and soon was far enough up the trail to barely hear Otto's screams. But when the three riders returned there was no doubt what was hanging on the other Indians saddle. Sickened Tuck kept his eyes downcast. No doubt the same end would befall him.

"Lean your haul there against that rock. I'll send one of the scouts back to fetch it."

Tuck eyed Peg Leg and frowned. Yeah, I bet you will, he thought.

"Tuck I'm talkin to you. Are you deaf?" Peg Leg Smith shook his head and grinned. "Hell if we were gonna steal your outfit we'd just shoot you and take it."

"You're gonna just scalp me anyway. Why not be done with it?"

"Oh that," he pointed to Otto's scalp. "Well yeah I can see where you might figure. No I was just following orders. Nothin personal. We didn't exactly kill him anyway just lifted his hair. Maybe he'll live through it. I've seen it happen."

"Following orders?" asked Tuck.

Peg Leg Smith nodded yes. "You see, I knew Otto way back. Well I'll just say I know why he was holed up way out here."

"Who's?"

"Who's what?"

"Whose orders? Why'd you first trade with him? Then come back and scalp him?"

"Stow them questions lad," Peg Leg snapped. "Just stash your pack and get up here with me." He slapped the back of his saddle. "Your Maw is waiting for you back at our camp. There's a mighty big surprise waitin for you."

"What? You gonna try and slave me too? My mother told me there were outlaws like you who stole women even children. That very thing happened to her once before. The Comanche stole her when she was young. Now you stole her again."

Fear made some go quiet, Peg Leg reckoned, but this youngin was spittin fire. "Young fella we didn't steal her. Otto woulda traded you or his own mother for enough whisky." Peg Leg was growing impatient. Again he slapped his saddle. This time a little too hard and his pinto pony shied and crow-hopped nearly throwing him.

The two Indians laughed and started to ride up the trail.

Almost choking on his chew, Peg Leg shouted, "Git to hoppin boy. Damn it, do what you're told. We got to get the herd movin."

He wondered what herd Peg Leg was talking about. "I'll walk," he said defiantly.

Even on one leg, Peg Leg came off his saddle in one bound. His stubby fingered hand snatched Tuck by the scruff of his neck. Instantly the wolf pup poked his head out and grabbed the fringes on Peg Leg's sleeve.

"Yowee! What in tarnation?" He let go of Tuck's neck. The pup let go of his sleeve.

"Don't hurt him. He's my dog. Ah, it's a wolf pup dog." Tuck reached his hand back and patted him. She licked his fingers and snarled at Peg Leg.

"Damn it boy, maybe you and that little nipper would prefer to ride tied down on your own travois? My Paint mare won't mind a bit—you might though—if she gets to kickin your brains out."

"We ain't never been on a horse," Tuck replied.

"Well it's about time." Peg Leg shoved him toward his horse. "Up the trail yonder there's plenty others you can ride and like you they ain't ever been rid either. Now mount up."

On up the trail the Indians laughed again.

Reluctantly Tuck stashed his pack but kept the quivered pup on his back. Peg Leg took him by the arm and swung him up behind. Up the canyon trail they headed. Soon the pup's nose was again resting on Tuck's shoulder but its eyes were watching the back of Peg Leg's neck.

4

"HORSE THIEVES AND OTHER RELATIVES"

"My Gawd." Tuck squinted and rubbed his eyes. There on the canyon's upper end was a place with small pools of spring water and several acres of thick grasses. Were his eyes playing tricks on him? The entire area seemed to be rolling in waves of black, white, gray, brown and chestnut. Then he saw clearly, the meadows were dappled with every color and size of grazing and resting horse.

How come all these horses, though covered with trail dust and on the thin side, were still in their light warm weather coats? Tuck could see right off they were not like Indian ponies. Even at a glance any fool could notice the difference. And when it came to knowing a bit about most four legged critters Tuck was no fool.

"Where did you get so dang many?" Tuck asked.

Peg Leg chuckled, "These be our Californee herd," glancing at his two partners. "By golly we tried to run em off but they done followed us here clean from them San Bernardino, Spanish rancheros." He laughed.

He didn't see Peg Leg wink at the two Indians nor could he take his eyes off the meadow. "Why I've never seen so many...must be hundreds."

"Humph," Peg Leg scoffed, "Near a thousand be more like it if you count all the foals. You can see them fancy Spanish breeds can't sleep standing up like Injun ponies. They're all tuckered out. We've been drivin em hard for two weeks. But with fair winds to our stern, before the snow flies, we should be in Santa Fee."

"Santa Fe?"

"You be backwoods ignorant ain't ya boy? New Mexico Territory, that's where."

"I'm not ignorant," Tuck glared. "Spring Willow told me all about Santa Fe, Taos and lots of other places. Said she had been there when she was a young girl, ten summers old when Comanche's sold her to Cheyenne's who before long sold her to some white—"

"Trappers," Peg Leg interrupted. "You're not speakin anything I don't already know."

"You know?" Peg Leg quit talking. Down through the grazing herd came a group of galloping riders. He waved them down. The Indian horsemen slowed to a trot and reined up forming a close circle around Tuck and Peg Leg.

All were dressed in gaudy buckskins outfits and straddling shaggy horses. Each well-armed they waved and gestured toward the ridge above, like something was urgent. Peg Leg raised his hand in silence and quickly spoke a few words in their tongue. Stopping their chatter in unison all heads swiveled and looked directly at Tuck.

Tuck thought; what are they gawking at me for? Figuring on what price I'll fetch, I bet.

"Walkara's." His name whispered amongst them.

Finally Peg Leg twisted in his saddle, his head facing Tuck. He spoke in English. "Boy, Chief Walkara's waitin for ya."

The entire troop grinned and nodded. Peg Leg then said with a degree of pride, "He be your grand pappy," spoken like Tuck didn't understand," your Maw's Pa. And we don't never want to keep Chief Walkara waitin."

Tuck finally managed to stammer, "My mother? My...mother's father?"

"Now you got it. Your grand pappy, Chief Walkara. He be Top Captain of most all the Ute Nation."

"Yes mother told me she was Ute but never said her father was some kind of big chief."

"Way back when she was little he wasn't so important but these last ten or fifteen years he's the one what dang near got all the bands of Ute pullin together. Now Walkara holds plenty respect. Among other things he is the greatest horse thief in the whole wide west."

"Horse thief? My mother's father? My very own grandfather, a horse thief?"

"Right on all counts, and lucky that you and your maw are first in line as Walkara's blood kin."

"I know my mother was just a girl when the Comanche stole her. Does she know about her father?"

"She sure do, now. And she ain't forgot how she was rustled while he was off buffalo huntin on the staked plains. Utes were at war with them stinking Comanche pirates over the rights to hunt buffalo. Those coyotes sneaked into their village and grabbed up a slew of wimmin and children. Over thirty years ago, and they're still fighting."

Peg Leg said, "Enough jabberin," in Ute gave a command, "Let's git." He spurred his paint mare into a gentle lope. The rest followed.

Over the sound of galloping hooves Tuck yelled in his ear, "How come you know so much about Spring Willow and Otto?"

Peg Leg only answered. "Yah...yah," he cried, digging his heels into his horse's ribs.

Startled by the horse's lunging power, instinctively Tuck gripped tight with both legs. In a few strides he thought, this is awesome. Never had he dreamed he might some day run with such hair-raising speed. He soon got the rhythm of it. As they sped toward the far side of the herd just above the ridge, he saw a wisp of white smoke coiling skywards.

Peg Leg gave his pinto mare its head—pounding strides increased to a flat-out tail twisting dead run.

Tuck grimaced, his eyes watering...winds whipping his face. For a moment he felt as though he might fall.

Peg Leg sensed his plight. "Hold on!" he cried.

Tuck clutched Peg Leg's stout shoulders with both hands...white knuckles...his long black hair shook loose streaming in the wind. Jaws clenched, he held his breath. From deep in his throat swelled a wild cry of freedom right in Peg Leg's ear, "Why this is most near like flying."

Two teepees were silhouetted against a blue southern sky, tawny and smoked-stained buffalo hides stretched taut over a dozen or more lodge poles. The tallest was decorated with bright yellow and red horse and hawk designs. Sitting in front, a group of costumed Indians waited next to a large campfire. Roasted remains of a pronghorn antelope hung on an iron tripod hook alongside the fire.

Dressed in fine white doeskin, Spring Willow rose from the circle. Arms outstretched, she reached toward the approaching riders. A new smile spread across her painted face. With moist eyes, she waited.

Peg Leg jerked their horse to a halt, waved a greeting and dismounted in one graceful motion. Turning to Tuck he deliberately ignored Spring Willow, giving Walkara proper respect. He said, "Like I told ya, here's your grand pappy," and then whispered, "Dagnabit act like you're happy, youngster."

But Tuck's eyes were on his mother.

He slid off the saddle, leg muscles trembling from holding on for dear life during the all-out dash back to camp.

"Greet your grand pappy first...your maw understands," said Peg Leg.

Tuck's eyes didn't have to search. Seated in the teepee's open doorway was a large man, hawk nosed and elaborately dressed. Groomed waist length partly gray hair was interwoven with many eagle feathers that spoke of his chief's status. His penetrating eyes were fixed on Tuck's eyes.

Spring Willow said to Chief Walkara, "Father...my son, Mitakoye Tokehe, your Grandson." She motioned for Tuck to approach.

Despite trembling legs but shoulders squared Tuck moved around the circle of seated onlookers toward Chief Walkara. His mind churned, what should I do? What should I call him? Chief...Grand Father...or what?

Walkara rose to his feet and in a sweeping gesture his right arm motioned toward the bearskin door-flap behind him. In a voice like heavy waters, "My Son, my casa es su casa, Welcome," proudly mixing his limited English with his nearly fluent Spanish. Spring Willow unfastened the door. Walkara entered first and Spring Willow shooed Tuck through the opening.

Cautiously Tuck turned and stepped into the teepee. Inside half the space was taken up with sacks and boxes of trade goods. An incense of smoked meat and burning sweet sage filled his nostrils. The trade goods looked the same as those Otto traded for back at the cabin. Stacked up against the trade goods was a cache of several rifles. Black shaggy buffalo robes covered the floor.

Walkara seated himself. Tuck began to do likewise but Spring Willow, with a disapproving glance, took his arm and pulled him erect.

She whispered, "Wait for—"

"Sit, my Son," Walkara said. Ute words familiar to Tuck as words from his mother.

Replying in Ute, "Thank you Grandfather."

Spring Willow nudged Tuck with her elbow. She whispered, "Remember what you have been taught."

Tuck did what his mother had taught him—respect toward parents and leaders. "Yes...thank you...Grand Father," he spoke in Ute dialect and seated himself at Walkara's left hand.

Walkara smiled hearing well-spoken Ute from his Grandson's lips. He said, "My son there is much for you to understand," he looked toward Spring Willow who nodded in agreement. "Your mother has cared well for you?" Walkara asked?

"Mother did care well for me...yes—"

A stormy look crossed Walkara's face, "Only your mother's pleas kept me from doing very bad things to...I will not call him your father...the man, Otto."

"He treated Mother badly."

"His shame is greater than that my son. There are those who would cut him into little pieces for all his evils."

"Grandfather, if you wish me to know...I'd like to hear of all my fa— Otto's shameful ways."

And so Walkara spoke, explaining that evil which Otto did. "It was 'Flat Tail' [Beaver] that first brought Otto's kind to our mountains. Soon there were more 'white eyes' than 'flat tails' for them to trap. Pelaje de companias, the American Company, and Rocky Mountain fur companies fought each other for the pelts. Some said partners in the Rocky Mountain Compania hired Otto to kill the two owners of the American Companias. He did that—no brave thing—shot them both in the back and took their hair."

"He was paid to say Blackfoot murdered them. But to Otto we were all just, 'savages'. And instead of the Blackfoot he pointed all those evils at the Ute Nation."

He motioned, "Many of our people were killed and driven from their places because of Otto's lies."

Tuck imagined Walkara was looking right into his heart and seeing a heart half white and half Ute. He almost said, I do not lie, Grandfather. He didn't.

And Walkara continued, "Then at a Green River rendezvous truth found words in whiskey. Otto's boasting spirit betrayed those lies. Like a blind bear he roared and made war with his own demon, waving scalps of the two dead men for all to see. His only friend, Peg Leg Smith saved his life. Put him on the fastest horse." Walkara stopped. He had finished the story.

"Peg Leg, his friend?" said Tuck.

"Yes perhaps his only friend."

For a moment Tuck sat with head bowed until he glanced up at Spring Willow, and then asked, "And what of my mother, Grandfather? Others have told me but will you? Tell me if it pleases you."

Walkara looked at Spring Willow. She nodded approval.

Walkara began again, "Many moons ago, a few winters before the white trappers came to our land, Spring Willow was stolen by Comanche.

Two winters and she was traded to the Cheyenne. Ten winters later she was sold at Santa Fe to Otto. That was the first summer after Otto fled from the murders.

"Spring Willow was the age when she became a woman. Se hizo florcita, or as we say in our tongue, First Flowered."

"There were men in Santa Fe who knew she was my daughter, but did nothing to help. That is the way it is in the slave trade." He sighed deeply. "One month later I was at the very same place selling my own slaves. Only then did I learn of her fate. I did not know it was Otto who bought her. Anyway it was too late to follow."

"How did you find us here, Grandfather?" Tuck said.

"It was Peg Leg who noticed smoke from Otto's cabin and rode to see what it was. He did not know my daughter, but he did know, Otto. I can understand old friendships and why Peg Leg took Otto food and whiskey in exchange for, he believed her to be Ute, but did not know she was my daughter...your mother. He still did not know who she was until he brought her back to our camp.

"When he told me where she was found and with who, I forgave Peg Leg for taking food and whiskey to Otto."

"Seeing Spring Willow again for two passing of the sun my heart had only room for happiness."

Walkara's expression and voice change, becoming as a threatening force, "But I also understand old hatred," his fists clenched, eyes blazed.

Tuck stiffened, Spring Willow held her breath.

Then like a passing thunderstorm, as quickly as it began, Walkara's entire posture changed, saying, "So after much smoke and prayer last night, this morning I told Peg Leg to go and bring me Otto's hair. You see Peg Leg is one of my best Lieutenants and also my friend. He said he would do as I asked. Now, time and Otto's hair, have paid the old debt." And again he fell silent.

Voices outside, those around the campfire, droned on. Inside the teepee, for the moment, the three of them sat in silence.

Then as sometimes happens, the exact instant outside voices pause, Tuck, in a voice loud enough for all to hear, said, "Grandfather, is it true what Peg Leg told me? You are a big horse thief?"

In and outside of the teepee silence slapped every ear red.

5

"GETTING THE HANG OF IT"

Walkara's head snapped up as Tuck's 'horse thief' statement cut accusingly.

At the same instant inside his quiver the pup started to squirm up and out.

The chief's eyes popped wide open, "Uuhhaaai," he cried rearing back.

Spring Willow too let out a muffled cry, "Eeeiii."

For a frightful moment in the teepees dim light it looked as if something unnatural was growing from Tuck's neck.

Walkara grabbed his knife.

Hearing the commotion Peg Leg poked his head inside the door flap.

Tuck couldn't see the pup's head or its pee matted puppy fur standing on end. In the excitement of their galloping horse ride Tuck had forgotten it was jammed to the bottom of the soggy quiver. But he could smell and feel him struggling up out of the quiver to free himself.

To Walkara and Spring Willow the pup looked like some devil-headed spirit dog clinging to the back of Tuck's neck. Hoisting itself farther onto Tuck's shoulder he let out a haunting yowl.

Tuck reached up and pulled him gently down onto his lap. "He's just wet and hungry and I'll bet he needs to pee again."

Arm outstretched pointing at the door, Walkara snapped, "Not in my lodge...*out*!"

Startled by Walkara's reaction, Tuck struggled to explain. "I shot—. I mean to say, I killed—" His voice dropped to a whisper, "Her mother. "Except she was hurt...and the pup was blind and I—" His eye's flashed back and forth between Spring Willow and Walkara, "forgot he was in my quiver...and...." Tilting his face toward the pup his voice trailed off and his jaw hung slack.

What he wanted to say was, what in the heck is all the fuss about. But before he could the pup licked him right in the mouth then twisted its head toward Walkara and snarled.

Scowling with disgust Walkara spit, wiped his mouth and again shouted, "Out," jamming a wagging finger toward the door.

Spring Willow reached out a hand attempting to calm her Father.

Peg Leg said, "By golly lil' nipper wolf pup done come up out of his possum pouch'." He grinned, "An sounds like that pint-sized banshee is speakin its piece too."

Walkara fumed and glared at Peg Leg his arm still pointing toward the door.

Peg Leg grimaced, "Oops, excuse me folks," and ducked his head back outside.

Head and eyes still downcast Tuck jumped to his feet and pushed his way through the door flap. "Well, excuse me too."

Halfway out he lifted his head, glaring back he paused, jutted out his jaw and spouted, "Reckon if my pup's a problem you can always put him in your Injun stewpot." He slammed the door flap closed. With all eyes watching, the pup under his arm, he walked stiffly past Peg Leg and off in the direction of the horse herd.

As Tuck passed by Peg Leg whispered, "Chief don't never allow no dogs in his lodge. Bad medicine."

At that moment Tuck cared less.

Inside the teepee a few moments later: "As you said Father," Spring Willow soothed, "there is much to understand...for the boy too."

Walkara waved her words away with a fist clenched as tight as his face, "I know Daughter...I know." He dropped his chin on his chest, a sigh escaping his lips.

They were quiet for several minutes. Walkara broke the silence. "Daughter, it is not just your son. In the past our ways did not change. My father and his father's father all knew the same ways. We all knew the 'Path'." He raised his head, "Now," he shook his head and sighed, "Now everything demands words and reasons. It is always, 'porque—why'. Before, no such words lived in the Ute language. Is it not our way to just say, yes—no? That is enough."

"Yes...Father."

Weaving his way through the herd the pup at his heels Tuck headed for the nearby spring. The sour/sweet smell of horse was thick on the ground and he watched where he stepped.

Most of these horses were like none he'd ever seen. Those horses, mules' and oxen that had come this way with westbound settlers were either heavy work stock or big-footed wagon haulers. Those few the Paiutes rode were short coupled, roman nosed, pig-eyed mustangs. But these here were long legged, arched necks with large glistening eyes and flared nostrils.

None seemed nearly so spooky or skittish as Indian ponies. As he approached they just parted a little. He could reach out and touch them if he so chose. Pointing their ears at him, snorting and nickering, letting him pass close enough he could feel and smell their warm breathe. A dark checkered gray with long black mane and tail and a white-socked blood bay, both mares, followed close sniffing and blowing at his footsteps stirring up little clouds of dust.

Their nearness made him a little nervous. Increasing his pace they did the same. He broke into a jog.

Enjoying his seemingly playful company they too increased to a trot. Tuck thought he knew a bit about horses, in reality he didn't. And he was not playing nor was he sure of their ultimate intentions. His heart pounded. The hair on the back of his neck tingled. What if they're planning on stomping me or maybe run me right over?

Holding tightly to the pup he sprinted. The two horses stayed right at his heels. Fearful at first, but soon getting angry and finally he'd had enough. Stomping or no stomping he jammed to a halt, turned suddenly and threw his clenched fists up in their faces. He hollered, "Yah...yah!" Bucking and tossing their heads playfully they galloped past him one on each side brushing close enough for him to give the gray a swift kick in the ribs. Tuck's chest heaving and choking on their dust he reached down hoping to find a rock to throw at them.

He heard laughter. Off to his left on the trail leading up through the meadow a mounted rider looked in his direction laughing. A young Indian and his pony were dragging Tuck's travois. Seemed he found something humorous about Tuck running from horses.

Tuck turned and glared. "Hey Injun," he yelled, "what you laughing at?"

"Hey Breed!" the young Ute started to yell something stronger back.

Tuck cut him off. "Easy to see I was just having sport racing them."

He set the pup down, hiked up his britches and made both hands into fists. Nobody else was going to push him around today.

Anger also stung the Indian's insides. Lies, why do whites always lie? He wasn't laughing as he walked his pony in Tuck's direction. "Lieutenant

Peg Leg sent me to fetch your outfit." Black eyes flashing he glared down his high-bridged nose at Tuck, "Breed," he sneered again.

Tuck sneered back, "Breed huh. Well Redskin you can just drop my outfit right there."

The young man's expression did not change hearing Tuck's words of disrespect. His eyes barely narrowed. He reached for his knife, turned sideways in his saddle and deliberately cut the rawhide holding the travois. It slammed to the ground roughly scraping the sides of his horse. Startled the horse pitched and bucked unexpectedly throwing the young Indian on his face.

It was Tuck's turn to laugh. Slapping his thighs he affected his loudest hee-haws.

The young Indian still grasping his knife threw it down and charged attempting a flying tackle.

Tuck braced himself.

At first there ensued a great deal of head twisting, wrestling and rolling in horse droppings. Then they parted each circling looking for an opening. Though he'd never been tested Tuck fancied himself a fist fighter. But none of his punches found their mark. Not fighting with his fists the Indian lad seemed full of tricks and cunning moves.

A circle of curious horses formed around them ears pointing, glistening eyes protruding they joined in the fun and went off whinnying and bucking.

Again, lunging at each other, they both struggled for several more minutes both ending up having the other mutually clasp tight—head to butt in leg-lock scissor holds.

Tuck finally yelled, "If ya know what's good for ya—"

Ouray, the young Indian, squeezed all the harder.

Tuck grunted, " I'm Chief Walkara's Grandson."

"I know that. So what! I am Ouray. My Father is Walkara's older brother." With all his strength he twisted and squeezed Tuck's head between his thighs he snarled, "Someday I will be your chief."

"Someday ain't now." And Tuck clamped down with all his might on Ouray's head. So they grunted, thrashed and struggled but neither would cry uncle.

From between Tuck's thighs Ouray gasped, "Okay...okaaay...we both 'strike coup'. He released Tuck's head. Ouray admitting, "You are strong, Breed."

Still holding his grip deciding if he wanted to continue Tuck lay there on his back panting, "You...too Injun."

From what Spring Willow told him he knew what 'coup' meant and not knowing where the pup went he decided he too had enough and relaxed his grip. It was then he became aware of the tug on his pant leg. The pup's jaws locked tight, its eyes bugging, ears flat and neck bristling and his tiny teeth embedded firmly into Tuck's buckskins.

He sat up kicking to free his pant leg. Grabbing the pup by its neck he jerked him loose and began to brush off the weed stickers and horse droppings. Seeing his filthy clothes, bloodied nose and bruises he thought, by darn maybe it wasn't so bad back at the cabin.

He lamented, "Damn it all, first Otto wants to knock my head off, Peg Leg fixing to whip me, Grandfather pulls a knife, horses try to stomp me, we're fighting like bearcats and my own pup commences to chew on me," ending with a dramatic sigh.

Ouray had to clamp his hand over his mouth to keep from laughing again. His eyes wide and sparkling in between his fingers he chuckled, "Welcome to Ute country, Cousin." Seeing the pitiful expression on Tuck's face it was no use and he busted out laughing.

Perhaps in their long exhausting struggle Tuck's anger and the day's craziness diminished. Then too maybe laughter was contagious. Falling back on the grass, arms spread eagle, he peeked sideways at Ouray and grinned. At the same instant the pup latched onto his pant leg again. "Oh shit," he exclaimed in English. Frustration and confusion began to fade with the outlandish comedy of it all. Both of them spontaneously united in a back slapping chorus of howling laughter. Even the Pup joined in.

Before long their suspicions their waned and turned to curiosity. Similarity in ages, Ouray was two years older but Tuck a head taller, they began to find a common ground. The rest of the day they spent sizing each other up, asking and answering the other's many questions.

Tuck asking, "Where did all those horses come from? I mean, Peg Leg said, below the mountains in San Bernardino, California, but that's a long way." Isn't it?

"Not a long way for Walkara when the rewards are so great." Ouray threw out his chest, "We Utes are the best horse thieves in all the land."

Tuck couldn't help recalling Otto's words, almost nothin's worse than a damn horse thief. But he kept his mouth shut. Anyway, Spring Willow was Ute and apparently she didn't care. He would withhold judgment.

"Do you know what they call your Grandfather?" Ouray stood and began dancing in a slow circle flapping and swooping with his arms, "El Gavilan, The Hawk of the Mountains, and we," thumping his chest, "soar with him." Ouray continued the dance, kii-yiing and howling like a coyote. Pup seemed to find him funny and commenced hopping around in circles yapping.

Eyes wide with excitement Ouray put his face right up into Tuck's, saying, "My cousin let me tell you of the best raid ever." Seating himself he began to explain. "The greatest of all horse raid, the one before this, the famous one. Sadly I was too young to be included. That one was said to be the greatest horse raid in all the land. Three thousand fine Spanish horses in one bold sweep—using only fifty men and capturing three thousand prizes. It was easy," he laughed, "The rancheros knew we were coming again. Fearful of us and forgetting their pride they asked the hated U.S. Army to protect them and capture Walkara.

"Haugh," Ouray leaped in the air, "Easily, we are the better soldiers." He slapped his thighs with glee, "The stupid army waited at the top of the Cajon Pass expecting us to riding in from the northeast." He could hardly contain his excitement. "The fools didn't know we were already hiding in their foothills below the pass."

Drawing his knife he crouched and humped his back as though stalking, his voice a whisper, "Dry Grass Moon was full and a strong breeze blew down the canyon toward us. They could not hear us coming." One opened hand above his forehead as though gazing off into the distance, he said, "Peg Leg scouted ahead, returning with the army's position—two-hundred men. Hah! And most of them were sleeping. Others in a thin single line watched north. Hah! From the south we came stampeding right through their ranks with the big horse herd." Pausing to catch his breath, he shouted, "Before they could fire a single shot or saddle up we were far out onto the Mojave, heading over the Rojo Mountains, past Little Lake and into the big river valley beyond."

Tuck asked," Well, were you there or not? I can't tell by how you tell it."

So, into his storytelling Ouray ignored Tuck's question and went on.

"We didn't lose a single head. It was the longer way home, but usually turns out to be more than worth it."

"More than worth it?" Tuck asked.

"Like this time too, yes we captured a dozen slaves." He sneered, "Lousy Diggers, six women and six young girls."

"Diggers?"

"What some call Paiutes and Monos. They work hard but they are poor and stupid. Fit only for slaves. Strong as burros but in Santa Fe they will bring much gold from traders."

"Where are they now?"

"In the other teepee. They are too cowardly to try and escape."

Tuck thought, women and girls cowardly? Where would they go out here anyway? These folks do think a bit different.

Tuck said, "I have learned much today cousin."

"That is good," Ouray said.

"Do you know what the first thing I learned was?"

"What is that?"

"Don't take my wolf pup into Walkara's lodge."

"You didn't?"

"I did, and I thought Walkara was fixing to skin me and eat my pup."

Again they had a good laugh.

Later that evening after they returned to camp, and Tuck thought no one was looking, he peeked into the captive slave's lodge. Such a difference from the way Walkara's men dressed.

The Diggers dirty and barefoot wore only tattered reed skirts and capes of woven rabbit fur for warmth and bedding. In the shadows from under heads of uncombed filth hair looking like frightened rabbits their small round eyes set in wide round faces stared back at Tuck. As far as he could see their only bonds were the fear and threats of torture or death. Tuck jumped, hearing Peg Leg's voice right behind him.

"You and that Nip pup move along. Best mind your own business."

So the wolf pup got his name. Tuck patted her head, "*Nip*, yeah that fits."

A few days before they left, Ouray as his teacher, Tuck began riding lessons. The checkered gray mare, the curious one with the long black mane and tail, became Tuck's favorite mount. The name he gave her, Desert Wind.

Walkara announced it was time to pack up and leave.

Tuck rode Desert Wind from dawn to dusk, doing the thing he now loved, being glued to the mare's back. He rode first with a saddle and then began learning the more difficult skills of bareback riding.

The flexing muscles, rippling power and warmth between his legs was good but the best thing—running at full gallop—the rousing sensation of swiftly covering great distance. With thundering wind in his face he always imagined it was almost like flying. He had little time for anything else including work.

They journey eastward and the need for water took them near to Ruby Lakes where Tuck got his first glimpse of horse-trading. They slowed only long enough to sell a few of the lesser quality horses to a wagon train of whites heading for the northern pass over the Sierras.

Walkara warned them it was too late in the year to attempt a winter crossing. Despite the warning they climbed up into their wagons alongside their women and children. With little trail to follow the wagon train pushed its way slowly through the endless miles of bitterbrush.

On the trail east everyone had duties to tend to. Walkara dressed in all his chief's finery, leading the herd astride his prancing black stallion, appeared preoccupied with his responsibilities and seemed unconcerned about Tuck. Tuck saw little of him and only occasionally did he get to visit with Spring Willow.

Often Ouray acted like he didn't know him. Tuck wondered why it was so?

Nor did he understand why Walkara sent Ouray to tell him he was to ride drag at the back of the herd. After that, Tuck on Desert Wind, Nip, as the pup was now called rode draped across his lap. Riding 'drag' the three of them spent most of the time plodding along in choking dust clouds. Only once in a while Tuck did get to chase a stray or two. For those not doing their part Walkara had his ways.

Tuck moped and grumbled, "Everyone thinks I'm no good for nothing." Pouting, he was grumpy toward everybody. They left him alone to figure it out for himself.

Finally late in the season under the icy-blue of Sleeping Bear Moon they rode into Taos. That night it snowed up to the horse's knees.

Nip the wolf pup, which by then had tripled in size, still rode in front of Tuck slung across his saddle blanket. Nip didn't mind but Desert Wind's natural instincts, and the stronger smell of a growing he-wolf, was taking some getting used to.

Those captive slaves, the stronger one who lived through the march, were being left behind at Taos Pueblo. There Walkara met the man trusted to trade their slaves to the highest bidder. He and Walkara greeted each other like brothers.

The man's name was James Beckwourth. Walkara introduced him around.

Right off Tuck realized the man was different than any man he'd ever seen.

Tuck offered his hand. Beckwourth's large green eyes looked down intently, almost curiously into Tuck's silver-blue eyes. The corners of the man's mouth turned up slightly but he didn't offer to shake Tuck's hand. Besides being tall, even taller than Walkara, his features and skin tone were somehow different—black hair in long braids—course like wool. Dressed in full beaded buckskins more like Cheyenne he walked and talked with a peculiar swagger and confidence

That same morning they continued south a three-day ride to the much heralded, Santa Fe. Tuck could hardly wait.

7

"TWO OF A KIND"

Tuck hadn't forgotten Beckwourth's snub back up at Taos. He was sick and tired of getting the cold shoulder and anyway this guy was nosing into his plans. Though his plans were still a bit sketchy. Right now all he figured on doing was keeping a blank face. His so-called friend, Ouray did that to him all the time. Why not give what he'd been getting?

Over the talkative Beckwourth's shoulder the lights of Santa Fe beckoned. The fire flickered low. Tuck glanced up but made no move to add fuel. He hoped without a warm fire the uninvited man might leave. But let the fire die and it wouldn't be the least bit pleasant for Tuck either, even with Nip curled up in his lap. Both were already cold just sitting there waiting. The pile of broken branches was close at hand. Reconsidering he shivered and sighed then laid a couple big branches on the dying fire.

Beckwourth droned on and on. Tuck aimed not to listen. But the man's deep throaty voice chipped away at his thoughts. Not exactly the words but the rise and fall of his tone. Tuck's was drawn to the sounds, tranquil and not all that unkindly. The word 'Breed' and 'blue eyes' and the chuckle following got his attention.

"What? Blue eyes?" Tuck's eyes narrowed. "You talking about me?"

"Don't get your dander up young fellow. I was speaking about me and you. Seeing we have that in common."

"Why's that? Your eyes near as I remember sure ain't blue."

"See, that's what I mean." He pointed both index fingers at Tuck's eyes and then back at himself, "Mine are green but you noticed them too."

Here he was getting drawn into an unwanted conversation. "Naturally I'd notice. Except for folks on the wagon train it's been weeks since I saw anything but dark ones. Anyway my Father's eyes were blue just like mine."

"Your father is a white man, right?"

Tuck waited a minute before answering, "Of course."

Beckwourth continued, "So were my father's eyes blue."

"Then I reckon that makes you a 'Breed' like me?"

"Not exactly. My mother is not Indian." Quickly Beckwourth got to his feet, packed the food back into the saddlebag and walked to his horse.

Suddenly he turned and spoke hesitantly, "When I first met you, you being so tall for your age, I believed you to be older. Walkara' s son, not his Grandson." Both hands, palms up, he shrugged and declared, "I'm not sure why now but seeing that your eyes were so light blue I expected you to figure you were more white than me."

"Oh," Tuck replied simply. Beckwourth's words about blue eyes, not Indian and his strange talk about being more white didn't register on Tuck. So he nodded like he understood then put more wood on the fire.

"And you?" Beckwourth asked.

Tuck had to hand it to him. He'd not say quit when it came to gabbing. Again he waited a couple of minutes before responding. At least here was someone to talk to. Seems he's not leaving so why not? Dropping his guard he joined in.

"My mother Spring Willow is full blood Ute. You know, Chief Walkara's daughter. By now more than likely you know that?"

It was quiet for a while. Beckwourth picked up a stick and stirred the coals. Finally jamming the stick into the fire, he lifted his head watching the sparks swirl into the darkness. "Tuck did you hear me? My mother is not Indian." He looked directly at Tuck. "She is a Negro and a slave." No instant reply, he repeated, "Negro—slave—understand?"

Tuck did not know how to respond.

Beckwourth said, "Can you understand, I'm from Virginia and my white Father brought me out west to get away from the stigma of having a mulatto son? Dixieland's no place for, Sir Jennings's, bastard son to be labeled a nigger." Beckwourth returned, sat down and threw wood on the fire.

He continued, "Way back in the eighteen twenties I met your father Otto Schultz, Peg Leg Smith and a bunch of other young men who signed up with General William Ashley's Company. It was them and me who brought beaver trade supplies to these parts and started the tradition of the Great Mountain Man Rendezvous. And everybody knew it was me who saved Robert Campbell's hide and his men's too," he pointed north, "when the Blackfoot had them surrounded in a patch of willows up yonder near the Great Salt Lake. Even so most whites still don't accept me."

Tuck wondered how did Beckwourth know Otto was his father?

Beckwourth went on. He tugged at his braids and said, "Until I let my hair grow long and tied it into these braids it was nigger bushy as a buffalo's head. Fact is the Sioux call me Tutanka Hat, Buffalo Head. Some think me Indian."

"So who cares?" asked Tuck,

"Well I know Walkara and his men don't mind one way or another. Because I can speak Crow, Blackfoot, Spanish, a little French and perfect educated English. And that comes in handy for our trading purposes."

A big white-toothed grin spread across James' face. His voice changed, "An, sho nuff, ol' Jim kin peddle boots to a rattlee snake. An I kin swap some white boss-man outta his poke fo a hot crotch Injun slave gal." He threw back his head and roared.

At Beckwourth's last comment Tuck stiffened, 'Hot-crotch Indian slave' didn't sound so funny? Just what does he mean? For Tuck's young ears there was a gang of words in Beckwourth's talk he'd never heard before: Mulatto, Dixie, nigger, stigma. Tuck frowned. Seemed it was a one-way conversation, so he said, "My Mother was a slave too. So, what?"

"Now Tuck, I was not referring to a good woman like your mother, Spring Willow. You see my Mother and her Mother's mother were all white man's slaves too. All that side of my family will more than likely always be slaves. Just Darkies, a commodity bought and sold from far off Africa."

"Maybe they can all escape too?" Tuck wondered what kind of lingo *'commodity,'* was?

"Too many niggers, and no place to go. No, Darkies are what they are. That's the way down South. But I'm a manumitted slave and lucky to be my own man out here on the frontier."

Tuck still couldn't figure out what green eyes, or blue for that matter, had to do with anything. And what was it Beckwourth said, 'man-united'? For a while they sat quietly and stared into the fire.

Tuck asked, "What if like me you went back to your Negro family?"

"I don't think I could. You must understand how most folks are. You are either one of them or..." he snorted, "For me and you I think it's like being betwixt the devil and the," he pointed at Tuck's eyes, "deep blue," he pointed at himself "green sea." Again he laughed at his own words.

Tuck couldn't help but laugh along with him though he didn't understand for sure what Beckwourth was driving at. Far as he was concerned he wasn't one of anything or anybody. Beckwourth nodded toward the lights of Santa Fe, "That town down there can be friendly enough in daylight but at night I wouldn't recommend you go waltzing in without an armed partner, someone to cover your backside. Down in Santa Fe there are some who would just as soon skin you as your wolf pup."

"Well, I wasn't planning—"

"Yeah, I know...I know. You were just going to take a look from up here, right? Then walk all the way back to camp—"

"Didn't figure on—"

"You can come back here in the daytime. There's always manana so why walk back? Concho my stallion can easily carry two men"

"Two?" was all Tuck said, but he liked being called a man. He got up, kicked snow on the fire, picked up Nip and stepped over to Beckwourth's stallion and stood there waiting.

Riding double back to camp the moonlight gave everything a ghostly blue quality. Only the crunch of Concho's hooves gave meaning to the silence.

A couple of chilly hours ride and the teepees came into view. "Beckwourth here!" he called out in Spanish. A mounted guard appeared from the shadows down by the stream. He waved a greeting.

Tuck knew Spring Willow was in one of the teepees, maybe asleep, maybe awake worrying about him? He doubted that. She was home, 'one of them.'

Nip felt right at home stuffed up under Tuck's buckskin shirt. Tuck slid from the stallion's back. The snow was ankle deep. He remembered Walkara's words, 'famous horse man,' that seemed possible. But, 'fearless Ute brave'? He stood there not knowing for sure where to go.

From beyond the stream he thought he heard Desert Wind nicker a greeting in his direction. Heck more than likely at Beckwourth's stud. Just one more thing to tell him nobody cared.

8

"CHOICES"

Almost a month had passed since his late night return from the Santa Fe trek. Tuck had muttered to himself, "Humiliated, by my own actions, running off from camp like a child. A man would have at least taken his horse, or a real man wouldn't have run off in the first place. Maybe stayed and fought?"

Anyway, there had been two snows since then and he reckoned it smart letting Beckwourth bring him back. The crisp clear days drifted by. At least now he had someone to talk to. Though mostly he just sat and listened to, 'Sir James' as Beckwourth playfully liked to be called.

Beckwourth said, "If you plan on going back with Walkara to Ute country, get as many horses as you can. In the Ute nation they are the measure of the man. The more you have the more you're looked up to. If that's the life you're looking for?"

And to show Beckwourth it wasn't, Tuck traded a good horse for a used two-man canvas army tent. It sagged under the snow load and he was constantly up at night tightening the ropes and tent pegs. The hole he cut in the top didn't always let out smoke from his fire quickly enough. But at least Nip could be inside with him and they both had a snug place to sleep and store his outfit.

Then without consulting anybody, the very next day he traded another horse for a handmade rawhide-oak pack saddle, a bag of lead shot, powder and a rusty battered, what the Spaniard he did business with had said, was a genuine Army model 1799 'Horse' pistol. At night by candlelight he cleaned and polished till it gleamed almost like new. Then he loaded it and kept it under his bed robes.

Time was drawing close. Tuck had to make a decision.

By early spring most of Walkara's horses were traded or sold and the now wealthy raiders were talking about riding north and home when the weather cleared. The successful Ute warriors now spoke only of returning to the Mountains of the West Central Rockies. The Wasatch and Bear River Mountain ranges, their forested canyons and beaver filled streams and rivers empting icy sweet waters into the endless horizon of the great inland sea. Home during celebrations they would be heroes being begged to tell of their great exploits of bravery and cunning.

But Tuck did not feel a part of it and he confided that to Beckwourth.

For reasons of his own, Beckwourth sometimes kept important news to himself. He'd heard certain rumors in Santa Fe. And there was no way for Walkara and his band to know, even as they spoke, several Mormon wagon trains were rolling down those beautiful pristine canyons and into the heart of Ute country. Only thing he said to Tuck, was, "I have a feeling Walkara's home is not ever going to be the same."

So to avoid thoughts of loneliness Tuck kept himself busy hunting and occupied listing to Beckwourth's never ending tales of history and the frontier.

That evening late in spring, Beckwourth pointing at the setting sun said dreamily, "The West. Now that's where a man can really be free."

Tuck wondered which West he was talking about but he didn't think he should ask, seeing he figured they were already west of most everything. Still he was drawn to the unknown possibilities.

Tuck's thoughts drew him from listening to asking questions. "Tell me all you can about the West."

From Tuck's point of view Beckwourth knew more than anyone. On sunny days Beckwourth sketched rough maps in moist sand alongside the stream explaining how thus far the western frontier had pushed mostly around the Central Rockies both north and south of Ute's tribal lands. Explorers, pioneers, hunters, trappers and men who look and take only what lay at their feet. "Just a few others like me who gaze at distant horizons and dream of wealth, even empires. You see not all men crave freedom and wealth, the elusive elixir of life." Beckwourth's face glowed hearing his own eloquent words. Having Tuck's ear was an added pleasure.

Using the rounded bottom of an old fire blackened clay olla pot as a globe to depict the earth, he said, "Look Tuck. See here how Europe's bulging cauldron of humanity boiled over across the Atlantic Ocean and spilled into the ample waiting fry pan of eastern America, then into the blaze of western expansion. An entrepreneurial menu of never before consumed sights, smells, free lands and of course its hapless indigenous peoples."

Tuck's head spun hearing those unfamiliar words about this new world of which he knew nothing.

Whenever he had a willing audience like Tuck, Beckwourth could always talk loud and long. Tuck got goose bumps seeing Beckwourth stand gazing east poised dramatically, hand over his heart as he spoke, "This America, unrestrained for almost three hundred years, of who's appetites millions are satisfying themselves from seeds they haven't sown, harvests wrenched from weaker hands and mouths of those with fewer, less penetrating teeth." He prophesied, "In less than fifty more years there will be nothing left but scraps and crumbs falling from the nation's table into the collared throats of these poor unfortunate and soon to be domesticated heathens."

The words tickled Tuck's ears. Fascinated with tales of the America, he eagerly absorbed each lesson.

"How in tarnation did you learn so much?" Tuck asked.

"In Virginia. Sir Jennings, my Father...sire, if you will, taught me the history and civilized ways of Colonial America and its white Europeans. And except for my father's carefree indulgence with too many Negro ladies and had he not consumed excessive bottled spirits, he was a man of vision.

"When he and I headed west one of his favorite sayings was, 'There is a divinity that shapes our ends, rough hew them how we will.' My boy, that is Shakespeare, I believe."

"And now that I have had the best of wilderness life as well and have grown to love the Indian way it grieves my spirit to envision cities like Norfolk or Washington sprouting on the banks of the Great Salt Lake. We, at least you, will someday certainly see all this land overrun with those who would tame and fence it for their own. Some say, it is divinely ordered. I doubt that. None-the-less, I am 'rough hewing' my remaining years. I will not be yoked by any man, directly or indirectly."

Tuck's head swam with the wonder of Beckwourth's words and images.

Other days Beckwourth traveled back and forth from Santa Fe a few times with stories of excitement and danger—enough danger to give Tuck considerable pause. According to Beckwourth, in cantinas during late night hours, it was not uncommon to see blood run free from the sudden flash of a knife's blade and outside in dusty dark streets the occasional burst of pistolas, thuds and screams as they find their mark.

He promised soon he would ride there with Tuck. He brought Tuck a trophy the last time he returned to the Ute camp—a small white embroidered kerchief.

And Tuck pressed it to his nose. Curiously it held a beguiling scent of summer wild flowers.

Raising his eyebrows Beckwourth watched the entranced expression on Tuck's face. Beckwourth laughed and teased, "Don't worry, there is an ample supply of beautiful young senoritas. And as far as hostile knives and guns, have no cares my friend, I will cover your backside." It was Festival and Fandango time in Santa Fe. Beckwourth pledged, "I avow we will have a night to remember."

One late afternoon when sunset's orange and gold shadows were long across the valley Tuck saw his Grandfather on his black stallion leading an exceptionally handsome white side-stepping horse out through the meadow's few remaining islands of snow and then disappear for several minutes into the cover of green cedars at the valley's far edge. Tuck watching anxiously caught glimpses of Army blue, rattle of gun metal, and the clatter of shod horses.

Soon Walkara returned astride his prancing black stallion, sitting erect an expression of humor and contempt etched across his dark hawk nosed face. A U.S. Army courier s pouch swung heavily from his shoulder.

As Walkara rode past Beckwourth, Tuck overheard him scoff, "Fifty silver dollars," Then snicker, "Stolen California horse, ha ha. No matter to General Kearney he wants only the best."

Daily columns of mounted troops both Mexican and American rode past their encampment. Tuck watched and wondered. Where did they come from and where were they going? He watched Walkara work his trade magic with both sides—selling fine horses impartially—and in doing so he wisely kept unsavory sentiment and hostile guns from being directed toward his people.

And most interesting, all those who passed were now echoing rumors, the United States just made a treaty with Mexico purchasing more than a million hectares of New Spain including Santa Fe and clear down to the Rio Grande all the way to Texas.

Walkara reviled the very idea of anyone buying Mother Earth especially the lands of his people. But with the weather clearing and all the 'California' horses sold he prepared to leave for the free lands of home.

Tuck sat alone watching the heavy spring runoff cut and reshape the stream's sandy banks. Winter's fallen leaves and twigs dislodged into small swirling eddies some caught the current swiftly moving south. Others trapped, around and around...going nowhere eventually sinking to rise again downstream, bobbing and spinning toward their next destination. He yearned for some spirit force to catch him up, spin him around and send him in one direction or another.

That day came. Lodges were pulled down and rolled onto travois. The Ute band busied itself with provisions enough to see them homeward. Spring Willow, the only woman in the group, scurried between piles of furs and canvas wrapped supplies.

It was not like Mother. Never had Tuck seen her giving instructions to men, and surprisingly shouting orders at them. Tuck wished she would at least glance in his direction. She didn't. At least he hadn't noticed. Nor did he recognize the anguish in her heart, silently hoping he could become one of them. Head bowed he rose and turned toward his tent. Sagging and smoke stained it stood where it was first erected.

Close by his side walked Nip, now almost thigh-high. He never left Tuck's side. Tuck, always sharing in his kill, he grew round and full with a heavy winter coat of shimmering silver fur. His now wide set, slanted golden-yellow eyes never let Tuck out of his sight. Puppy teeth were replaced with inch long fangs that could snap the neck of a rabbit in one jerking twist. Others, including Beckwourth, had learned to give him a wide birth.

In the midst of all the confusion of the camp packing and until Beckwourth rode up and began talking to him Tuck felt almost invisible.

"Are you packing up too?" asked Beckwourth.

"Can't we start into Santa Fe right now before the fiesta is over?" Tuck blurted.

Beckwourth wouldn't answer until their eyes met. He searched Tuck's face and with measured words, he said, "Certainly...we can. If, you're so inclined."

Tuck looked down and cleared his throat, "I'm...so inclined." He said, "I'm ready, but first I've got to get my horses." He turned and jogged down to the stream wadded across and soon returned leading Desert Wind, the blood bay and the three others. "Can we sell these three in Santa Fe? I'd rather have money." Beckwourth dismounted and walked around the three appraising them.

"You have a good eye for horseflesh. Their conformation is excellent. Twenty dollars, each...easy."

"Good," and Tuck ducked into his tent and returned with the

packsaddle. A soft sheepskin smoothed out across the bay's back first and then he swung the packsaddle into place. The blood bay didn't flinch.

Beckwourth expected the mare to shy and when she didn't he commented, "You've been working with her I see."

"Yep," was all he replied. Within minutes everything Tuck owned was balanced and cinched tightly to her back. The heavy 'Horse' pistol was snug in his waistband. In his beaded buckskin sling the Hawken was conspicuous across his back. Pouches of shot and gunpowder hung from side straps.

Watching Tuck work deliberately and swiftly Beckwourth realized he'd been thinking about this for some time. He thought, it looks like he means business.

Tuck said, "He don't like it none," as he slid a rawhide collar over Nip's head. "But I don't want nobody thinking he's wild."

Wild? Beckwourth thought, Mister Lobo is a lot more wild than tame.

Tuck bounded to Desert Wind's back. "Let's go."

"Whoa, there, Tuck."

Tuck reined up. "What?" he snapped.

Beckwourth thumbed in the direction where Spring Willow busied herself for the journey. "She's the only Mother you'll ever have."

"So?"

Beckwourth jerked his body erect shaking a finger in Tuck's face, "*So?* What I wouldn't give to see *my* mother one more time. Least you can do is bid your mother farewell."

"She don't care none," he smirked halfheartedly, "Let's go."

"By God you're a cold one Tuck." He rode close enough to take Desert Wind's reins in hand, yanking her head toward Spring Willow, he ordered, "Now get yourself yonder. You're her only youngin. Don't confuse her duties and feelings for her people as not caring for you. She cares enough to let you make your own choices. That's the way it is. Haven't you learned that yet? None of them are going to try and change your mind."

Tuck set silently for a few moments, sighed and handed the bay's lead rope to Beckwourth. He turned his mare and rode toward his mother.

Bending forward over her tasks, her back toward him, she heard him approach. Her long graying hair hung down concealing her face.

"Mother?" he waited a moment. She stood erect but did not turn around. "Mother..." he paused, "I am going to try and make my own way."

She nodded, turned and reached inside her blouse taking out a pair of fully beaded moccasins. Slowly she walked to his side and handed them up to him. In her native tongue she spoke, "Timpanogos village on the Spanish Fork River will be our home. You are always welcome."

"I will come and see you...Mother—" His voice broke.

Her head bowed, she nodded again.

Tuck couldn't see Walkara and Peg Leg Smith sitting on their mounts back in the trees watching. Peg Leg's hand rested on Walkara's slumped shoulders.

10

"CALABOZO"

Dusk, and up the arroyo the three of them sat talking next to their small campfire. Tuck eyed the folded saddle blanket next to the flickering firelight with its stacks of glittering gold Eagles, newly minted U.S. ten dollar gold coins.

A white and indigo Navajo blanket from Beckwourth's pack covered Christina's shoulders and breasts—her nakedness hidden—with a damp bandana Beckwourth's wiped her face free of dust and sand. Tuck couldn't decide which to look at.

To Tuck, sitting opposite, Christina's creamy smooth skin had exposed itself like the soft underside of a doe's belly. Her eyes round and dark, the eyes of a yearling fawn. He knew the word beautiful but he'd never seen anything so...she was even more than that. When he did have the courage to look, what he glimpsed was too overwhelming to look at directly. If he held his gaze he feared she might look back into his eyes and see every wrong thing about him. Maybe even things he didn't yet know about himself. He kept his eyes down staring toward the fire, his hand unconsciously stroked Nip's fur.

"So you didn't know you had over a thousand dollars in gold coin?" Beckwourth asked.

She looked down, stammering, "When I...when, aaah...I aparted, removed it...out from under the Governor's bed, there was not time to count it. And lucky for you we did not have time to practice shooting the rifles we...aaah...aprioritized from the Norte Americanos soldiers. They were on their way to search mi casa. We packed in haste and fled mui pronto."

"Appears like Tuck and I should be grateful for that," he chuckled. "So when you shot at us were you just aiming at the trail?"

"No." She answered sheepishly, "We wanted fine swift horses. There were Ute Indians in the big valley north of here selling good horses. We needed at least three more to speed us to Mexico. Then when you came along...why not?" She shrugged and gave an embarrassed little smile, "We decided...why spend any gold? Lead is much cheaper. No Senor, we aimed to kill you."

Sorrowful eyed she look first at Beckwourth and then Tuck. Tilting back her head, satiny hair cascading over her shoulders, she stared up into the darkening sky. Then in a childlike voice, "But it was not meant to be. I guess we were poor revolutionarios and worse shooters."

Tuck watched and listened. From her moist lips, Christina's voice...to him, sounded like the delicate song of mountain quail. Moonie-eyed, Tuck and Beckwourth glanced at each other both obviously enamored. Tuck fed the fire. It was quiet for a while.

"I'll untie your feet, if you behave yourself," said Beckwourth.

She said, "Oh Senor James, where would I go? What could I do? I'm just a young senorita now with no one to help. And everyone in Santa Fe, those cowardly Nuevo Mexicanos, and that old cavrone Governor and the powerful gringo army will be looking for us—" her voice broke, "That is... just me...now."

Beckwourth cut the rawhide restraints off her ankles and loosened her wrists. "Doubt if they will find us up this little draw. We'll keep our fire low," he said.

Though both hands were still tied she reached up and tenderly touched the scratch on his cheek. "Oh Senor, you are so kind and—" she didn't finish, just batted her eyes and smiled sweetly.

Fumbling for words Beckwourth said, "Yes Mam," glanced meekly at Tuck, "ummm...aaah," searching for something right to say, "Now that we buried your brother and your friend, the vultures won't—" in midsentence he cleared his throat and stopped abruptly. "Excuse me Senorita, for being so thoughtless." His voice trailed off grimacing at his own crude remarks.

Even Tuck frowned. He'd never seen Beckwourth so befuddled. But Christina didn't appear to notice and just kept babbling in her sweet childlike voice.

She explained the failed plan. "They expect us to run south...to Mexico." She lowered her chin to her chest. All her tears spent, she spoke mournfully, "Our Plans were to join the Revolucion. The gold was to buy an army and win back Nuevo Espanna from greedy Americanos. But that is now a dream as dead as my Companeros."

She shook her head from side to side, "A 'Land Treaty', only 15,000,000, in silver and gold." She looked up her eyes filled with contempt, "Those estupido Spaniards sold our homeland," she raised her bound hands north, "from the great Shinning Mountains," then pointed south, "and it is said, one thousand miles clear to the lower Rio Grande...Santa Fee, too"

"That's quite a parcel of country but mui mucho dinarro grande, si?" said Beckwourth.

"Dinarro si, but how can you sell your homeland? Can you sell your own Madre?"

Beckwourth raised his eyebrows and cocked his head with a little shrug. "Some do," he muttered.

She pouted her eyes reflecting the fire's blaze, saying, "And that nasty old Governor, he and every politico from here to Mexico City each got a sack full of that sucio, foul, 'Treaty' gold. "That," nodding toward the coins she raised her finger tips to her lips tittering, "That was the old lecher's cut. He promised me." Her eyes pleading, she said, "Senior James, please do not give the gold back to that pinchi porko."

That night, with a leash of doeskin, Beckwourth tied her ankle to his. Nobody slept much and Tuck was the one who had to tend the fire.

In the dark, Tuck lay with arms folded behind his head gazing at the heavens. The moon seemed to hang in the same place for hours. His thoughts were mostly of Christina. She was much smaller them him and not more than five years older, if that. But she seemed so much more...well, more of everything he ever thought a girl...woman could be. Now everything around him seemed to take on new dimensions. Even their campfire danced magically within its glowing embers and wispy swirls

He tried to sleep but it was no use and finally dawn's marbled sky began to glow in the east. He smiled, in the west, the moon was setting like a sleepy cat's eye in-between two ominous flat black clouds that blanketed the western horizon. One cloud changed into a puma's head—its open mouth swallowing night's fading silver saucer.

Unlike Spring Willow, he wasn't much for omens or signs but the image gave him goose bumps from head to toe. Before meeting Christina he thought he knew just about everything. Maybe he didn't? Just a few feet apart he turned his head toward Christina. Was she was looking right into his face? It seemed so. Slowly he closed his eyes, hoping she couldn't tell his eyes had been open.

A warm, but uncomfortable glow stayed with him. Between his legs his buckskins felt tight, blankets too heavy and too warm. Turning his head toward Nip, and dang if he wasn't staring at him too. But it was only Nip who nuzzled him and licked his face. "Ugh," he threw back his blankets, sat up and straightened his clothes making sure he didn't look at Christina. Sliding his Hawken onto his back he checked for enough shot and powder. Picking up Desert Wind's bridle he muttered, "Need fresh meat," and walked gingerly out of camp.

They now had eight horses total. With hobbles enough for only five they left the stud Concho with Christina's pinto mare and Desert Wind free to roam. Concho would not let the mares stray. Concho snorted at Tuck as he approached Desert Wind, shaking his head and mane, pawing as if demanding permission for Tuck to touch her. One warning snarl from Nip and he went back to grazing.

Tuck's usually gentle touch was missing as he jammed the cold iron bit hard into her mouth. Desert Wind jerked back her head.

"Whoa, damn it!" He leaped, flinging his left leg over her back locking his thighs tightly, heeled his moccasins into her ribs and started galloping up through the pines. Slopes of the San Juan Mountains began to rise steeply and soon angled up sharply. Disregarding Desert Wind's need to warm-up, he spurred her on; her breath came in short grunting gasps as she dug her forelegs into the steep mountainside. Within the hour they reached the snow line high above Santa Fe.

Miles later, his emotions spent, he finally eased her to a stop, sliding off and landing heavily on his feet, legs trembling in ankle deep crusty snow.

Desert Wind stood gasping and her sides heaving, head down, neck and flanks covered in frothy sweat. She staggered a few steps and coughed once—drops of crimson expelled from her nose splattering on the virgin snow.

He leaped to her side. "Oh girl!" he exclaimed, "I done caused you to flounder." And there was nothing much he could do but hot-walk her slowly in the snow, his arms around her neck, whispering constantly in her ear. Finally she stopped coughing blood, cooled down and fortunately her breathing returned to normal.

Relieved, he collapsed in the snow on his behind, his head hanging between his legs. Nip nuzzled his way onto his lap, tail flagging and whining he licked his face. Desert Wind's reins in one hand he threw his free arm around Nip, not knowing why, he began to weep.

Beckwourth's words, spoken the first time they talked, rang in his ears, "Nothing's worse than a man feeling sorry for himself."

Was that what he was doing? Maybe so, but hell he couldn't even unscramble any of the goings on between his ears. And what he felt between his thighs was most nearly driving him loco. He pushed Nip off his lap, dropped the reins and flopped on his back into the snow.

Hand stuffed into his pants. Eyes closed, his mind filled with images of Christina his groin ached with passion. He tried to resist the need for physical satisfaction for a moment. He couldn't and eventually he moaned, "Oh, oh, oh, Christina." His whole body feverish he lay there panting on the snow.

Below, the morning's sun-shadows slid across Santa Fe soon bathing the bustling pueblo in bright daylight. Tuck rose to his elbows. He gazed trance-like at the scene below. Rolling over and laying his forehead on the cold snow he grabbed a handful and rubbed it behind his neck and around his face. "Whew," muscles flexed, toes dug into the snow he pushed up from the snow, jerked his knees under him and sprung to his feet. He stroked Desert Wind's nose, "Got to walk you back girl. No hunting today. You are more important."

They zigzagged their way slowly back down toward the camp far below. A good three hours later he neared where he figured their camp should be. *Gunshots rang out*! Reverberating sound waves pulsed up through the pines. He froze, motionless. All senses alert.

Through the trees sounds of mixed voices shouted angry commands in Spanish and English. Christina screamed. He began running downhill in great leaping strides. He knew right where their camp was, but where was it? "Oh no!" he wailed. "I plumb come down *too* far north." Over the next crest more sounds—many horses moving—came on the crisp mountain air. Tuck, moving fast, still took several minutes before the startling sight below came into view. He jammed his feet to a sudden halt concealing himself in dense brush. He crouched low...watching.

Two columns of solders, eight in each, rode in tight formation. One column Mexican the other U.S. Army, rode away down the arroyo. In front they herded all five of the captured horses. Beckwourth and Christina, their hands bound behind their backs, rode wedged in-between the two columns. In camp, their fire still blazed high, all their supplies were torn open and scattered. He leveled the Hawken at the departing company but knew it would be foolhardy to try.

He wanted to kick himself for not taking his Horse pistol with him that morning. Their camp now vacated he returned quickly and searched through the scattered packs—the *gold* wasn't there either. The soldiers had all the horses and the guns. What he did find though was his quiver still full of arrows and his old orange wood bow. They hadn't bothered to take them and now that he was down to only one gun they might come in handy. With the wind gusted strong up the arroyo and before leaving to follow, he kicked sand on the blazing campfire.

On the way to Santa Fe, Beckwourth, in his best form, told the solders what happened. Well, not everything. He told of the attempt to steal the horses. Not mentioning Tuck at all. And saying Christina was his only companion when the two horse thieves met their deserved end. Explaining neither he nor Christina knew anything of stolen gold.

Tuck trailed at a considerable distance. This was not the way he expected to enter Santa Fe.

It appeared none of the solders believed Beckwourth. Christina kept her mouth shut. Some of them knew her. The territory jail was still under Mexican control. The Comandante listened to their story and then threw the both of them into a small single, one room adobe building. "Calaboso mue pronto, manana you both will be shot." He smiled as he slammed the heavy door.

"Hold on there, Comandant, the feller is American," said the U.S. Army Sergeant.

"And tomorrow what will he be? Manana, I will show you Mexicano justice." The comandant laughed.

The solders unsaddled their mounts and led the horses into a cedar-post corral, then piled their loot next to the windowless one room 'calaboso'. The Mexican soldiers looking at Concho's fine saddle began arguing among themselves who deserved it most.

"Silencio!" yelled the comandante, "venga aqui...vamanos!" They followed him quietly toward the governor's court house, leaving two soldiers, one a Mexican with a thick black mustacio and one lanky tall American, standing guard at the jail's oak door. And each carrying one of Beckwourth's newly acquired U.S. 1795 flintlocks.

Staying back a hundred yards, up to that point Tuck hadn't heard a word they said, but he did see his friends getting thrown in the Calaboso. Lying flat on Desert Wind's back he rode as close as he could without them seeing him, hoping to overhear their conversation. Tuck heard nothing.

What could he do? Of course he was just hoping and guessing. Seemed only reasonable, if the Mexican soldiers brought back the gold the U.S. Army's rifles, Tuck's horses and their belongings, why didn't they just call it even and let Beckwourth go? He didn't have anything to do with stealing none of it. Then maybe they could trade all the other horses for Christina and the three of them could go off to California or someplace mighty nice like that.

Tying Desert Wind to a nearby juniper, he crawled on his belly as close as he dared. Nip right by his side mimicked his movements. For what seemed hours he lay there listening...the two guards wouldn't speak to each other. A third soldier, a short, smiling Mexican, moseyed up and handed the other an open, two liter bottle.

"Bueno." The mustached guard took a long swig, started to hand it back when the other nodded toward the U.S. soldier. The Mexican guard grinned and offered the bottle to the Americano. The three of them sat there guzzling Tequila until the bottle, except for the worm, gleamed empty. Their talk grew louder and gestures more vulgar.

The chubby Mexican, who brought the bottle, raised his arms as though aiming his rifle, twisted up his face, closed one eye "Ka-pow, ka-pow!" he blurted. All three of them roared with laughter. The American rose staggering to his feet, made a circling motion around his neck, stood on his tiptoes and lolled out his tongue, gagging. The three of them slapped their thighs and hooted and hollered.

"Manana, manana," they taunted, while pounding on the jail door. It was then Tuck understood.

'Tomorrow!' Tuck had only tonight to figure out what to do. There were three of them. The Hawken only fired one shot at a time and when it went off the whole compound would know it. He had to do try something... but what?

Just before dark the rotund Mexican guard stumbled to his feet weaving his way toward the larger adobe building south of the jail.

Now the odds were better. In the distance as the skies darkened, warbling concertinas, wailing fiddles and strumming guitars filled the clear night air. It wasn't long before sounds of laughter, shouting and stomping accompanied the rollicking music that helped conceal his movements.

"Some fandango we're having, huh Nip," he whispered.

Then from outside the jail door the single Mexican guard said "Adios mi amigo," struggling to his feet he staggered in the direction of the fandango.

"Don't ferget to come back and spell me...me-meigo," the American slurred after him.

The odds were getting better all the time.

11

"UTE COUNTRY"

In a gliding swoop overhead a hoot-owl lamented mournfully. That could mean bad medicine? But, for whom? Bad medicine or not, it was now or never. Whites of Desert Wind's eyes rolled as she watched Tuck and Nip crawl back to her side. "Easy girl," he whispered. Hands damp and trembling he untied his quiver and bow. Not since he joined up with Walkara's raiders had he hunted with anything except his Hawken. Had he lost his touch?

The U.S. soldier, his head hanging, sat slumped back against the jail door. Tuck approached with Nip at his side, his moccasins barely whispering. He kept the jail's north wall between himself and the soldier. There was no way to tell if the guard was passed out or sleeping, hopefully both.

At the adobe's corner he paused, his heart thumping in his chest. Slipping an arrow into position he forced himself to relax. Taking a deep breath he and Nip stepped silently around the jail's corner. The next thing that met the woozy soldier startled gaze was the snarling, Nip. Lips curled back, yellow eyes glaring. Squealing like a wiener pig the guard threw his hands over his face and tried to stand. The stench of his own urine filled the air. Nip lunged. The fear-paralyzed soldier lurched backward slamming the back of his head into the massive brass lock on the jail door. He fell in a heap without uttering a word.

Tuck stood there for an instant his arrow at the ready. It wasn't necessary. Leaping to the door he called, "Beckwourth, it's me. I'll have you out of there in a jiffy."

Tuck tugged at the lock. Where was the key? Rolling the unconscious soldier onto his back he searched his uniform...nothing. He scoured the ground nearby...nothing. The sound of loud music and boisterous jollifying became annoying drumming in his ears. The guard began to moan and stir. Tuck quickly yanked the man's jacket over his head and clubbed him with his own gun. Taking no further chances, using strips of rawhide, he tied the man's hands behind him and the jacket tightly around his head.

A scattering of gravel from Nip's paws hit Tuck's legs as he unexpectedly charged off into the darkness. One brief cry, "Iiee-mmmfff." Tuck turned just in time to see Nip clamp his fangs around an approaching man's gaping mouth. The Mexican guard, the one with the large black mustache reared back his jaws spurting blood, Nip's teeth holding fast, the man collapsed in a struggling, kicking, but muted heap. Tuck leaped to Nip's side and with a sharp rifle blow to the guard's head quickly dispatched him into unconsciousness. A single heavy iron key hung on a brass ring from his waistband. In seconds Tuck had the jail door open wide. From inside the pitch-black jail Christina emerged first her eyes filled with fear.

Right behind her Beckwourth chided, "What took you so long?"

Moments later, Tuck and Beckwourth, heads together, whispered briefly. Quickly they saddled their three horses and loaded the bays pack saddle.

"All of them? You're sure?" whispered Tuck.

"But of course," answered the smiling Beckwourth.

"Won't twenty horses make too much noise?" said Tuck.

"Those loud Mexicans are have too much of a good time," replied Beckwourth.

"Pronto, pronto, mui pronto," Christina hissed.

POW! A single shot exploded from over by the fandango.

Christina squealed, "Dear Blessed Mary."

"Just celebrating," Tuck whispered.

Then quietly as possible the three of them, under cover of the boisterous fiesta time fandango, herded all the other twenty-some horses out of the compound heading northwest, the way they agreed. The same way they'd come before. Tuck wondered why Beckwourth had insisted that route? Once clear of town they urged the horses into an easy lope. An hour later Beckwourth reined up at the mouth of their arroyo.

Staring at Beckwourth, Tuck exclaimed, "Why in the heck are you stopping? We sure as hell can't stay here!"

"Hold your horses, youngster," Beckwourth smiled, "Wait here. I'll be right back." And he spurred Concho up into the shadows.

Tuck was still tongue-tied when it came to speaking to Christina. So they waited in silence while Nip kept the other horses milling in circles.

Long minutes pasted—Beckwourth returned. In hand, lifting a familiar looking but soot covered, partly burned leather bag. "Bonanza, the gold coins! Whew still hot," he chuckled, juggling the bag back and forth between his hands.

"Still hot?" said Tuck

"Well, it was like this. I'd heard the soldiers coming. Before they saw us I had just enough time to dip the bag of gold in the water bucket and then chuck it into the fire-pit. I heaped branches on it like nothing was wrong. They rode up shooting in the air, shouting and giving us orders."

Tuck said, "Dang, all the while I cussed you for making such a big smoky campfire. Figured that's how they discovered our camp." They both laughed.

Beckwourth said, "No time now to fetch what little is left of our outfit. We have the important things—guns, horses, tack and our, Bonanza," he said again, patting the bag and slipping it carefully into his saddlebags. "Anyway, from now on we can *buy* whatever we need."

Christina looked worried and kept glancing back toward Santa Fe. She cried, "Sir James, they will easily follow our caballo's hoof prints."

"Not until morning's light, Pequeno Nina. And if we get a move on by nightfall tomorrow we will catch up with Walkara. Mexican and U.S. soldiers know better than to follow after him into his own country."

They pushed the herd back into the easy distance-covering lope. Beckwourth's promise, '...a night in Santa Fe to remember,' and it surely was. Tuck grinned realizing that in two days they rustled almost twenty more horses and now owned a thousand dollars in gold coins. Not to mention I struck four coups. Not bad considering. Maybe Walkara isn't the only one that's so grand. Another thought pleased him, and maybe Ouray won't be thinking he's such a dandy. Alone he galloped to the front of the herd. Erect and proud he rode whistling and thinking of those times he ate dust when being ordered to ride drag. Just before dawn he located the 'Old Spanish Trail' and found Walkara's raiders two-day-old tracks. Before long their own tracks were hidden among the many. The eastern sky began to lighten.

Beckwourth thought, doesn't that lad beat all. He shook his head, amazed. A pretty little lady turns him topsy-turvy, but fighting and killing doesn't discomfit him at all.

After wading the Rio Grande to the far banks of the Rio Chamus they spent the rest of the day following the Old Spanish Trail. They pushed the herd and themselves to the point of exhaustion. No stops for food and only time enough for the horses to drink. Up through the scrub oak, juniper and pinion pine to the fir forested heights of the San Juan Mountains they moved. Finally they crested the Continental Divide.

Just ahead Tuck saw campfire smoke spiraling up through the tall pines and the aroma of roasting meat filled the evening air. Out of sight, off the trail Walkara and his raiders had made camp. Walkara was rarely surprised and one of his scouts had seen the trio and their horses coming and hour before. They began to prepare a feast. Spring willow waited, her heart filled with happiness.

As they entered the circle of lodges, "*Hola!*" Tuck cried loudly just to show he'd learned some Spanish. "*Hello,*" replied his mother and ran to his side.

Everyone crowded around to see the horses—especially the horses with U.S. brands. They touched and poked the brands, hooting and hollering. In the midst, astride Desert Wind, Tuck sat proudly his head held high.

Beckwourth and Christina pushed their mounts through the throng and rode to the campfire to greet the seated Walkara.

That evening after feasting on buffalo calf, everyone insisted Tuck and Beckwourth tell of their courage and boldness, stealing the army's horses, the killings and the gold. Such great coups! Hearing it once wasn't enough and they had to repeat the tale many times. Each time they told it more vividly until finally Tuck leaped up and went stomping around the campfire displaying their coups in pantomime to the delight of everyone. The campfire was heaped with wood, its radiant glow and sparkling embers reached into the star-studded sky. Throughout the night, triumphant howls of jubilation echoed through the mountains.

In the distance, on night winds through the tall pines ghostly sounds came. Nip's ears pointed in their direction hearing howls of his own kind answering.

Later, and only to Walkara, did Tuck tell how much gold they had.

Throughout the evening's festivities, Spring Willow, no longer the only woman, kept a watchful eye on Christina. Spring Willow saw fear in her young and beautiful eyes and sorrow when she lowered her head at the mention of the killings. In addition several of the wild looking Ute braves had their eyes on her. Tuck didn't miss any of the gawking. After all, the horses were his and Beckwourth's, and as far as Tuck was concerned so was Christina. Even though she would fetch a handsome price, maybe ten good horses, he just hadn't figured out exactly what to do with her. Anyway, he had horses, lots of horses. And to sell a pretty captive like Christina shouldn't be that hard. Why then was he angry at the rude stares and glances of other men toward Christina? Another thing bothered him—Ouray was not around to hear and see his honors. Tuck wasn't about to ask why.

The next day Ouray and three others rode into camp with fresh game and good news. The trail for the next fifty or so miles was passable. Stony faced he and Tuck greeted each other.

In many places the trail to their homelands was narrow and treacherous. Often moving single file and even then there was always the chance of a pack animal or for that matter anyone, slipping and tumbling to the bottom of some perilously deep canyon. However the hazards of this direct passage home were well worth the risks. And after swinging north to miss the perils of the almost impassable Colorado River Canyon there now remained only the Green River to cross before entering familiar territory. Tired but victorious, Walkara leading, they all arrived safely at their last camp before bidding fair well to each other.

That night, Walkara took the time to sit with Tuck. Spending more time than ever before, he explained, "Our Ute Nation is not like any other. Many of my men have family clans spread out in several locations. We are not so tribal as the buffalo hunting, plains tribes. They are always moving and making war. The Ute's way places much value on small family clans. Each family clan, except in times of horse raids and buffalo hunts, lives on its own hunting, gathering and farming."

"Some say that makes the Ute Nation weak. My son, you need to know my greatest desire is to bring all the Ute people into unity. I see many things are changing. Ute's, need to speak with one voice if we are to stand against the whites.

"Not far beyond Green River there is a fork and another trail turns toward California. It is a long journey riding hundreds of miles across the Great Basin—for years, me and many braves have stolen many fine horses—through Cajon Pass into Southern California and back again."

Tuck already knew most of what Walkara was saying. Still he listened carefully and with respect.

Walkara rose to leave. "Today we will camp where the trail divides. One turns left, the other right, north to where our ancestors have lived forever." He rose and walked away.

Since leaving Santa Fe, Christina never let Sir James out of her sight. Their relationship was obvious to all. Had it been with any other man, Tuck could not have accepted it and then he did only by keeping his distance. These were hard lessons and Tuck was not blind. He sensed something in the air. Then at the camp where the trail divided Beckwourth took Tuck aside and explained he and Christina were going on to California.

"My friend you are welcome to come along," Beckwourth said. "Months ago a trader told me great quantities of gold have been discovered."

Tuck briefly argued with him, "We already have enough gold," though his feelings were not about the gold. Beckwourth smiled and said, "No one ever has enough gold."

All that they could divide, they did. But their friendship and feelings for Christina could not be divided. Beckwourth insisted Tuck take half the horses and half the gold. Tuck countered, insisting stubbornly, Christina deserves at least a third. And so, avoiding eye contact, they shook hands and agreed. Tuck quickly turned away.

Watching him walk away, Beckwourth stood with hands outstretched, as if to add something more, but didn't.

Several days earlier Tuck had given Christina his blood-bay mare. Now Christine was in her saddle, the bay gnawing at the bit ready to go. Tuck climbed to the ridge overlooking their camp and watched them depart. Long after they disappeared into the forest, he remained, staring at the horizon.

Spring willow watched it all happen and pondered it in her heart. Though her feelings said, go comfort him, she knew the Ute way was best. "Heavy snows, like sorrows, make deep roots for strong trees and men." The next morning Spring Willow packed to go north, to the lands of her people. Tuck approached. "Mother, let me help you." And he lifted a heavy bundle from her.

Later the same day as they rode north he loped Desert Wind up beside her. "You were right about many things, Mother." He took his place by her side and behind Walkara.

Ouray accepted that for now, knowing his time would come.

Cool morning breezes at their backs—the sun touched warmly on their shoulders. Straight ahead north the hazy peaks of the awesome Unita Mountains shined in the noonday sun like silver gatekeepers. To Tuck's left the snowcapped Wasatch Range. Somewhere on their westerly side, on Spanish Fork River not far from Utah Lake was his new home.

12

"FRIENDS AND OTHERS"

"Mother, who are they?" Tuck asked. A small swarm of women, their faces beaming came scampering up from the village to greet them.

"His wives...it is to his honor to have many." Spring Willow whispered, "Look there," nodding. "The tall very old one following is Deer's Foot...she is your great grandmother."

He noticed, yes, she is tall just like me.

Crops of corn and squash surrounded the many lodges of the Timpanogo's Ute Village. Several horses grazed peacefully in meadows alongside the stream. Tuck wasn't sure what he expected, but this scene of peace and plenty wasn't it.

The wives, some of them younger than Spring Willow, came waving their arms and scurrying in their best doeskin dresses joyfully crying out his name, "Walkara, welcome...welcome...The Hawk returns!" rang through the village. Lodges emptied and grazing horses raised their heads whinnying. Everyone, men, women, children and dogs ran to greet their returning Chief.

Walkara motioned Tuck forward and handed him the reins of his stallion. He dismounted surrounded by twittering, giggling wives. New clothes were brought forward. Promptly the wives escorted him through the maze of well-wishers pushing and pulling him down to the stream and there in relative privacy, a rare smile on his face, he was bathed and preened.

"Is one of them your, Mother?" Tuck asked.

"My Mother died while I was taken captive, but that was long ago. Then Walkara had but one wife. Now," she sighed, "see for yourself."

"And your brothers and sisters?"

"None. I am his only child. Great Spirit does not answer his prayers for children."

"No others?"

"No, Mitakoye Tokehe," sounding impatient, "you are his only son... grandson." Her lips parted as if to continue, she gazed up into his face.

"What is it Mother?"

She placed a reassuring hand on his arm and then looked away putting her other to her mouth nervously. "Oh..." a tone of indifference, "He told me, he is away so often, some of his women have children, but they are not of his loins." She lowered her eyes, "We...that is...Utes allow for that...sometimes."

Tuck had never seen Spring Willow blush before. Otto told him some Mountain Men took more than one squaw, but this was something he'd never considered. He wondered if Beckwourth did? If Tuck had known the answer to that he might not have let Christina go so easily.

"So, you do have brothers and sisters?"

"*No!*" she snapped, "others might be of his lodge, but...I said, I am...I mean, you are his only man-child." She raised her head proudly, "Those words spoken from Walkara's own lips." Tuck knew Otto was his father, but he reckoned '*blood* kin' was what she was aiming at.

Lifting her hand, she touched Tuck's cheek, and frowned, searching his eyes. "Some here might not agree."

He thought for a moment."My light eyes—right?"

She nodded, yes.

"Beckwourth forewarned me. Him and me, both be Breeds, 'twixed n' between."

"It is so." She paused, "It will take time. The People will watch you closely. They will see you are indeed Walkara's blood."

Tuck watched the old silvered haired woman approach alone, her hair swinging left and right, up and down, apparently busy disputing something with herself. Despite age her posture was erect and her stride long and sure footed.

Tuck's watched her closely. His eyes scanned his own tall torso with its long legs hanging down past Desert Wind's sides. Otto was a big man, but short legged and barrel-chested. Spring Willow, though lean, came only up to his chest. Her face was more oval like Walkara's.

But this old weathered and skinny woman reminded him of his own long jawed, angular faced self. As she came toward them he noticed her walk was like the long legged elk he'd seen grazing in mountain meadows. Except for being a woman, her gate was almost identical to his.

She drew close, first stepping in-between Tuck and Spring Willow's horses. Before Tuck could tell her not to, surprisingly she spit on her hand and bent over and whispered something to Nip and then wiped her damp palm across Nip's snout. For the first time, Nip gave ground and moved to one side.

Deer's Foot pointed a long callused finger at Spring Willow and said, "Who was it took you away?" Her face suddenly twisted in tortured memories. Uttering a lamented wail she answered her own question, "Those Who Always Fight Us, killed my Tall Elk, took you and stole you away. Where have you been, Little Girl With Dancing Feet?"

Spring Willow had forgotten her childhood name. Tears brimmed her eyes, "Yes Grandmother...the Comanche. But I'm back now," she said softly.

Deer's Foot turned and faced Tuck, staring long and hard. Her eyes like small obsidian stones set in amber. She spoke, "You...bad boy...it is about time you came home, too."

Tuck and Spring Willow exchanged surprised glances.

"The lodge is waiting for you. Everything is there, like you left it. Let's go." Deer's Foot turned and trotted toward the large central lodge.

Nip started to follow her. "Hey," Tuck called. Nip hurried back to his side looking guilty.

Tuck's eyes followed this strange but fascinating ancient woman. Deer's Foot hustled right past the large central lodge and around behind it. There stood a well-worn, darkly smoke-stained, buffalo hide teepee, heavily decorated with painted symbols. Around the circular door-flap opening hung carved bone, fur, feather effigies, a Spirit Chaser and other totems. The flap itself was covered with deer hoof bell-rattles that, when opened, sounded like clattering stones tumbling in swift stream water. She shook the door flap four times, chanting something under her breath. Smoke puffed out from inside. She stooped and stepped in.

Popping her head back out, she said firmly, "Dancing Feet...Tall Elk, get in here."

Spring Willow whispered to Tuck, "Her son, Tall Elk was killed during a buffalo hunt." She motioned to Tuck to go in first. "Everywhere Spirit talks to her spirit. She is strong Medicine now."

"How do you know these things, Mother?"

"Walkara prepared me. I am to be her caregiver. She is very old and needs someone to help her but it must be done with much respect. Do as she says."

Inside through the haze he saw things piled almost shoulder high.

Medicine Bags and parcels of old leather and fur occupied most of the space. Hanging on the center smoke pole high above the small smoldering fire hung two bead-eye dolls. One wore a skirt, the other leggings. Their miniature buckskin clothes black from years of rising smoke. A narrow path only wide enough to get from the door to the fire and to her sleeping pallet was the only area not stacked high with dusty ancient looking things.

"Mother," Tuck whispered to Spring Willow, "there is no place even to sit. Where will we sleep?"

"We will not. Walkara wants you to lodge with him...for now. Only I will stay with her."

He began to protest, "But Nip and—"

"Make loud talk," Deer's Foot cackled, "Drums of summer and the eagle's cry live in my ears."

"Grandmother," Spring Willow shouted, "Tall Elk will—"

"Why are you shouting?" scolded Deer's Foot, "I can hear you." Slightly lowering her voice, patiently Spring Willow began again, "Grandmother..."

But the old lady seemed not to hear and stepped over close to Tuck squinting and poking at him as she looked him over from head to toe. Putting her hand on top of his head, "Tall Elk, you are too tall now. Go lodge with the other young men, but..." Her eyes twinkled, "you can leave the wolf pup with me. He talks to my spirit."

Tuck stood there with his mouth open. Spring Willow nudged him with her elbow and nodded toward the door.

He said, "C'mon Nip," turned and stepped quickly through the opening. As he walked away he could hear Spring Willow's voice searching for the right volume. He snorted and wagged his head thinking, that old women hears as good as a...his first thought was wolf but he didn't want to admit that. Nip by his side he marched off looking for his Grandfather. "Wherever I lodge it will be with Nip, and that is that," he muttered.

Walkara's bare feet soaked in the icy mountain stream with his back toward the approaching Tuck. On the grassy bank surrounding him his wives happily took turns combing his long salt and pepper hair. Eyes lifted, the women became silent noticing Tuck and Nip draw close.

He turned and seeing Tuck waved him to his side. "You have met Deer's Foot...my Mother?" a mischievous glint in his eyes.

"Yes, Grandfather." But he would not let his face portray anything.

"Your new home, how do you like it?"

"Grandfather, if this is to be my home where will I lodge?" Placing his hand on Nip's head.

Walkara was prepared with the correct answer. "My Son...I too listen to Great Spirit. Your Nip is not just a dog, but a brave and fearless companero. Without his help..." he paused and shrugged, "well you know what I am saying. There is much room in my lodge and," he waved his hand over his head in a sweeping circle, "and all I have is yours to share." The women looked at each other, put their hands to their mouths, nodding and whispering among themselves.

That being settled, Tuck's attitude made a turn for the better.

The next day Ouray left to be with his clan on Bear River. Peg Leg Smith headed for Fort Bridger located on the Black Fork of Green River there he hoped to find a few old mountain men to reminisce with about old time rendezvous and drink up some of his horse money. Tuck again assumed his role as hunter. During times of mountain solitude and silence his thoughts often drifted to Beckwourth and Christina's life in California. But he had reconciled his Breed status; this was his home and his people. He set about learning Ute ways and proving he was worthy to be called, the Son of Chief Walkara.

Walkara had suggested they all go visit the whites at Salt Lake. Though Tuck was curious about the white men he kept his distance from Mormon settlements springing up on the flat tillable lower areas. Let Walkara do the visiting and talking, he believed.

Though curious about white men's ways he kept his distance from the Mormon settlements springing up on the tillable lower areas. Often he sat astride Desert Wind hidden back in forest shadows watching men dressed in black with their women in long dresses and bonnets working side by side as they cut Mother Earth with the plow and divert her clear streams into muddy irrigation ditches.

He avoided their mounted hunting parties and almost daily he heard rifle shots approaching closer to his village. Wild game migration and their feeding patterns begin to change. Now and then in the distance, in the meadows where Walkara said he used to keep horses, he caught sight of small herds of fat cows grazing. White man's buffalo, the Utes called them.

Months passed and golden leaves now hung on the trees and the chill of winter was in the air. Tuck figured it wouldn't be long and some Ute will help himself to a Mormon cow. He understood their thinking. After all whites have plenty, so it seemed only right to help themselves seeing as our wild game is being scattered and harder to find.

Tuck listened as the Elders spoke of the problem but talk alone would change nothing. Eventually a few Mormon settlers, despite Brigham Young's policies of co-existence would resort to defending their livestock. Gunfire might be exchanged and perhaps escalated to open hostilities. "Indians who steal the occasional cow or sheep are few," Walkara complained to Tuck. And Tuck remembered when Beckwourth had said, "Manifest Destiny beliefs will ferment waiting for the right circumstances to justify hostile actions against the heathen savage." It seemed to Tuck, that time was near at hand.

"Walkara...Walkara," two young Ute brothers from a neighboring clan came shouting and galloping into the village. One of them slumped over his horse's back holding on for dear life, blood streaming from a gunshot wound in his shoulder.

Warning shots had been fired before but Walkara gave strict orders to the people of his village not to touch anything of the white man's. There were rumors other Indians had, but they were none of his own. Though once he did share a tasty beefsteak with his neighboring half-brother, Sowiette. But to his knowledge this was the first time someone, Indian or white, had actually been shot.

"War...this means War Path!" the people of his village chanted. Walkara took the two men into his lodge and let his wives doctor the wounded one. When the truth was known, both men had been caught stealing a cow. And not having guns of their own, they each loosed one arrow in the direction of approaching settlers and fled. A random rifle shot hit the younger man.

Walkara held 'Pow Wow' with clan's Elders, including Deer's Foot. It was agreed, Chief Walkara would ride back with the older brother and attempt to parley and make peace with the white farmers. The cow thief was reluctant—but Walkara's option, if he did not agree, was even less desirable. So taking food for two days, they set out to locate the settlers.

Arriving at the place of conflict neither cows nor settlers, were to be seen. Farther down in the valley, near the shores of Lake Utah, Walkara found their small settlement. It too was absent of life and it looked like those who had been there made a hasty retreat, livestock and all, north toward the large settlement near the Great Salt Lake. Walkara was undecided whether to pursue their mission, but not being one to quit, the two of them continued north.

Already the wagon trail was cut deep into the earth and they rode at a leisurely walk until the outline of large buildings began to show through the tall sage.

From inside the settlement noises of busy hammers and saws reached their ears. Walkara and his companion drew closer. Now from the settlement, silence...next the implications of unfavorable shouts and screams. But Walkara kept riding forward whipping the young man's horse to keep it moving and occasionally the young man too.

Then those unfriendly voices erupted as one and confused sounds unscrambled on the evening air, *"Injuns are coming!"*

"I believe they must be talking about us," grumbled Walkara.

The cow-thief trembled pleading with Walkara to let him run away.

Walkara said, "No we have nothing to fear. Captain Brigham Young and I spoke once before, he is a good man...a Holy Man." Well Brigham Young was no doubt better than most when it came to common sense and getting along with savages. But Walkara knew his savages could have—when Mormons first arrived in their land—easily run him and all his Saints back across the Rockies, had the Utes been at all unified.

Walkara also believed, like a coyote circling a baited sweet smelling trap, the Indian's own curiosity could get the best of him. Flashy trinkets, trade goods and things that went boom were mighty tempting.

On this particular day Brigham Young could be of little help seeing he was up visiting a new settlement several miles away on the north shore of the Great Salt Lake. And by the time the panicked settlers from Utah Lake, along with their cows, had reached the capitol swearing exaggerated tales about multitudes of warring heathens screaming down out of the Wasatch Mountains to scalp them all, nobody was of a mind to parley.

Walkara was no fool and when bullets started flying and dust puffing up all around he reckoned it might have been a little hasty just the two of them coming in alone. Finally one of the slugs, lobbed at them from a distance of about a half-mile, got lucky and stung Walkara's stud on its flank. Then there was hell to pay before Walkara, an excellent rider, got him under control but almost ended up in the dirt. While Walkara was yanking leather trying to get his stud's head up from between its front legs and keep its hind legs on the ground at the same time the cow stealing Indian was already a half-mile away—scared into near panic—bent low over his horses neck running flat-out heading south back toward home.

A hazy lemon sun was setting in the west casting long shadows. And with as much dignity as he could muster Walkara turned his still crow-hopping stud and followed his companion's rapidly receding dust cloud south.

There would be other times to parley.

13

"CROSSING THE LINE"

At sundown that same day a grand celebration took place in Salt Lake City. Considering what sort of celebration is allowed—under the guidance of 'The Word of Wisdom'—without alcohol, coffee, tea, smokes or chew. None of which could be seen flaunted, openly.

That evening when President Brigham Young drove his black, shag-top surrey back into town he was greeted by screeching fiddle music, loud singing and cheering in the street in front of the yet to be completed construction site of the new temple. Seemed every 'Saint', and some not so saintly had turned out.

Things quieted down a bit when the scowling Brigham was first spotted just down the road reining up in front of his house. Him feeling disrespected when none of his pretty young wives or his several children came running out to greet him. So, he made a whip-popping U turn in the middle of Temple Street's wide road and trotted into the midst of the frolicking revelers demanding to know what was going on. Then, in his bull like voice, he reminded everyone it was still 'Sabbath' and tomorrow there was a heap of work to be done.

"But, President Young, we whipped 'em! We run the whole passel of 'em back to where they come from!" A grinning towheaded young boy stepped up carrying an old flintlock longer than he was. "Was me that shot the Chief." A trickle of chew dribbled down the lad's peach-fuzz chin.

Unconsciously Young wiped his own chin then thrust up both hand for silence, demanding to know, "You shot, who?"

"Walker...Walker, Chief Walkara!" the lad and several of his pals cried.

"Oh Lord," Young gasped. "What in the name of our Prophet Joseph Smith did you shoot him for?"

The story started big and got bigger. Folks from Utah Lake swore there was a hostile band of at least a half a hundred painted warriors that swooped down on them hell bent on stealing all the women and children and maybe even a few cows.

"I thought we shot at least half of 'em back at Snake River Meadows," said, old brother Kimball.

Young's eldest wife stepped regally through the crowd, "Brigham," she stated firmly, "these brave Godly soldiers," she gestured toward a group of older, bearded sawdust flecked followers, "with nothing but meager hand tools, defended our sacred Zion."

The men cheered raising saw, hammer and axe, shaking them proudly. Brigham hollered, "Wait a minute...wait a minute now, sea gulls and grasshoppers I can believe, but whipping Chief Walkara's raiders with hand tools and children—"

"It was that fancy Chief Walkara...you can bet on it," one of the crowd shouted. "On that grand black stallion of his—"

"Yep, Chief El Gallivanting', it was," chimed Sister McGregor. "Rode right into town, proud as a peacock."

Another man from the crowd shouted sarcastically, "Mister President, he t'was riding the same piece of horse flesh you had your eye on when you invited the spyin' heathin' to visit us last fall."

Seemed there was nothing much more to say, so Brigham led them in a prayer for the heathen deceased and their lost souls. It was agreed that in the morning they would lay work aside and go count and bury the carcasses. None of course was found, either outside Salt Lake City or near the meadows.

"See, they done come like wolves in the night and dragged off their dead," Elder Bennett noted.

With so many positive witnesses it was generally agreed the number of dead certainly must have exceeded twenty and Elder Hancock duly recorded it in the archives.

A chill was in the air and it was getting on toward Barking Bird Moon before Walkara found out he'd been killed. He reasoned, his usually friendly Mormon brothers must be particular about Utes coming to town in the middle of one of their secret 'go-to-meetin' temple building ceremonies. After all, some of the Ute's own ceremonies were sacred and bad medicine too, if an uninvited stranger butted in.

Walkara reckoned they all ought to parley and set the record straight. This time he would ride into Salt Lake taking the best looking of his wives and Tuck and Spring Willow too. They could speak English. And like himself, Mormons seemed to take as much pride and pleasure in their many wives as he did his best horses and wives.

While he was at it he would bring some extra horses along. Maybe there was a trade in the making? Owning a white Mormon wife might be a big help?

The following morning there wasn't any end to the prettying up. Walkara was the last one ready. Single file they started to ride out of the village.

Out from between the aspen and into the middle of the trail, Deer's Foot stepped and threw up her arms shouting, "Stop!"

Right off Walkara knew he'd forgotten to check with her as he'd promised. The last time, when he came back from Salt Lake making excuses, she forbid him to go again unless she said it was Good Medicine. He'd forgotten...she hadn't.

"Yes Mother...I wondered where you were," he fibbed. "What can you tell me?"

For a minute her toothless mouth twitched without speaking. She then plopped down in the middle of the trail, took out her pipe and motioned Walkara to come sit by her side and smoke. He looked around—all eyes were on him. He shrugged and gave in to her wishes.

Forgetting to light the pipe she began to scold him, "Since you been a little boy you have a slippery tongue," she leaned forward as if to hug him then gave his ear a good yank. "You must walk your talk."

Right before Tuck's eyes his proud invincible grandfather, head bowed and child-like, appeared to shrink alongside the old woman. Everyone watched and waited.

"Spirit's timing is always right," said Deer's Foot. She sat erect with her legs crossed and palms resting on her thighs. Lifting her face to the sky she closed her eyes and took a deep breath looking as if to speak. Everyone held their breath.

Blinking she opened them again and whispered, "At first I believed I had nothing to say—only to scold you for not seeking my council but while I was back in the trees doing my business Spirit spoke to me. So here it is, maybe you can figure it out; Red spotted salamanders will rise from the salt. A dark north wind will blow them over the mountains. They fall from the sky. Our people eat them but they grow sick and die." She took a long drag on the cold pipe, nodded and said, "That's it." She rose and walked back to the trees. She stopped, holding one finger in the air, turned and added, "No more wives."

Walkara looked to the sky...nothing but tall white clouds. He would keep his eyes open for red spotted salamanders. Now how to ride into Salt Lake without stirring up a beehive?

A few settlers from Utah Lake had returned home, though now they all carried guns while farming. Walkara again gave orders to stay away and give them plenty of space.

But occasionally he would ride alone to the ridge above their farm in full view. His idea at first was to let them see him as friendly. But once they caught sight of him they dove in a dust kicking panic for the safety of barn or cabin.

Like prairie dogs, Walkara chuckled. From then on when he was bored he'd ride to the ridge and holler just to watch them scatter and try to hide. See they all know of me, he boasted to himself. It was sport and he fully expected the farmers to return the challenge. No matter what he would never let his people see him run and hide. The settlers never did show up at his village and he was a little disappointed. He reckoned, Mormons don't know how to enjoy fair fights.

So as far as going' to Salt Lake he figured it best to stay to the mountain trails. It would take a little longer but they could approach the town unseen from the east down the big canyon, camp one night and come into town in the morning. Tuck and Spring Willow would go in first. His friend Brigham would not be inhospitable to his only daughter and his grandson.

The mounted armed 'Temple' guards patrolling the mouth of Emigrant Canyon didn't quite see it that way. If Tuck, when he heard Nip growl, hadn't yelled in English, "Mother look out!" All of the five-man patrol was fixing to blow them both right out of the saddle. Seemed hearing Tuck's shout in English the Mormons didn't want to shoot anybody's mother and lowered their rifles.

The Patrol approached keeping their rifles at the ready. Tuck sat erect looking them right in the eye, saying, "Chief Walkara brings Captain Brigham fine horses and comes to make peace talk."

"You talk pretty good yourself young fella," the nearest rider quipped, "but it seems you are a liar. There ain't no more Chief Walker." They whispered amongst themselves. "Is there? Anyway, that's what folks tell." And they looked around nervously. "He is dead isn't he?" Tuck said, "My

Grandfather, Chief Walkara, is alive." Tuck turned and pointed back up the canyon. "This woman by my side is his only daughter and I am his only grandson. Walkara waits for us to return so we can all enter your town in peace."

The Patrol continued whispering amongst themselves but slid their rifle in to their saddle scabbards taking their aim off Tuck and his mother.

"Walkara waits," Tuck exaggerated, "with many, until Captain Young comes to parley." Tuck nodded at Spring Willow and then looking straight ahead and together they rode right through the Temple guards toward town.

Glancing back over their shoulders the Patrol fell in behind them, muttering, "Did ya see those eyes? He ain't all Injun, I can tell that. A breed is more like it. Female, looks pure squaw to me. Grandfather, he sez. My, arse." Almost in chorus, "President Young will know what to do." They hung back but kept a close eye on Tuck and Spring Willow.

From their canyon campsite Walkara could see dark rainsqualls building up over Salt Lake. For a few moments he saw, coming up over the Wasatch Mountains, a glowing red morning sunrise that lit slanted sheet of rain to a fiery crimson. Walkara watched the signs carefully. These were red drops but they were falling down not up. How could this be Deer's Foot's vision?

Just in case, as rapidly as he could, he and his wives mounted up and followed Tuck and Spring Willow's tracks. Quickly he located the shod hoof prints of the Patrol's five riders. None of the tracks were smeared and there was no blood. He smiled and thought, good there is no trouble. The signs read of a peaceful meeting.

Then clearly he saw the two unshod tracks heading toward town with the Patrol's five shod following. His plan had worked. Waving to his wives, his arm making a motion to be silent, he put his caravan into a brisk walk. Within minutes the Mormon riders came into view.

Walkara could see that Tuck and Spring Willow knew he followed. But the guards had no idea he was following them. His blood stirred for battle but the needs of his People to live at peace was great. And anyway the white Mormons owned many things he was curious about...including white women.

At the mouth of the canyon, the trees that once stood so thick you had to ride single file, were gone. All of them chopped down and Walkara and his women found no place of concealment. So he reined up and watched

Tuck, Spring Willow and the temple guards approach the town. Walkara could hardly believe his eyes. In the distance green fields seemed to stretch on forever and where once the Mormon's had only wagons, corrals, small shelters and cabins. In months buildings taller than any he'd seen in Santa Fe or even California blossomed from the sage brush glistening white in the morning sunlight. "Look at all that!" he exclaimed.

He concluded, Great Spirit must favor these Mormons. What else could it be? Brigham Young himself had said, God certainly loves us more.

It must be true. Then and there Walkara decided he wanted some of all that too. But he and the women would watch from what little cover they found back up the canyon.

Before the bright morning sun rose directly overhead here came Brigham Young riding out from town. Tuck came with him, riding alone by his side.

Walkara smiled. Wise, Captain Brigham, he keeps my daughter as hostage. I would do the same.

Once in town Tuck had tried his best to reassure Brigham that Walkara's intentions were peaceful but he felt he wasn't completely successful. And considering all the rumors of hostilities he understood Brigham's caution. Tuck hadn't been surprised at the doubtful whispers about him being Walkara's Grandson, or his fluent English and the color of his eyes. No one dared asked what they wanted to ask. Tuck expected not to be treated friendly but Brigham Young ushered he and Spring Willow right into his big house and introduced them to all his wives and many children.

The thing that amazed Tuck most was how almost instantly Brigham's wives began to fuss over Spring Willow. Everybody talked a mile a minute, touching, ooohing and aaawing about Spring Willow's beaded doeskin dress and all her quill, shell and silver adornments.

At first Spring Willow looked like a frightened fawn. But when she cautiously answered their questions in English their cries of joy turned her fear into a shy, guarded happiness. Soon she was reflecting their smiles.

Approaching the canyon Brigham fully expected to see a swarm of painted braves by Walkara's side. He rode into the clearing between the town and the canyon. It was time for Walkara to show himself.

What a surprise when Brigham saw only women on horseback—he knew then Tuck told him the truth. Perspiring, his tense hands and his frowning forehead relaxed. As if to a close friend, he waved and cried, "Hello." Walkara did likewise.

While they waited Walkara had rehearsed his wives so they might greet Brigham Young with a friendly, Hello Captain Brigham, but their, "Low Cap Ham," salutation, sounded like it needed a lot more practice. Side by side the two leaders sat astride their mounts and faced each other. Young smiling, reached out his right hand. In the Indian way both men grasped each other's forearm, leaned forward and patting each other's backs. Dismounting, the two of them walked up the canyon to a place of privacy.

Walkara was heard saying, "It is a good day to talk."

They were gone for a couple of hours. Tuck grew fidgety sitting there with all those women. Back at what Brigham laughingly called the Beehive House, Spring Willow, happy as a lark was forming a new opinion about white folks.

After the parley was over Brigham headed for town. The odd thing was, before he left he patted Walkara's black stallion and Tuck could have sworn he heard Brigham say, "I'll take good care of him Brother."

Now facing his band, and for the first time Tuck could remember, the usually confident Walkara looked stunned—like a man bested in a trade.

A nervous Mormon crowd waited at the edge of town for their President to return. Tuck waited for Walkara to speak to him.

"Tuck Mitakoye Koneke," Walkara wide eyed and breathless confessed, "I am now a Mormon...a Ladder Day Saint."

Tuck thought his Grandfather sounded more perplexed than pleased. With a great sigh Walkara sat down an began to speak. "Old plates...big angels...the Spirit man Jesus...my new," for an instant he fumbled for words, "all...my...wives, sealed to me forever."

Walkara went on and on talking about what President Young told him were Great Spirit's special promises to all Mormon children.

Then, like a man in a trance, Walkara got up and walked over to his stallion and began whispering—gesturing apologetically, to what had been his favorite horse.

14

"FAIR TRADE"

The small makeshift jail looked out of place behind the imposing Mormon Temple's construction site.

"Get her feet out of those stocks," Brigham ordered. "Then take her in my house get her prettied up and be quick about it."

The armed guard fumbled for the key. He replied obediently, "Yes Sir, Mister President."

Brigham kneeled next to the unkempt, raven haired, green-eyed girl sitting on the floor with both feet locked tight in hastily carpentered wood stocks. "Now listen carefully to me Missy Ann." Brigham's tone was fatherly but stern, "You shot and killed Bishop Anderson." He cupped her chin in his hands, putting his face close to hers, "I don't know if you're a Jezebel or not? And, while putting a lovely young lady like you in front of a firing squad, might make Bishop Anderson's wives satisfied, yet to do so would be a poor witness for all Latter Day Saints." Brigham Young realized they had been in this new Land of Zion for almost three years and had nary a serious problem until this one came along.

Brigham mused, Lord a mercy she is a beautiful young thing. I'd of taken her for my own, if...? He felt himself getting aroused. So to keep his mind focused, he continued talking, "Missy Ann we cannot have crime of any sort here in this blessed land, especially murder." Although he was still a bit heated up and wanting her for himself, he figured he'd found a way to get rid of the problem and gain a something too. He added, "Yes, retribution has its place. That I know. Maybe like you said, Bishop Anderson did have it coming."

The guard unlocked the stocks.

Missy Ann said, "That be the first honest thing ya spoke Brigham." She spit out, "He sure did have it comin."

"Just by, not marrying you? Come on now. He would have eventually."

Kicking her feet, she cried, "He promised-promised-promised! Then just because." She grinned. "Well Brigham you know." She patted her belly, "He gave me the boot and this—me in a family way. The no good lout."

Brigham addressed her sternly, wagging a finger, "Miss Kelly, ever since we left Nahvoo you've been sleeping with one married man after another. Being Irish and orphaned and sixteen is no excuse. I'm surprised the fair women of our ward haven't taken it upon themselves and run you off, a long before this."

Missy flipped her hair back and laughed, "You should talk Brigham. T'is just grand for one man to have many wives," she tittered, "and gallop a few on the side but heaven forbid it be the tuther way round."

"It's not a laughing matter young lady. I must do something with you—"

"What do ya have in mind...again, Mister President?" She smirked and pushed out her firm young breast toward him.

"Oh...Missy, you are impossible." He had to look away. "Look, I'm going to lay it on the line. You have two choices, the firing squad or leave town with some...well, a friend of mine. In fact, a Brother—a recent convert to our faith."

"A nasty old man, no doubt." Removing her feet from the stocks she hiked up her skirt if full view and swung her legs free and buttoned her gaping bodice right in front of Brigham. Taking Brigham's sweaty hand she got up and brushed off her black frock. "An where be he takin me?"

"Missy Ann, I'm glad you're willing to be reasonable."

"Hell, it's an easy choice," she threw back her head and laughed, "Either way, getting hitched to your friend or the firing squad, I'll be gettin plugged." She stood defiantly. "So what be the catch?"

"Oh, w-well," Brigham stammered, "next to me he's the most influential man in these parts. Yes he is older but he's a fine specimen of a man with several lovely wives."

"Say now Brigham Young why ain't ya lookin me right in the eyes when ya be telling me all this blarney? What's really goin' on?"

"Well, I guess you ought to know. His name is Walker. Least that's what most white people call him."

"White people?" she exclaimed, "I ain't seen no darkies since we left—"

"No darkie. He's thee biggest Ute Chief in the Rockies," Brigham blurted. "But the richest most respected Indian I know."

"To hell with you! I druther ya shoot me." Missy plopped back down and thrust her feet back into the stocks.

"Then you leave us no alternative?"

"Shee-it!" she lifted her head, eyes skyward considering her options.

Kicking free from the stocks she jumped to her feet. Stamping her foot again, she cried, "If only me old Paddy was here—"

"I'm sorry your brother died, Miss Kelly, but—"

"Ooooh...shee-it," she moaned, lowered her head and began to weep.

Prudently, Brigham placed his arm around her shoulders and said, "Walker promised me he'd treat you like a good Mormon wife. Look, maybe later he'll trade you or something?" Clearing his throat he added, "And he traded me the best horse in the whole United States." Immediately the look on his face said, I wish I hadn't said that.

"Trades horses and...?" she paused, hands on her hips and squished up her face, gazing into Brigham's blushing face, "I'm wise to your ways Brigham Young, ya son of a bitch, ya traded my arse for a harse, didn't ya? Brigham bowed his head, "Take it or leave it. Either way you're leaving town. You should be grateful." Then the wise Brigham said, "Then again maybe you're not women enough for a real Chief?"

Her green eyes narrowed and she clenched her jaws. Glaring at him for several seconds..."Best horses, eh?" Young knew Missy Ann loved horses, "Then by gad, maybe I'll be givin' your big Chief a ride he'll always remember."

So the deal was set. Brigham and Missy Ann agreed not to mention her being in a family way. Brigham could breathe easy now. A good trade, Walkara's fine black stallion for the beautiful little Irish wildcat, Missy Ann...and child. Although Walkara would not know anything of her being nearly three months along.

Brigham whispered to the waiting guard, "You didn't hear any of this understand?"

"You bet, Mister President."

"Now take her into my house and let my wives put on the finishing touches."

Head erect, eyes wet and glistening, Missy and the guard marched out of the jail down the boardwalk in full view of everybody, up the steps, through the etched glass and mahogany double doors and into the President's house.

Hearing of the trade, Brigham's wives were aghast at his solution, but knew better than to disagree openly. Brigham's wives knew, never would anyone in Utah admit what happened to the pretty little murderess and Brigham saw to it that her name was officially stricken from the genealogy of 'Saints'. After all, Brigham was not only President of the Church but also a

Living Prophet. And whatever he said was directly from the Almighty. And a trade was a trade...fair and square.

Later, after the trade and he'd gotten Walkara 'saved', Brigham brought the chief's entire entourage into town and to his very own doorstep. Brigham guided Walkara through the many rooms of his spacious house. Brigham said, "The Holy Bible says: "In my Father's house are many mansions." Walkara couldn't help but gawk. Finally the tour was over and it was time to present Missy Ann.

Brigham's wives had done a miraculous makeover on, Walkara's wife to be. Missy's face was scrubbed to a shine, her long black tresses brushed to a silky cape cascading over her shoulders. Her plain black frock was cleaned and ironed, white lace collar and cuffs added. In her arms a bouquet of white lilies. They presented her as one would a young debutante.

Walkara was more than pleased. As was, Tuck. Walkara mussed, a beautiful white women but with the wary eyes of a treed puma.

Spring Willow stepped to Missy's side and extended her hand, "Welcome to our family," she said in almost perfect English.

All the wild-eyed Missy Ann could do was blow her nose on the kerchief she'd been given by the wives and bob her head up and down in reply.

Brigham got out his big black Bible. Administering the wedding ceremony, but not going to any great lengths reciting long vows, just, I do's, he pronounced them, "husband and wife," and, "Sealed forever in eternity." Though during the entire ceremony, Missy Ann and Walkara stood across the parlor from each other.

There were no tears, no applause, no ring, hug or kiss. Slowly those present at the wedding, more like a wake, quietly traipsed upstairs or out of the house.

As the wedding party exited one of Brigham's older wives handed Spring Willow and Tuck two well-used carpetbags, whispering, "It's not much. Just some clothes and things for Missy Ann and Chief Walker."

Outside the front door waited Walkara's other wives and the black stallion. Walkara had removed the silver adorned bridle and saddle. Brigham was about to complain. Then thought it best to escort the wedding party to the edge of town rapidly as possible, avoiding any further delay.

This was not the time to do more trading, so Walkara kept the extra horses he brought. And without even glancing at his stallion he picked and saddled the best horse among the others for himself and Missy Ann. As was Ute custom he and his bewildered new bride rode double all the way back to their village.

To Walkara, Missy smelled like a mountain Spring meadow. To Missy, Walkara and his horse both smelled alike.

Lines of noisy geese streamed south in the moonlit sky as the bride and groom rode into the sleeping village. After turning all the horses to pasture they trudged silently into Walkara's lodge. Usually a Ute wedding meant celebration. And Walkara decided, tomorrow there would be a big Pow-Wow. He would send messengers to all the neighboring clans. In the manner of his people they would have a Sacred Ceremony. Tomorrow night, they would do things right. Only then would it be good with the Spirits.

Several times before when he took a new wife he had a big Pow Wow and everybody had a good time. Maybe this time, with the white Mormon woman, Great Spirit would give him a child?

The next morning in the early light of dawn, Missy Ann was nowhere to be seen.

15

"CARPETBAGS"

In minutes the village churned like a pissed on anthill. Nobody slowed down long enough to remember to look for Missy Ann's small, hard sole shoe prints. And when they finally finished running all over there weren't any tracks left. Not that there were many to begin with.

Sometime earlier, before dawn, Missy Ann, lying awake next to the sleeping Walkara, had sensed no guard was posted outside the lodge. She'd raised herself quietly, gathered up her clothes and slipped silently through the door flap. She quickly dressed outside, fearful a fierce brave might run her through with spear or arrow. Nip slept close by but just lifted his ears and gave no alarm. The coast was clear—all Missy Ann knew was the nearby stream headed back down to the valley. Somewhere, in that great expanse, there must be a farm or settlement, even a wagon train west. Find someone... anyone, not aware of her tarnished past.

Leave no tracks to follow, she'd reasoned. Tired and weak from jail, the long ride and no sleep, she managed to skip from rock to rock, grassy spot to grassy spot, toward the stream.

Deer's foot was stone deaf when she chose to be. Though there were times everybody swore she could hear quail tiptoeing through tall meadow grass. To her, night or day, the sun and moon moved when she decided. Sometimes in the darkness sounds of her songs and chants were heard drifting through the village. Often before dawn she was off to nearby mountains gleaning roots, berries and herbs. The tinkling clickety-clack of her deer bell covered door flap was the only telltale sound of her coming and going.

Missy Ann, now fully dressed and in spite of stock bruised ankles, stiff muscles, saddle sore and being three months pregnant, finally made it to the stream. Whispering, "Leave no tracks," her only thought. Legs trembling she rested for a moment pausing before she waded in. Bending down, her fingers touched the icy waters—cold as anyone could imagine, almost taking her breath away.

Some distance below the village in the cold stream wordless singing mingled with the stream's burbling chorus. By moonlight Deer's Foot bathed neck deep. Between the stream's grassy banks her reedy flute like voice seemed to rise from several directions.

To Missy Ann, Mormonism was fey daft. But now, and according to her upbringing—Fairies, Leprechauns and Sprites...they were something wonderful. An Emerald Isle's lass could believe in the likes of them. Missy Ann hoped she was hearing what her dear departed Mum told her was a, 'Boon, Water-Sprite'. Water Sprites always brought luck and *'Oh Lordy'* she needed a bunch—but would she, could she, be touched by Irish luck right now?

Touched she was. A sudden gust of wind pushed against her back. And luck she got. Perhaps, bad luck? Off balance, her foot slipped—barely time for a muted cry—the stream much deeper than she reckoned. In seconds only her thick black hair floated on the surface of the dark shadowy current.

In a minute or two Missy Ann was spinning, rotating and being swept downstream past Deer's Foot. Only her floating hair reflected in the moon's eerie radiance. Always watching, Deer's Foot's spied the strange sight—spontaneously her long fingers grabbed for it. Unconscious in heavy in wet clothing Missy Ann's limp form swung in an arch almost pulling Deer's Foot off her feet but she managed to hold tight and gradually tugged Missy Ann to the bank.

In the waning moonlight Missy Ann's white face glowed a ghostly pale. For a moment Deer's Foot stared wondering why this bone-white spirit child was dressed all in black? What manner of omen could this be? She put her ear to Missy Ann's chest and pushed. It gurgled like a deer-gut water bag. Good spirits are not supposed to drown—maybe this one is bad? But if you know how, truth is easy to see—this was just Water Spirit's trick. Deer's Foot scolded the unconscious the girl. "You think you want to join Water Spirit? *No*, you cannot. It is *not* your time." She put her face close to the girls mouth, listening. Thin blue lips hung open without sound or breath. No matter. Deer's Foot turned her over, slid the body around, and put Missy Ann's face and head pointing down the bank. Chuckling to herself, she straddled and rode slowly up and down in the middle of Missy Ann's back. Missy Ann coughed, retched, began to moan...and at last breathe.

Deer's Foot jumped to her feet. Not wearing a stitch, like a long legged, loping strip of jerky she trotted back to her teepee and woke Spring Willow. "Quickly, come see what Spirit brought me."

Side by side they hurried to the unconscious, but alive, Missy Ann. Deer's Foot dressed and together they carried her back to their teepee.

Spring Willow tried to explain who the girl was, but for reasons of her own, Deer's Foot chose to hear none of it. Piling several cedar and sage branches on the fire, Spring Willow removed Missy Ann's soaked clothing. But Deer's Foot was the first to notice the three-moon roundness of Missy Ann's white naked belly and the tautness of her pink tipped breasts. Neither said anything as they covered her with warm furs. No one need know about that, especially Walkara. She was still unconscious or asleep when those in Walkara's lodge had finally realized she was missing. Spring Willow had heard all the ruckus, and fearful Walkara might display reprisal toward the girl, she sat silently tending the fire watching Missy Ann and Deer's Foot sleep. It was almost daylight, what should she do? Remembering how often Otto beat her when she tried to run away, she trembled. Surely Walkara would not do such a thing seeing they promised Brigham and the Mormon wives to look after Missy Ann.

"Mother," Tuck stuck his head inside the flap. "The Mormon girl is—"

"Hush." Spring Willow put her finger to her lips and pointed to the mound of furs and whispered, "In here, she sleeps." She motioned Tuck to enter. "Is your Grandfather angry?"

"He is surprised and sad. Sad mostly about his horse but I do not think him very angry. Slaves are supposed to try and escape...though not new wives."

Missy Ann began to stir. She coughed and let out a low moan.

Tuck crept to her side just as she turned her face toward his. She opened her eyes and looked directly into Tuck's silver-blue eyes. She cried, "Oh, me Paddy...me Paddy ya come back, ya come—" and she began to retch again. Tuck pulled back. She clawed in his direction and in-between her gagging, cried, "Don't go...me only Bother...don't die." And she collapsed back onto the fur pallet. Spring Willow came close and took her hand. The hand was hot...much too hot. "She burns with the fever." Spring Willow turned with an uncertain fearful look and said, "Go tell your Grandfather." Tuck rose to do as bid.

"No, not yet." Deer's Foot got up and began rummaging through her medicine bags, singing, "Willow bark...where did I put you, Willow bark?"

Several small leather pouches hung on lodge poles. Each one painted or beaded differently. She had cared for her family and clan for over a half a century. To her doctoring was a deed of spirit. She knew each Medicine Spirit: powders, leaves, herbs and roots desired to become a part of a Ute life. All she needed to do was find the right combination of Good Medicine and she could sing them into the bad sickness.

A hundred times, maybe a thousand, she brought the Healing Path to sick ones. But these were Ute ways and maybe white eyes could not receive life from healing spirits? In all her years she never doctored a white person.

Walkara was busy forming a hunting party when Tuck and Spring Willow emerged from the teepee. Walkara mounted a horse he deemed inferior—his face like cast-iron—scowled at everyone.

"My Father," Spring Willow called.

"Not now. We go to bring back the," he sneered, "as Young promised, the good Mormon one."

Spring Willow with head bowed approached him. Her voice low intended only for Walkara's ears. "Father, your...new wife...she sleeps in Deer's Foot lodge."

She could see at this point he was angry and, at his best when that way, showing no emotion only glared accusingly at Spring Willow.

Hands clasped in front, head bowed and looking submissive as possible, Spring Willow said, "Father, the Mormon woman is sick with fever." Walkara grunted indifferently.

Making the circle crazy motion around the side of her head Spring Willow said, "Your new wife, she is not here in her mind." His face didn't flinch.

"Father," she pleaded, "at this moment Deer's Foot doctors her." Turning his eyes west toward the valley, Walkara sat motionless gritting his teeth. Finally he sighed, dismounted and turned to the other waiting riders, growling, "Put the horses away." Head held high his large moccasins stomped a dust cloud as he retreated back inside his own lodge. Immediately shouts thundered from inside and out tumbled all his other wives, scurrying, scattering and squawking like a gaggle of spooked geese. Directly the two carpetbags came flying out the door.

Spring Willow stood quietly watching the children come swooping and shouting and grabbing the bags, sprinting into the woods and laughing. It made her feel good to see happy people.

Onlookers cheered the children and laughed at the goings on. "They will make good horse stealers—maybe better than," they teased.

Spring Willow wouldn't show it, maybe for different reasons, but laughter also welled up inside her. Too many wives now, and still he wanted more. Corners of her mouth turned up. She shook her head and went back to help Deer's Foot.

"It is mine...no mine...give it to me." The children playfully fought over the contents of the carpetbags. Eventually the goods were divided, though the largest of the group naturally got the most.

They were not new clothes. In fact one of the bags contained only soiled bed clothes. In the other the older children found white men's clothing. Both boys and girls dressed up in the men's rolled up coats, pants and shirts and went parading through the village much to the amusement of the adults.

The smaller children, even some toddlers, simply wrapped the soiled hand stitched pillow cases, flannel sheets, towels and cleaning rags around themselves and marched along behind.

Hearing the laughter Walkara poked out his head and roared for silence. Giggling and screaming, the children scattered in all directions.

Same day, back in Salt Lake: One of Brigham's wives, "Oh my we sent the wrong bag." She looked in the bag on the floor filled with church ladies used clothes intended for Missy Ann. "Heavens, we gave them the bedding from the children's sickroom by mistake." Later they swore, "An accident...truly an innocent oversight."

Tuck watched the children scatter, heard his Grandfather's undignified roaring and those of the village laugh. Disgusted, he shrugged, what woman could be worth all this fuss? With his Hawken slung across his back, Nip by his side, he went looking for Desert Wind. A long ride in the high country, a good hunt, was needed.

Walkara's big wedding pow-wow was going to have to wait.

16

"CRYING FOR HER CHILDREN"

Spring Willow noticed red spots beginning to appear on Missy Ann's stomach and her fever burned for three more dark cloud covered days. After only a few more spots appeared, Missy Ann began to feel somewhat better. The fever seemed to respond to Deer's Foot's medicine and vomiting came only in the early morning.

Daily life in Walkara's lodge returned to near normal. For the next few days Walkara seemed compelled to tell everyone who would listen of his new God and Jesus his Son.

Everyday Deer's Foot burned sacred sage and prayed—she, watch and waited, asking for another vision. A long week passed. The north wind blasted through the mountains, temperatures dropped and lodge fires were built high. Quaking Aspen leaves turned golden-yellow and in the early mornings a frosty silver crispness lay on swiftly browning meadow grass. In the pastures horses grew heavy with thick blankets of dense hair. Everyone, including Deer's Foot, saw the signs and agreed it would be a long, deep snow winter. In a Dream Vision, Deer's Foot saw them once more—the red salamanders—no longer falling but slithering everywhere.

At the beginning of the week when Yellow-grass Moon was thin like a knife's cold edge the first of the Ute children stopped playing. Throughout the village at night there was no stillness. Children cried and their coughing was without end. By the end of that week every child in the village had fever and red spots and not just a few. The children were soon covered from ankles to scalps—puss filled, pimple like red spots, crusty and painful.

It happened so fast Deer's Foot had almost no time to prepare. She ran from lodge to lodge, doctoring and singing until her voice became raw and hoarse and there was no more medicine.

Death Spirit's voice came on the unrelenting north winds howling through the Timpanogo Village. Death first called the children, though they seemed to struggle long to survive. For the adults, men and women alike, within ten days fever convulsions broke off life like so many red leaves falling to earth from canyon oaks. In the new snow's first dusting, bodies also began to fall.

Toward the end of the second week Tuck thought about going to Salt Lake for help. Otto had told him of the white man's spotted plagues: Chicken Pox, measles and the dreaded small pox. But Tuck did not know which disease this was. Not that it mattered...there was nothing anyone in the village could do.

Tuck was saddling Desert Wind when he heard the clatter of shod hooves. No sentry was left to sound an alarm. Brigham Young and two other men came riding into the village undetected, as everyone in the village was either too sick or tending several who were. Many had already fled to neighboring villages to try and escape but only to spread the red spot sickness.

Brigham rode in, thoughtfully not on the black stallion, a broad smile on his face. "Greetings my red Laminite Brothers," he called out. Referring to Mormon belief, red men were a lost tribe of Israel. He'd eagerly expected a village full of likely new converts. Had the weather not been icy cold the stench of death would have told him why the village was almost empty.

Tuck rushed to his side. "The people are sick with the spotted fever. Many are already dead. Many are dying. Can you help?"

"Small Pox?" Elder Hamlin, one of the riders asked fearfully.

"More than likely measles, just like our children have been laid up with lately," answered Brigham.

"But plain old' measles, that ain't much of killer sickness," the other replied. Brigham was silent for a minute. Tuck and the two men waited for him to speak. He stared at Tuck. His eyes took on a fearful guilty look, "Oh my...seems I have heard tell these poor savages have no resistance to measles." He soulfully asked Tuck, "How are you feeling young man?"

"Me? I'm fine. I was poorly for a couple of days, but now, like Missy Ann, I'm feeling fit."

"Anybody here, not sick?" asked Brigham.

Tuck's eyes looked gaunt and empty. "My Mother is just coming down with a cough. My great grandmother seems to be holding up, as is Chief Walkara. And like I said, Missy Ann is fine, except for the heaves in the morning."

Determination in his voice, Brigham said, "I'm going to go look in on them. Which lodge?" Tuck-pointed and Brigham rode toward the central lodge. Muttering, "Oh dear God...there must be something I can do."

"Best stay out Mister President...ain't only measles ya might have to worry about." His companions yelled after him. If one thing Brigham Young had it was an honest compassion for the sick, physically and spiritually. He recognized his own hard driving businessman's mind and obligations as leader but he felt it was his responsibility, saying again and again, "I will shepherd this flock." To him that meant tending wounds of body as well the soul. And in that regard, few men were his equal.

After spending the morning appraising the situation he sent the other two men back to Salt Lake for help. It would be three days before they returned with a doctor, several volunteers and mules loaded with food and supplies.

Distressed, Brigham wondered if they had come the first day would it have made any difference.

When death became more familiar than life, Spring Willow died. Holding Tuck's hand, like she'd said farewell that day leaving the horse camp in Santa Fe, she smiled up at her only child. Her last breath gasping, "Tuck Mitakoye Tokehe." The other hand clasped tightly in Walkara's. Her last thought's...a vision of a many roomed house, high on Sacred Mountain.

Not counting those who fled, within a month only Tuck, Missy Ann, Deer's Foot and Chief Walkara remained alive in the village.

Deer's Foot, with Nip curled up at her side, sat by silently. This time none of her medicine brought life.

Deep snows began to fall silently and Walkara's whispered lamentations replaced the cries and death songs that once echoed through the canyons, filling the mountains, and covering the land of the Ute. In new white snow crimson fires now burned, not for warmth but to send the dead on their way. And, as Brigham Young mandated, "To consume lodges and belongings tainted by disease." In the span of a few weeks, from Bear River Mountains in the north, all along the Green River and south to the western rim of the Grand Canyon over two-thirds of all the Ute Nation was gone. Walkara often wished he could join them. Sadly, as it often is with those who look only to their God for reasons, Brigham Young's well-meaning reply to Walkara's question, Why did this happen? Was, "Because of your sin."

According to Young, if Walkara wanted God's curse from off his people he could steal no more horses nor capture any more slaves to own or to sell. Walkara and his people must accept 'the faith' and, although little remained, give ten percent of all the Ute owned to his brothers, the Latter Day Saints. What else could he do? Blinded by guilt and grief Walkara agreed.

A few who had fled the village early on eventually returned to the village. Missy Ann's boy baby was born on a clear sunny day in spring. She seemed reconciled to life among these people. Some things she found good. Deer's Foot's medicine and spirit-path fascinated and intrigued her no end.

Walkara was very proud of his Son, though the baby boy had black hair, his skin was as white as his mother's. From birth, Walkara saw something that appeared not right about the baby's measles weakened limped gray eyes. Because the daylight hurt the baby's tender eyes, he seemed happier during evening and morning shadows. Walkara called him Little Gray Owl. Secretly, Missy Ann called him Travis, after Paddy, her dead brother.

Had it not been for Missy Ann, her humor, outspoken ways and charming odd talk, Tuck in his grief might have left for California. Besides enjoying Missy Ann's company he liked being the go-between when she occasionally spoke with Walkara, or more often with Deer's Foot.

Deer's Foot oddly accepted Missy Ann as a blood sister, even as a novice of doctoring and medicine. As one who is usually bold with questions, Missy Ann learned quickly. Too, she felt a certain power that came from talking in both languages and understanding the mysteries of Spirit Path. As though born for the task, she rapidly acquired Ute ways and their language. Now, being the only wife of a Chief, gave her a feeling of security. Nobody dare ask her about her past. Walkara kept his promise, treating her as well as any Mormon wife—considering. By the following spring, Little Gray Owl began jabbering in both languages. Middle of summer, before Comanche Moon when it was usually time to hunt buffalo or go on a horse raid, Chief Walkara's hair changed from gray to pure silver. His once erect swagger turned to a stoop shouldered shuffle.

All those things that once gave him prominence among the tribes were questioned and seemed of little importance. His once famous horse herds grew sparse. Without slave trading and tribute from his neighboring clans there was no gold, silver or wealth to flaunt. He felt his authority wane.

Grief and guilt began to turn to blame and anger toward the Mormons for all the ills of the Ute people, particularly his own personal losses.

In the north, where the plague hadn't been as serious, the word among the Ute was that Ouray was growing in strength and renowned. "After all," he complained, "it was El Gavilan who did not listen to the vision's warning. His not listening brought red spots that slayed our people. Walkara should accept that as being *his* burden. It is Walkara's great weight to carry."

At Salt Lake, the next spring, the first Sunday in April, and President Young preached from The Book of James: Chapter 4, verse 1. "From whence come wars and fighting among you? Come they not hence, even from your lusts that war in your members?"

On Spanish Fork at the Timpanogo Village Walkara sat alone by his fire. Lurking in his members he saw enemies, not uncommon to old men who have lost battles. He saw not with words but through eyes of bitter feelings, reckless of desperation, fear masked as anger, and pride posing as self-importance. He vaguely understood those things about himself and yet there was nothing he could do to change the situation or the way he felt. For almost twenty moons those spirit enemies festered inside his sullen heart. Because of them—the Mormons—he now had but one wife and she would no longer come to his bed at night. His horses, no more did he have the finest ones. And most unfairly, the people blamed him for the sickness. The God of the Mormons promised plenty, but that too was a lie.

Walkara's conclusions: While there is still more of us than them— before white eyes, devour all that belongs to the Ute, something must be done. The white man to our face calls us brother, but behind our back, savage. They, that murdered my braves. Them, who brought the sickness. Those, that spoke of a God of love and giving—then took everything that gave the Ute power over their enemies.

While he was still Chief Walkara, The Hawk of the Mountains, he who stole more than four thousand horses from the Spanish and defeated the U.S. Army. He would lead his people to victory. It would be war! Walkara's war!

Whispered first to a few in his village the lust for war grew slowly. Walkara rode personally to scattered nearby villages and fueled fires of resentment each man held toward the Mormons. From those places others were sent out to fan flames of war in distant villages.

Though his face was haggard and his hair like silver, Walkara's swagger returned. His head now held high.

Even Tuck's heart pounded at talks of war. Most of the time he believed there was good reason. Wasn't Otto like almost every other white man, a liar and bad—wasn't his mother an Indian honest and good? Missy Ann hoped the men of the village were only talking big. She remembered when her dear old Irish Father got drunk he was always a big talker. He'd boast and get mean just like the Indian men of the village were now doing. But nothing ever came of it. And without whiskey why now would anything worse happen? Still, she worried and feared for her new baby's safety.

Tuck and Missy stood just outside Deer Foot's teepee, Tuck said, "Seems to me the Mormons need a good butt kickin. All-out war if need be. And if we all stick together we can give it to 'em. What do you think?"

Missy Ann jumped at the opportunity to speak her piece. "Now that ye asked," standing on her tiptoes, right up in Tuck's face, "D'ya believe such drivel? Ba goom, Tuck if that happens we'll never stand a chance. T'is misbegotten foolishness. Over them mountains they's thousands upon thousands of 'em. If ya think measles brung the glooms, them Mormons will hunt us down, whittle away at us and then we'll know nothing but a life of want and woe. Mark my words, Tuck."

She said no more. To do so, in many eyes, might have put her on the side of the enemy.

Inside the teepee Deer's Foot lit her pipe and sought Great Spirit about what she just overheard.

17

"WALKER'S WAR"

"Gathering of The Twelve," Salt Lake City.

Brigham Young called an emergency meeting of the Latter-day Saints highest apostolic leadership. Not long after Brigham was appointed Governor of Utah Territory the dry desert air whispered of rumors. The first thing on The Twelve's special agenda: "Walkara intends to make war."

Before Brigham could utter a word, "Governor Young, why in heavens name would Chief Walker even consider trying it?" Bishop Berry asked.

Brigham anticipated the question and began reading his prepared response, "When a man like Walkara believes he has lost everything that defines his good name—when those thing of pride and power seem stripped from him—like a bear cornered in his den or a mountain lion trapped in a tree...you tell me, will he...can he accept defeat?"

Bishop Richards interrupted, "Hell no, but you're talkin about dumb animals. What I mean is, Walker is no dummy." Brigham continued, "That's true. But like any wild animal believing his passing is eminent, more often despite the obvious, will fling himself at their adversary—"

"Hold on there, Governor, what are you gettin' at?" said squint-eyed, guilty looking Bishop Kimball. "Nobody sitting around this table been caught acting like Walker's enemy."

"That's right Governor. When have any of us meant him any ill will?" said Bishop Allred.

"Oh, I'm sure—like me—none of you have," Brigham said with a bit of cynicism.

Then the questions and comments came fast, "So what's he got to gain?" another of The Twelve asked.

Brigham replied, "I suspect satisfaction is pretty much it. Getting in one last blow. Odds of survival mean little to Walkara now."

"Do you think many others will follow him?"

"He's the greatest chief they have ever known—first one to ever try to unite the Ute Nation. You know how his people are. They respect and obey him like deity," Brigham completed reading his written statement.

"But Brigham, he's beat down already—whipped before he starts. Most folks west of the Rockies know that."

"Perhaps some might, but Walkara would never admit it. Deep down, a man in his position more than likely knows that, and—"

"Scuse me, Brigham," interrupted Bishop Bennett, a bearded, gray headed, older man.

"Yer out of order, Bishop Bennett," another reprimanded.

"What order? Well meb'e so, but them Sioux Injuns east of here was dang sure out of order when they butchered my wife and child. And I ain't forgetting that." He waved the stub of his right arm.

"I know, Bishop...I know," Brigham said compassionately.

"Young," Bennett pleaded, "I ain't never raised a weapon agin another man, black white or red but by...the Good Lord...I'm itching to. If ever I see one of them crazed savages coming at me or my new family, they's gonna be hearing from the talkin end of my old Kentucky flintlock and, sorry Brigham, I ain't gonna take time to preach the gospel."

"Well John, that's why we're here discussing this," Young soothed.

"Hells bells, Brigham!" John Bennett jumped to his feet, "Either it's like the good book says, It's God's will we take Dominion over this here land." Now is it, or ain't it?"

Muttering continued around the table, "True. That's true...Amen... Dang right. It's our destiny. Could be. Amen...again" until a majority consensus was reached.

So Brigham called for a vote. At the highest level in Mormondom, the unspoken was finally voiced. "Co-existence didn't necessarily mean racial or for that matter, religious equality." The second motion, "They ought to prepare for war, just incase." Both motions passed unanimously.

Walkara started numbering braves—those he knew he could depend on. What matter if there were far less than he hoped? This victory was going to be his, not because of numbers, but because Great Spirit was stronger than the Mormon's god and *Great Spirit* was on the side of the Ute. He asked Deer's Foot to go make strong medicine—a Vision Quest—asking spirits of his dead ancestors to come and fight by his side.

"I will my chief. I will, I will...I will." She pointed to Little Gray Owl and then at Walkara. "You take care of him." With little preparation she took Missy Ann by the hand and they walked to the top of Santaguin Mountain. For three days they fasted and sought *Great Spirit*.

Missy Ann couldn't understand exactly what Deer's Foot was beseeching Great Spirit for. But clearly it seemed different than what Walkara had asked—to Missy Ann these wailing chants sounded something like somebody's breechclout was too tight.

Together, eyes closed, they lifted their arms to the sky. But Missy Ann kept one eye slightly open, peeking just to be sure she was doing exactly what Deer's Foot did.

By the end of the second day without food, Missy Ann could hardly lift her arms. And she asked Deer's Foot if it made any difference to Great Spirit if when she lifted her arms it could be from a laying down position? She didn't get an answer and the old medicine woman kept going strong.

Three days past swiftly. Hiking back to the village famished and weak was no easy chore. And had she known Deer's Foot, for emergencies only, had a pouch full of pemmican tied off under her skirt...well.

Well anyway, they made it back just in time to hear Little Gray Owl throwing a conniption fit. Walkara sure loved that boy but at three years of age he ran the Chief around in circles. Between the two, the only one knowing the word 'no' sure wasn't Walkara.

Brigham took great pride for the relative peace in their valley, realizing the rest of the Western Frontier was pretty much up to its scalps in lead-shot, gunpowder and tomahawks. That is, everywhere else the flood of predominantly white traders, settlers and the U.S. Army seemed hell bent on eradicating the red man and his culture. So, up to this time Brigham's Indian Relation strategies were a testimony to Mormon policy and tact. And he darned sure wanted to keep it that way.

Walkara regretted his hunger for wealth, and desire for the things of his white guests...and their women. Gray Owl was happy and the white Missy Ann was no different than his Indian wives. Walkara expected the whites to learn some Ute ways and change some of theirs. Mormons didn't quite see it that way.

Walkara's thoughts of past victories—when he and his raiders never failed—were what allowed him to even consider, War Path. In those old memories his thoughts soon grew to actually considering doing something as grand as war against the whites. War would be more than bold—beyond brave. His tactics always worked when stealing horses, even when hunting buffalo. Come in quietly from two sides early in the morning when clouds of sleep fogged the thoughts of their query. How difficult could that be? He ordered, "When Wolf-kill Moon is fully awake, we meet here." Walkara sent couriers with that message to all he considered Brothers.

Light snows of winter were already gone when the other eleven, Heads of Clans, began to arrive. There was much talk and much passing of the Pipe around Walkara's lodge fire circle.

"This will be a good year to hunt the buffalo," an older one suggested.

"Better we hunt our enemies," a muttered reply.

"When we drive out Mormons we put fear into every Comanche's heart," from another.

"There will be plenty time for our people to feast then." And most heads were nodding in agreement.

All of the men speaking boldly were much younger than Walkara. He had done a good job filling their hearts with war. Tuck, sitting just beyond the circle, remained quiet. Those men, who rode in with them, the ones older and gray headed, held their piece. Walkara seemed attentive and listened to all the debating, but in his heart, behind his eyes, he rode leading the charge to war mounted on his new black stallion. He would gather up all the Mormon's big black books and burn them to warm his lodge and take anything else he wanted. Tuck and Walkara's eyes met. A brief glance, but in his Grandfather's glance the question spoke clearly. Are you with me?

Slowly, deliberately Tuck removed his knife from its sheath, his eyes flashing, he thrust it deep into the ground. "This is our land," was all he said.

Walkara nodded, "It is *so*." And to the gathering, "Go and prepare your braves for battle."

Outside, those waiting and listening heard the first words of war. Like a flash of lightening all eyes blazed and hearts pounded for War Path.

Back inside, Walkara concluded, "One moon and seven days, when the night sky is black, at sunrise we will strike. I will send messengers to your villages with the war plan." Spontaneously, inside and out, War cries erupted.

Missy Ann off by herself down in the meadow stood near the grazing horses. Hearing the shouts, she and they lifted their heads...the horses whinnied as cries for war spilled from the lodge and into the throats of all those listening.

Fear griped Missy Ann's heart hearing Nip's plaintive howl lead a chorus of his own kind afar off in high places. Horses tossed their heads, throats blaring shrill screams and they began galloping and bucking in circles. Had war actually begun?

In moments War Drums began to throb. The people heaped logs on the fire until flame and spark leaped to the heavens. Two rotating dancing circles formed, one inside the other, around and around. In the outside circle painted braves stomp-danced in unison chanting and shouting war songs. Arms raised, they thrust their weapons skyward.

Missy Ann realized she had been wrong—it was going to get worse. She left the meadow and stood in the shadows watching. Women dressed in their finest beaded doeskins, in pulsing, shuffling lock-step, encircled by every old and young man, all cried to War Spirit for victory.

Watching, she knew this scene had been acted out many times before. And throughout the moonlit night, as in centuries past, nearby pines reflecting the fire's glow seemed to sway to the beat of the war drum. Pearly moonlit peaks silhouetted against the stars, in kindred spirit, echoed back. Missy's ultimate thought—how can I help?

The following day Missy Ann asked Tuck, "D'ya have a horse I kin ride?"

"You ride?"

"T'is the Blarney a stone? Never ya mind...if that pale nag ya straddle be yer best—"

"Desert Wind? Why she's the best in the village, now."

"Me Paddy wouldn't give ya two-bits for her."

Tuck just stared at her for a moment and said nothing. Then twisted his mouth with a, "Humph," and asked, "Do the Irish even own horses?"

"Uuggh," she gasped, "Never have I seen such a country bumpkin. Ye never heard of, Morgans?"

"Morgan, who?"

"For suure, not Morgan le Fay, ya yokel...Justin Morgan and his fine horses. Swiftest in all New England."

"Not faster than my mare."

"Huulloo...yer long legged beastie is winsome, even a bit handsome but bred for looks not real speed." Tuck, tongue-tied for a moment, spit out, "Maybe...but that don't mean the likes of you know how to ride her."

"*Begorrah*! Do ya need to see to believe?" In a huff she turned and headed for the nearest pasture.

"*Wait*...I'll get you one that's safe." Tuck picked up his leather lead.

"*Uuhh*," tossing her hair back over her shoulders, arms crossed, toe tapping impatiently, she stopped and waited.

Together they walked toward the lower pasture near the stream.

Tuck feeling civil, asked, "Truly, how did you learn to ride?" On the way Missy Ann explained: before her family got religion, her Father was Justin Morgan's groom and Travis her brother, Paddy as she called him, was one of the best jockeys in Vermont. Before she was five, Mister Morgan had her sitting in the saddle, silk cap and black boots, too big, but she loved every minute of it. By ten she was good enough to gallop on the training track, now and then beating Paddy in short unofficial races.

Then, one warm midsummer day, against Mister Morgan's rules, riding bareback and double, they raced through the countryside easily jumping several low split rail fences. Fearless, both of them urged the horse on. Stonewall was going to be their greatest jump. Through the air they sailed, both laughing, her arms wrapped tightly around her brother's waist... the horse failed at the height, slamming into Stonewall's top. Catapulting, they crashed to the earth. That was the day Paddy died. Missy Ann was only thirteen and vowed never to ride again. She hadn't until that day Walkara put her on behind his saddle and brought her to the village. She had no choice and the memory of riding double was almost too much to bear.

"What of your Mother and Father," Tuck asked.

She said, "The day they drove the Mormons out of Nauvoo, Illinois... the very night before, for no good reason they both were murdered." Brigham said we couldn't wait around and find the killers and maybe be murdered ourselves. Two years on the trail, with Brigham Young leading, we rolled into this new Promised Land. One year later Brigham traded me to Walkara."

With a breathless shuddering sigh she lowered her head. "I'm glad to be here Tuck. I be no angel. Ya see—bein alone was more than I could bear."

Tuck stammered, "You're...not...alone, now."

"Oh Tuck," sobbing, "Paddy died in me arms, his dear sweet neck broken and after that terrible night I'd never ever see my bonny Mum n' Pap again."

By the stream in silence they sat side by side. Tuck had the urge to comfort her, just put his arm around her trembling shoulders, but something stopped him and he just took her hand squeezing it gently. Even that was too much. Not for Missy Ann but at the touch Tuck's heart raced. Regretting his boldness, he released her hand.

Clearing his throat, he said, "So you can ride then?"

Wiping away the tears, she nodded, yes. Looking directly into Tuck's eyes, she said, "Granny...ah, Deer's Foot, whispered to me the real reasons for Walkara's war. Peculiar, I already figured the same."

Real reasons? Tuck wondered.

Missy Ann stood, blew her nose, brushed off her skirt and looked down at Tuck and with fire in her eyes, and said, "And a plan of me own I be havin. If ya have any desire to know? So, now for once, listen ya big lunk. Lest ye be scared an Irish lass can outwit ya?"

He grinned. "Scared, no. But I've seen your plans before."

18

"GETTING EVEN"

"Missy Ann, it won't be safe," argued Tuck.

"Ha! Brigham won't know what hit 'im. When it comes to my play actin, Annie Lowry's, got nothin on me."

Obviously there was nothing Tuck could do to change Missy Ann's mind. And he had to admit Missy Ann was an amazing female and her plan just might work.

Placing her hand softly on Tuck's arm, she asked, "Will ya 'help?"

"Explain your plan to me, one more time."

"Okay. It's simple. I'll scrub myself shiny, pull my hair back in a bun and dress in the cleaned black outfit I wore the day I come to the village. Quietly leavin tonight, with the moon still full, no one will miss me till mornin."

"So, Tuck, you pick me any old swayback nag to ride. The loss of one old plug like that will save wolves the trouble anyway. "Then see, I'll dress up and be mounted befittingly. Then ride into Salt Lake City wild eyed and screamin, Help! Injuns are gonna scalp me."

"Humbly, I'll throw myself at Brigham Young's feet sobbing and cryin, I repent, President Young. I've seen the true light and the error of my ways. Please help me. There's a wee risk I might catch Brigham in a less than forgivin mood, but I figure, like most men wish for, rescuing a young maid in distress entitles him."

"The last part of my plan is a bit iffy but I know Brigham's stables are directly behind his big house. Should be a simple matter to convince Brigham, and for sure his wives, of my sincerity. I'll be explainin with fervent feelin's, that as part of me contrition, I should be sleepin in the stables."

Her excitement brimmed. "No way will Brigham Young be able to balk when I say, with all proper feelin's, Like our dear Lord, a stable will be the place of me new beginning."

"It should also be the stable where Walkara's beloved black stallion is bedded. So, do you get the picture, Tuck? If all goes well, by early the next mornin, the stallion and me will be long gone. In the stallion's place the old nag will be left standin. Then, what a good laugh I'll be havin. Ah begorrah, what satisfaction that will be. The stallion and me should be back to Spanish Fork trail by midday. "Try to understand, Tuck. Ya see, I just kin no more bed with dear old Chief Walkara but I kin give him back 'is tuther love." Again she touched Tuck's arm.

"So Tuck, will ya help me?"

"All right I'll help and I won't tell a soul. But tonight I'm ridding to the valley floor with you. And day after tomorrow I'll meet you there when the sun is at its peak."

"Agreed," she said.

"One more thing...if you're not there on time I explain it all to Walkara."

"So be it."

Going and returning, so as to avoid other Saints, Missy Ann would stay close to, but off the main road.

Tuck waited at the agreed upon location.

The entire plan went off without a hitch. About a mile from the Spanish Fork cutoff to the village, proud and happy, Missy Ann deliberately rode the black stallion at a lope smack down the middle of the main road.

Tuck first saw dust, then the single bareback rider. Yes, it was her sitting ramrod straight, her skirt hiked up around her thighs and smiling pretty as spring's new bloom. Spying Tuck, she waved both hands over her head in a joyful greeting. Like Walkara, she'd tied off the reins using only knee pressure to guide the big stallion as she pleased. The lass could ride after all, "Yeh-yeh-yeh!" she shouted, "I told ya—I told ya. Like takin candy from a wee babe." And she reined to a stop beside Tuck.

Grinning, she reached down the front of her dress and pulled out a shiny brass object. Tilting her head coyly, "How do ya like me new horse?" And she held the small rectangular plague up in front of Tuck. "See," she giggled, "What's it be sayin'?"

"I can't read, you know that," Tuck laughed.

She smiled mischievously, her eyes flashing, "I unscrewed it from his stall door. Diablo. The devil, as Brigham called him. Kin ya imagine his holy Mormon highness tagged this sweet gentle boy, D-i-a-b-l-o...Devil. Now kin ya beat that." Clasping hands they laughed, their faces almost touching.

Tuck, imitating her in his best Irish brogue, their hands still clasped, said, "So tell me bonny lass, wha 'appened?"

With no intent—looking deeply into each other's eyes—in that instant, whatever it was, flowed freely. Then, like she'd burned herself, Missy Ann let out an almost imperceptible gasp, abruptly dropped Tuck's hands and turned Diablo toward the village.

"Wait. Missy Ann...ahh...I was only asking what happened in Salt Lake?"

Reining up, she turned and looked at him as if in a daze. "Oh...well...yes." It took a moment for her to regain her composure. "Brigham took it, hook line and sinker. Even come out to the stables in his nightshirt with his wee white candle to make sure I was comfortable in me hay pile." She brushed at her hair, evidence of straw still clinging. Brigham said I best stay away from the black stud. E's too mean and dangeroos. I said, Yes sir. An' before he left," she giggled, "he come up real close and asked if there was anythin he could be a do'n' for me?"

Tuck failed to see humor in that.

Her in front, Missy Ann and Tuck rode single file silently back up toward the village. She eventually asked, without making eye contact, "So, what'd ya tell em, here?"

"Nothing. Just like we agreed, you wanted to be alone. A Spirit Quest, I said."

"That's true," she chuckled, "this old stud still has plenty of spirit."

And she kicked Diablo into a gallop. Tuck raced to catch up and together they sped toward home.

A mile from the village Missy Ann reined up. "Wait, I want to turn him out in the lower pasture...watch him race toward his mares...hear his bellowin and snortin."

Dismounting she led Diablo closer to where the mares grazed. Nostrils flaring, his eyes flashed...ears up, he began to prance sideways until he almost pulled her off her feet. Tugging with all her strength she dug in her heels trying to slow him. Quickly slipping off his bridle she whispered to him then gave him a slap on the rump. Tail and mane dancing in the wind away he flew, bugling his homecoming.

Trembling, she said, "Did ya see it, Tuck? The stud's fire, in those magnificent eyes? Me Pap used to call it, The Look of Eagles. Her cheeks blushed as she swung up on Desert Wind, behind Tuck. Putting her arms around Tuck's chest, she pressed her cheek against his back.

Before Walkara saw Diablo he heard the stallion's bugling blasts. A few moments later Desert Wind, Missy Ann seated behind Tuck, came loping into the Village.

Walkara was already on his way, dashing through the lower meadow, his moccasins seemed to barely skim the top of the grass. Diablo gave him a quick glance of recognition, but for now the stallion had other things on his mind.

Walkara's lodge sat empty for the rest of the day. By dark, as the whippoorwill's cry rang through the aspen, Walkara still had not returned from the lower meadow. Then, as the moon crested the Wasatch, the clop-clop-clop of hooves came easily through the village. In morning's light neither Walkara nor Diablo was to be seen.

Taking a close look at Walkara's lodge Tuck solved the mystery. Above the lodge door buffalo skins, once tightly sewn together, were now cut open to a height of about seven feet. Hoof prints in the soft earth led right up into the door and disappeared inside. Walkara's vision was coming true and he wasn't taking any chances. Anyway, it was better than sleeping alone. The next morning Walkara made every effort to let the entire village see him leave dressed in his beaded buckskins, two white, black tipped eagle feathers in his silver hair. Diablo brushed and greased, shined like new obsidian. Circling the village once at a slow walk, then, with a shout, Walkara galloped up through the pines.

For the next three days they were gone. Returning home the fierceness of battle was etched in the set of Walkara's jaw and his eyes burned deep and black. Without speaking he entered his lodge with Diablo.

The next two weeks little was seen of Walkara or Diablo. Only now and then from inside his lodge came songs and chants of victories past.

When Walkara emerged, a rolled up badger pelt was held tightly in his hand. Painted on its smooth white hide was his plan for war. For the next two weeks, by messengers, the plan would be carried to distant villages. Preparations for Walkara's War were almost complete.

Walkara never questioned anyone about Diablo. Neither Tuck nor Missy Ann said anything. It was assumed the black stallion escaped from Salt Lake City and returned home on his own. Walkara's only comment, "Horses are the wings of men. As it was meant to be—my wings have returned."

By Tuck's count, the Timpanogao Village now had a returning population of fifty, sometimes at its peak as high as seventy-five. Before the plague, there had been upwards of three hundred men, women and children. Of the fifty plus souls only fifteen were of age to go to war and that was allowing for boys above the age of twelve. Would that be enough? Tuck wondered.

"We have the best," Walkara said to Tuck. "Over the years, Timpanogoe Utes have taken fine pieces of weaponry from raids on wagon trains along westward trails and in Santa Fe we traded a few horses for weapons. Walkara believed his raiders were almost as well equipped as the army."

He boasted, "My men own a half dozen Kentucky, forty-two inch flintlocks and twenty some muskets, U.S. flintlocks. Many, Model o-threes and over two hundred pounds of Best's gunpowder, gun flints and lead shot. Who can match that? My own best weapon is a handsome fusel, P. Bond's thirty-four plains rifle. I have hit many buffalo from a long ways off."

Walkara put his right hand on Tuck's right shoulder and said, "My son, I have seen what a great hunter you are." Tuck was taken by surprise by his next words, "You and I will lead the attack."

"I am honored, Grandfather."

Walkara said, "Have you noticed for several days now, my warriors have been carrying hand pistols in their waistbands? They are eager for war." As an afterthought, he said, "Oh yes, I own a good swivel gun blunderbuss, never used but I know it can fire a dozen or more musket balls at once." The village had firepower. Tuck was always impressed with Ute loyalty. If Walkara said 'war' then it was war. Yet the basic nature of the Ute was not to be under anyone's thumb and most of Walkara's small trained army of raiders were spread throughout the Wasatch, Bear River and Unita Mountain Ranges. Each Ute clan leader was powerful in his own right. But like Walkara's village, most of the clans were decimated and severely weakened as the result of the plague. Never the less, if Walkara said war, so be it.

Walkara gave instructions for the men of the tribes to spend the remaining weeks cleaning and oiling weapons. Busy fletching and sharpening new arrows, grinding the knife and tomahawk's edge until mirror like they would gleam in the sunlight, flashing victory.

His war plan was explained more than once, "Ute Clans located northeast of Salt Lake, those south of Bear River, will begin to attack settlers driving as many Mormons as possible toward Salt Lake.

"The second arm of mounted attackers will come mostly from the Uncompahgra bands (Ouray' s people) east of the Wasatch. Cresting the pass they will stream down Emigrant Canyon and Ogden Canyon and put Salt Lake under siege, circling and firing from a distance trying to spook the inhabitants. Those Mormons escaping our attacks from the northeast must flee south." Walkara would be waiting with his braves along the main road, south near Utah Lake. It was hoped the two other arms of his victorious army would join him there.

Walkara believed, "Then the only way for the Mormons to finally escape then will be to turn west and flee across the salty, hot desert." That would be fine with him. It was not important they be killed. Chasing them into the desert wilderness, maybe clear into California, would be acceptable. Then, sitting astride his black stallion, atop Granite Peak, he would watch the rolling dust clouds from the 'Saints' as they fled across the desert. And all would be well with his spirit.

Walkara's orders memorized, in the early morning as planned the first band of ten warriors attacked the small settlement of Wellsville. A larger band of fifty was enroute to Brigham City. Both units mounted on their finest steeds were well armed and bravely anticipating a fierce battle.

What Walkara had not planned on was sadly unexpected.

Governor Young also had given orders. "Fortifications must be prepared in advance. We'll build simple earthen covered bulwarks, each in our tradition and stocked with food, water and supplies. Set them in strategic locations and see to it they are heavily armed. And unfortunately for the Ute those preparations were true in every Mormon settlement, especially Salt Lake City.

There was no Mormon stampede to escape. Just volley after volley of shots that kept the Ute attackers at impotent distances. By noon several braves were killed or wounded. None of the settlers were even wounded. The same was true of the major attack at Salt Lake City by the Uncompahgre warriors. At the mouth of the canyons the warriors did manage to push the Temple Guard back inside the city but in doing so several key warriors were lost to wounds and death. They could get no closer than just beyond range of their muskets.

South near Utah Lake, Walkara and his small band of braves waited. The sun was dipping low in the west and now and then a yellow dust devil would come spinning across the sage flats down the road toward them but that was it. All was stillness. Where was the wave of escaping Mormons as Walkara envisioned?

"Grandfather," Tuck asked, anxious to fight, "what are we waiting for?"

In his frustration Walkara could only glare and growl at this foolish question. In silence they would wait. Soon the enemy will come stampeding to escape the terror of Walkara's army. The plan was right...after all...he sought Great Spirit and Great Spirit answered by sending his most famous battle horse back to him.

Through the cold and fireless night, they waited huddled together listening for sounds of the Mormon's retreating hooves and fleeing wagons. Then at dawn's first light the scout he sent up the road in the black of night, just before dawn he came charging back toward Walkara's waiting warriors.

Out of breath, he leaped from his mount and came running to Walkara's side. He spoke quietly but in an excited tone, a look of desperation covered his youthful face. "My Chief," he gasped, "The Mormons come!" Then the scout blurted so all could hear. "The Mormons they come alone, maybe one hundred armed men. None of our warriors pursue."

"That cannot be," Walkara bellowed. "None...*None*? But where are our braves?"

"My Chief, the Mormons do not flee. They ride with pride and strength, seeking in all directions...looking, for us."

Barely discernible in the distance a large rolling dust cloud formed on the northern horizon—rumbling sounds of many horses grew closer by the minute. Then they saw and heard the Mormons coming.

Walkara made the only choice a wise leader could. Shoulders slumped, his command came with great difficulty. He and his warriors must retreat.

Placing his hands on Tuck's shoulders he spoke, "We must warn the village! My son, you must stay behind with two others and hold off the Mormons as long as you can."

"I will die for our people!" Tuck exclaimed.

Walkara, paused and looked into Tuck's eyes remembering those days long ago when he would have said the same, but now, "No, my Son. Do as I say. Slow them...I realize now we cannot stop them...later you will be needed at the village."

"But Grandfather—"

"Do as I say." He pointed to a low tree covered knoll, "Quickly, set the canon (blunderbuss) there...be ready. Do not fire, too soon."

Walkara and the others sprung to their mounts, lying flat in their saddles up the trail toward the village they flew. If the Mormons cornered them at the village they might kill them all.

19

"EXODUS"

Tuck's hands trembled. He fumbled with stiff rawhide knots on the mule's pack- saddle trying to untie the heavy blunderbuss. Walkara said to put it on top of the low knoll. The soil was soft and the weapons narrow iron tripod legs sunk in the sand. Not knowing for sure how much, Tuck primed it with ample gunpowder and more than a pound of buckshot. Their canon was ready, though Tuck, nor any of the others, had ever seen or heard the dangerous looking weapon fired.

The Mormon pursuers reined to halt less than a hundred paces from where the canon sat primed and waiting. The riders circled, staring down at the sandy depression where Walkara and his braves had waited the night before. Excitedly they talked among themselves. Some gesturing up the canyon trail, others back toward Salt Lake. Those pointing up toward the village apparently were in the majority.

Tuck anguished, when was the right time? Fire too soon or too late? The instant the Mormons spurred their mounts toward the village Tuck knew it was time. Though uncertain, he set spark to gunpowder—an explosion roared like he'd never heard or imagined. Flames and smoke belched several feet from the mouth of the blunderbuss. The soft sand did not hold the tripod like he thought and the whole thing reared back and up with sudden force, throwing sand and debris in all directions.

Tuck and his two companions, their mule and three horses, all went tumbling and scattering in different directions. Every bird and critter for a mile around did likewise. And the explosion echoed up the canyon clear to the village. Walkara had said not to try and stop them, just slow them. Tuck thought, well I couldn't help if the canon did more than expected.

He saw the first half dozen Mormon riders go flying off their horses backwards. The rest, and there were forty not a hundred, bolted in all directions. Many of their mounts stung by the buckshot went stampeding and crow-hopping through the tall gray sage spilling their startled riders left and right.

"Reconnoiter! Damn it, reconnoiter!" a voice of authority emerged from chaos.

And while they were busy reconnoitering Tuck and his pals gathered their mounts and hastily retied the smoldering blunderbuss on the mule. Quietly as they could, they stayed in cover on the shadowed side of the canyon and headed for the village. Other than their pride, only three Mormons were actually wounded. Both men and horses were frightened to near panic at hearing the roaring blast in the morning's stillness. Reconnoitering, they spent several minutes just laying on their bellies all eyes searching the hillsides for their attackers. Eventually the unit's leader, Bishop Vanders, got courage enough to stand up behind the protection of his horse and searched the hillside with his pocket brass telescope. He decided the enemy's artillery had retreated.

Nearing the village Tuck saw the meadows were already empty of horses. Some lodges were being pulled down. The village was jammed with horses, everybody running and shouting trying to get their belongings together. Deer's Foot calmly loaded her shoulder travois with medicines and her paraphernalia. Walkara, astride Diablo, was shouting orders.

There wasn't much time, but just before entering the village Tuck stopped, untied and set up the blunderbuss. For good measure he fired one more blast down the canyon, this time using slightly less gunpowder. The entire village, surprised, leaped at the explosion's percussion. Diablo shied, Walkara ducked, but kept shouting orders.

At the mouth of the canyon the Mormons were making up their minds which way to go. At the sound of the second blast they stopped, listened and murmured amongst themselves.

Tuck decided he did not have time to again load up the canon. Leaving it where it lay he a raced to make sure Missy Ann and Little Gray Owl were safe and prepared to leave. Nip watched and waited by their lodge. Missy Ann was sitting in the middle of all her things. In her lap she held the black dress, her only store bought dress. Tuck did not understand the tears in her eyes, and perhaps she didn't either. Finally she rose and flung the dress into her discard pile, turned, shrugged and smiled sadly at Tuck.

Back at the mouth of the canyon the Mormons were still reconnoitering. Nobody could agree on the next move. All jabbering, "No doubt, there was at least a hundred of 'em shooting at us."

"We don't know what's up that canyon."

"Old Walkers got something up his sleeve."

Now the majority of opinions to fight were mostly negative.

So Bishop Vanders, decided, "We'll get more men and come back later."

The Timpanogos were as ready and packed as time permitted. Any moment Walkara expected Mormon gunfire to rain down on his people. It was time to move.

"Grandfather, where will we go?" Tuck asked.

"We must crest the Wasatch before dark."

"And then..."

"Southeast to a place where I believe no white man has yet come. My Fathers once lodged there. It is called Fish Lake...six days ride from here."

Walkara gave the command to move out. In ordered unison, a hundred horses and mules, fifteen men, twenty-two women and a handful of children, most under the age of three, began to move. Walkara's once powerful and feared Timpanogos were reduced to but a remnant of their former glory.

Young men and boys drove the horse herd on ahead. All those riding, except Walkara, dragged heavily loaded travois behind them. Those walking were each hauling their own loads and brought up the rear. Five of the most well-armed mounted men acted as rearguard. There was no talking, as they left their lifelong home but many tears.

Deer's Foot knew of their destination. Her Father's Father, Cheyenne Chief Two Bears, in an age-old war over buffalo hunting rights once drove these same Utes from Fish Lake. Ironically, Deer's Foot, then a young teen, had been captured by the Ute and though originally treated as a slave, eventually was accepted as one of their own and married Walkara's father.

Deer's Foot, with great wisdom, illuminated the past and a bit of the future to Missy. She'd never heard Deer's Foot talk so much. Missy Ann put the words to memory. "Cheyenne, it's been said, were called the beautiful people, being taller and more fair than other tribes. "The Cheyenne's manner of dress, their beaded buckskin, were copied by others, also their lodges. The Cheyenne fought Ute, Arapaho, Comanche and others to possess the grassy plains and the buffalo. Depending on Great Spirit, that could change from winter to winter."

"Fifty winters, my eyes have seen war between our tribes become less. The Ute too busy stealing horses and capturing slaves left others to divide up the buffalo herds. Anyway, a few more years there will be no buffalo to war over. The white man is in the land to stay."

Walkara had no way of knowing till weeks later that most of western Utes were following his lead and streaming eastward away from the angry Mormons. Ouray's people quietly disappeared into those lands between the Wasatch and the great Shinning mountains, fleeing there to try to begin a new and safer existence.

During Walkara's and his people's trek to their new home, little wild game was seen and thankfully no white men. Sunset on the sixth day they reached their destination on the shores of Fish Lake. Scouting the area the following day, much to Tuck's dismay, evidence of white man's passing through was seen. Here and there on rocky slopes, place had been gouged from the earth with pick and shovel and there was not one flat-tail left in the streams. Grandfather was wrong again. It seemed seekers of the yellow metal and fur had been everywhere. For now, apparently they had moved on.

Cool nights of Birthing Moon passed and meadow grasses began to green, though little rain and light snows of the past winter left the earth thirsty. Walkara suggested they plant spring gardens but his people went about subdued and morose and found little celebration in farming or erecting new lodges. By summer solstice buffalo, pea and blue blossom grasses were short and already dried and brown. The birch and aspen leaves began to color. The people still walked in defeated spirits.

Ten new moons came and went. It was nearing that time of year and Walkara again spoke of planning a new raid. Perhaps to the High Plains for buffalo or to California for horses, but no one seemed to listen. Comanche Moon, the raiding moon, quietly came and went. Tuck spent as much time as they could away from camp hunting and doing his job well. But unlike the last winter, this winter all but buried their lodges in deep snow and survival depend on supplies of meat, smoked, dried and stored from his earlier hunts.

Other hungry Ute hunting parties came and went. All spoke of the same thing, there must be peace. Around the lake, long after white birch's leaves yellowed and long lines of water fowl journeyed south filling darkening skies with clamorous calls, a messenger came from the northern Ute tribes.

The messenger reporting to Walkara, said, "Chief Ouray says, Governor Young would parlay with Walkara." But Walkara did not reply and the messenger left.

Missy Ann had never known such a long hungry winter and it seemed it would never pass. Sadly, spring found most of the people gaunt and sick with coughs and there was no laughter in the eyes of the children.

Walkara hadn't needed chief Ouray to tell him to go parley with Young. Before all the snow was gone from the high country Walkara left for Salt Lake, leading five of his last and best horses—in his pouch a white handkerchief, borrowed from Missy Ann. Nothing was spoken as he and Tuck rode up through the Wasatch to the high pass. When they reached the deep snows that still covered the trail, Tuck, at Walkara's insistence, turned back.

"You are needed at the village," Walkara said. "I will return." And he spurred on.

Diablo, paced himself down through the snow toward Salt Lake. The five other horses, all heavy haired and shaggy, plunged down the mountain pass close behind.

By afternoon Walkara passed through their Old Spanish Fork home. He paused and looked around. The village had been picked clean. Memories hung heavily on his heart.

West of the Wasatch on the valley floor the snow was almost gone. Governor Young weeks before had passed the word, "If Walkara comes to talk he is not to be injured or threatened."

Three men reined up sharply in front of Brigham's mansion and breathlessly ran up the front steps, pounding on the door. Brigham personally responded to their insistent hammering, hurriedly opening the double, etched glass doors. All tried to speak at the same time.

"Walker's comin. And Brigham, he's ridin your black horse."

"He's got his rifle, too."

"And they's a white surrender hankie hanging from it."

Young immediately gave orders to saddle up his recently purchased, eighteen hands tall, copper chestnut, thoroughbred gelding. From its high back when he and Walkara reined up side by side, he would be the one looking down. Young rode out alone to meet him and to offer sanctuary in Zion.

At first sight, "Brother Walkara," Brigham shouted at a distance.

Walkara's eyes narrowed at the unexpected greeting as he lowered the white flag and raised his open right hand in return greeting.

Brigham Young guessed right. Walkara assessing Young's thoroughbred tried to sit taller the saddle. It didn't help much. On the spot, he dismounted and spread his buffalo robe on the ground and sat. Now they would be equal. He'd brought his Pipe, but chose not offer it.

Reluctantly, Brigham followed Walkara's lead, dismounted and sat.

Walkara promptly declined Brigham's invitation to enter the city. For the next hour, sitting across from each other, they parlayed there on the outskirts of the city. First off Walkara offered and Young eagerly accepted Walkara's five-horse gift. A short parley followed and peace was acceded to. Brigham said nothing about Diablo nor did he mention the cunning and excommunicated horse thief, Missy Ann.

Walkara flinched when Young invited him and the Ute people to return to Spanish Fork village. Inside, Walkara fumed. Who were these white-eyes to tell him to take back that which always was and always would be his.

As they spoke, riders left the city and came in their direction. Young noticed Walkara's nervousness and explained, "Brother Walkara they bring gifts for you and your people."

Walkara did not respond and got to his feet.

"Brother, just a moment, wait for them to arrive." Brigham tried to appease, "I am sorry for the long hard winter, it must have difficult for you and your people."

Again Walkara cringed. It was neither the first nor the worst winter his people knew, that was for Mother Earth to decide and no one else. How could this man apologize for something not of man's power? He would never understand the white man.

Brigham attempted flattery, "Chief Walkara I have been hearing some good things about you lately."

Walkara wondered what Brigham really wanted? Walkara grew even more cautious. Eyes like black pinpoints he probed sharp into Brigham's. And Brigham could not hold his gaze.

"What I mean is," Brigham cleared his throat wanting to get the conversation on things of religion "...religiously speaking, you have not captured any more slaves nor gone on more horse raids. Isn't that true Brother?"

Walkara understood Brigham's talk pretty good but answers needed to be reinterpreted in his head from English to Ute. Sometimes it was better not to answer too quickly or not at all. And he didn't.

"Our God will bless you for your obedience my Brother...Bible says,

The Almighty will open the windows of heaven and pour down unseen blessings upon you."

More snow? Walkara wondered. He'd heard all he wanted. The important thing was the parlay worked and peace agreed to but he did not agree to accept any more unseen blessing from the Mormon's God. He'd had enough already. With a grunt he rose and with a questioning expression pointed toward those heavily loaded pack mules the others brought. Blessings like those he could actually see.

Brigham urged, "Take them Brother...they're gifts from God and our Relief Society." Brigham lowered his head, stuffed his hands in his pockets and after an uneasy pause sniffed. "Please, bring our mules back later."

Walkara looked at the five good horses he just gave Brigham, then back at the mules Brigham just told him to return. Again he opened his mouth to speak but it was best he did not.

Brigham talked on, "I know it's hard times for you and your people, right now, Brother Walkara." He paused and with a full smile said, "But don't forget your tithes and offerings." In closing, Brigham stood there with that big grin and offering his hand to shake.

Walkara's mouth snapped shut and turned his back on Young's extended hand. By the time Walkara got back in the saddle he was almost ready to make war again. Not speaking, Walkara tugged on the mule's lead rope and headed back toward Spanish Fork trail.

As Brigham rode back to Salt Lake his men were muttering, "Got off pretty dang cheap. He don't say much does he? Most likely, stupid."

Walkara was tired and his eyes were heavy. He thought, I'll stay in our old village for a day and rest. Maybe I can shoot a rabbit for dinner? It never occurred to him to sample what the mules were carrying. The preserved fruits and vegetables and hundred pound sacks of stoneground grains, Mormon tea and fifty pounds of sugar, were for his people.

As he drew near the abandoned village the rage of war still hammered in his head. There was no feeling of satisfaction. Sounds of battle swirled and tugged in his thoughts. War cries stuck in his throat—his hands yearned to strike coup. Then Walkara remembered Tuck fired the canon somewhere close, just below the village. Would it still be there perhaps buried in the snow? He began walking Diablo carefully around and around in ever decreasing tighter circles, searching.

20

"STARS IN THE SKY"

Elbow deep and bare handed in the snow, Walkara tugged at it, *half* buried in mud, but...no, it was just a log.

Not leaving his search for the blunderbuss to Diablo's hooves, Walkara spent an angry hour grubbing around sometimes even on hands and knees. Finally, both physically and emotionally spent, his passions cooled. He fell back on the snow arms and legs spread wide.

Seemingly watching him from overhead, a Bald eagle soared effortlessly in sweeping circles. Walkara's eyes followed the eagle but his feelings were still snared back at the parlay. One word escaped his lips, a fist clenched disgusted utterance,

"Brothers."

Finally he relaxed feeling the snow's chill tingling through his body. The eagle had come closer and now soared just above him. Tilting its head from side to side it was close enough for Walkara to see its scaly thick legs, powerful talons and golden eyes. Mesmerized, he watched the eagle's every nuance. Its strength and mystery of flight touched his spirit. Walkara rose silently, face tilted toward the eagle, arms raised, hands open. Then filling his lungs he roared, "You are my brother."

Instantly the eagle's wings collapsed against its sides and it dropped headlong like a pointed stone toward him, screaming back...right above.

Wings extended, tail spread, back flapping to retard its descent, abruptly halting its dive. Once more it cried out, then swooping just overhead and pumping its mighty wings skyward, circling once it headed southeast toward Walkara's new home.

Walkara watched until the eagle was just a speck disappearing in the azure blue sky—he knew he'd heard the eagle scream, "The circle...the circle...the circle is broken." Walkara fell to his knees, rolled onto his back and lay still until twilight's cold brought slumber to his eyes.

Nickering and pawing impatiently at the snow, Diablo watched his Master. Walkara turned his head toward his longtime companion, a slight smile came to his nearly blue lips, "You and the eagle...you too, are my brothers." Struggling to his feet, mounting Diablo, he headed southeast up the canyon. He would eat another time.

An old man's stoop came again to Walkara's shoulders—tiredness camped in his eyes. For the next two years he grew more isolated. Never again did he look up and watch the eagle soar. Still, under his guidance, his people maintained their existence. Children stayed healthy and new babies were born. Gardens were planted. Wild game and food supplies were adequate. But things that once made Walkara and the Timpanogo, powerful, had vanished.

Tuck had ridden north. In the great grassy basin between the eastern Wasatch and the Rockies was an expanse of clear running streams, rolling hills, abundant grass and shady canyons. There, hunting was better. Though hunting was still good near the village, he was always curious of what lay over the next hill and the next. This particular day he and Nip drifted farther north than intended.

Nip came bounding back to Desert Wind's side growling a warning. Riding up and over a rise Tuck came face to face with a half dozen riders.

At first he wasn't exactly sure who they were, though it was immediately apparent they were Ute. One man was in the lead. It had been almost five years. Both had changed. Ouray was the first to lift his hand in greeting.

They rode close each sizing up the other. Ouray had not changed much, facial features, jaw line stronger and hawk like nose more pronounced. Hands holding the reins were now larger and more powerful. Astride a sidestepping, white spotted rump, black Appaloosa stallion, Ouray sat in a silver mounted saddle, posing ramrod straight, and his barrel chest filling his fringed buckskin shirt.

Ouray appraised Tuck, noting Tuck had grown even taller—now approaching six and a half feet. Tuck, as always, preferred riding Desert Wind bareback. Tuck now too possessed the chest and brawny muscular shoulders of manhood. Since his personal victory over the Mormons, Walkara bestowed the right on Tuck to wear two eagle feathers. Ouray wore only one.

It could not be avoided. Competition that began long ago, at this latest meeting, had not changed.

"Little Brother," Ouray gibed.

And the tone was set. But Tuck remembered Walkara's exhortation— do not to be provoked. And he spoke on even terms with his old acquaintance,

"Ouray, welcome to Ute country. What brings you to here to my people?"

All that Ouray would tell Tuck was he and his braves were coming to parlay only with Walkara.

Though Tuck didn't question, Ouray seemed to gloat over still excluding him from tribal affairs.

Tuck led them back to the village. Walkara greeted them, though passively. The old chief always had a nose for treachery and the rumors he had been hearing were not good. Up north, because of Ouray's complaisant ways, Ute clans were again on friendly terms with the whites. Walkara would never again compromise Ute ways with those of the invader. Walkara let Ouray know that from the start.

"But Uncle," Ouray pleaded. "I have seen them. At the big mines near our villages they come over Shinning Mountain as many as stars in the sky." Walkara spoke bluntly, "We will make War. And this time we will win."

"Uncle, we *can*not prevail against them. They are too many."

Walkara said, "What do the people say in your villages?"

"Fear. They are afraid. I see with my own eyes the wealth and power whites possess."

"Humph," Walkara grunted.

Ouray foolishly wagged his finger toward Walkara, "I warn you—"

As soon as Ouray gestured and spoke those words, Walkara grabbed for his tomahawk but did not strike...just motioned threateningly.

"Wait...hear me out," Ouray cried. "Even now there are no few whites who even care to let us live."

"Then it is better we all die fighting."

Ouray spoke boldly, "Old one you can say that but the young—"

"The young have no pride or respect." Walkara cut him short. "If I had listened to my elder, Deer's Foot, we would not be so few."

For a few minutes all was quiet around the fire. Thunder rumbled in the distance.

Heavy raindrops began drumming the sides of Walkara's lodge. Everyone sat, heads bowed in contemplation. "It will happen," Ouray spoke quietly. "Sooner or later, we will all have to accept their offer."

"Offer?" said Walkara.

Now all heads were up listening. Overhead the crack of lightning and thunder resounded across the skies.

Over the sounds of the storm Ouray voice rose even louder. "They promise to give us land of our own to keep forever."

"Uhgaa!" Furious, Walkara voice raised even louder, "*You* speak like a white-eyes." He swung his arm in a wide arc saying, "This land is already ours. *All* of it. It is not theirs to offer. Blood of our forefather's cries from the earth...it is so."

Walkara turned to Tuck and asked, "My Son what do you say?"

Ouray's eyes narrowed. His men watched him. Jaws clenched, he glared menacingly at Tuck.

Tuck did not hesitate to answer, "Grandfather, you are Chief of all the Ute. Only your voice speaks for all."

And the parlay was over. Not once had Ouray referred to Walkara as Chief. Ouray did not look again in Tuck's direction. The most dishonoring act, Ouray chose, was not remaining for the feast prepared in his honor.

Some of the younger Timpanogos left with Ouray. That too was a great insult to Walkara. One he never could or would reconcile.

For weeks, Walkara wandered the hills alone on Diablo. No one could approach him but Little Gray Owl. Sometimes Walkara would take him on the back of his saddle. Only then was there any light in his eyes.

Deer's Foot brought Walkara warm broths specially prepared from herbs to bring well-being thoughts to his spirit. Even Missy Ann tried to bring a smile to his face.

Tuck considered it the right of a man to be as he wanted and left Walkara alone to his own thoughts.

The day was cold, winds gusting from the north. Little Gray Owl pleaded with Walkara to take him along on his morning ride. "Papa, I will be quiet...please." But his pleas did no good.

Before saddling Diablo—at his side Little Gray Owl looking all forlorn—Walkara smiled for the first time in a long time. "Gray Owl, it is time for you to learn to ride your *own* horse. Perhaps tomorrow you will begin to ride by yourself?" Walkara saddled up and left the village alone.

In less than an hour, Diablo, but Walkara not in the saddle, galloped back into the village. Tuck grabbed Diablo's bridle. Both reins were snapped off. Tuck leaped on Desert Wind. Leaning close to the ground he and a few others easily followed the tracks. They found him lying on his back, face toward the sky. No wounds or marks and no broken bones—as though

Walkara simply lay down and went to sleep. Never again on this side of the veil would he ride his loyal Diablo to raid or go war.

Lamentation—not heard since the spotted plague—went out across the land. The Chief, Walkara, Hawk of the Mountains, El Gavilan, was dead. His People the Ute, when it was needed most, were without a leader.

They came from all four corners—those who agreed with him, and those who sometimes didn't. All grieved. All spoke only of their respect. Even Ouray returned. And a delegation of Mormons from Salt Lake came for the ceremonial Cry and the funeral to follow. Peg Leg Smith came from Fort Bridger with a string of fifteen fine Indian ponies.

The ponies were brought for one reason. Because of Walkara's greatness with horses, they were to be sacrificed in his honor, and for his use in the beyond.

Diablo was first to be sacrificed—the others like him went to their glory without protest. The funeral pyre burned for four days.

Peg Leg chose to remain with Tuck and the Timpanogos. Civilization had been crowding him too.

The year was 1856. Tuck had just reached his twenty-second summer. A few short years thereafter, he heard Ouray was named Chief of the Uncompahgre tribe, now largest of all Ute tribes. And just before the beginning of the Civil War, Ouray negotiated peace and a Reservation Treaty with the government for the sixteen million acres of land promised to the Ute.

After Walkara's, death no one ever again raided California for horses and slavery, west of the Rockies, became almost a thing of the past.

Though urged by others, Tuck never felt like he should assume leadership of the Timpanogo. He and Missy Ann became as husband and wife. When Ouray's treaty was made Tuck knew he could never go to the reservation or serve under chief Ouray. Most of the other Timpanogo did, and it became time for Tuck to leave the Ute. He, Missy Ann, Gray Owl, old Deer's Foot and Nip followed Peg Leg, now in poor health, back to Fort Bridger.

There had never been any cause for Tuck to spend his New Mexico cache of gold coins. Now it would come in mighty handy.

21

"BLOOD"

That night in Peg Leg's cabin, Missy Ann had tugged Tuck's face toward hers and said, "Ya bashful lad, look at me." She'd cupped his chin with both hands and pulled him close so her eyes were looking directly into his. "Ya remember that day when I come riddin Diablo in from Salt Lake? And for the first time ya touched me? Ya big galoot, with yer sweetness an teazin, ya set me poor heart to blazin." He just lay there staring at the ceiling.

She gently placed her hand on his mouth, he sighed and let their eyes meet. "Me love, t'is it hard for ya to love?" She had kissed him softly on each eyelid, "Its, okay." That was the night of the same day they'd ridden into Fort Bridger.

Peg Leg had said the fort wasn't much to look at, but not at all like Tuck expected. No guards, no stout gate to open, and it was almost full sunrise, and nobody was up or moving. Tuck had in mind a busy stockade, though Peg Leg told him the army wasn't using the fort any longer. Somehow he'd at least expected something that looked like a battlement.

Long ago, in one his better moods, Otto had described a fort he had help build when he and the Ashley Party first came into the unexplored western Rockies. Tuck remembered him saying, "Forts was for fighting Injuns and had twelve foot tall pointed tip log walls and iron barred, double stockade gates. Me and the other men notched slots into the logs from which to shoot."

That was nothing like what Tuck saw today. And as far as he was concerned Fort Bridger, well, it looked more like a rundown trading post. Just a dozen log cabins, blacksmith's lean-to, a livery stable, a few old weathered canvas army tents and falling down split-rail corrals. The main building, sod roofed, log walls with windowless board and batten add-ons stood at the fort's center. Out front, painted on a weathered plank, a sun bleached sign read, INN AND STORE. The only sentinel that challenged them—on top off the Inn's roof, a long spurred, wing flapping red rooster, strutted and crowed.

"That's my cabin yonder," Peg Leg pointed and then led them to the back of the settlement.

They'd tied off the horses on the sagging hitching rail, shoved open the leather-hinged door and gone inside. One large rectangular room and at the far end a yawning stone and mortar fire place, a raised stone hearth and three cast iron pots and one fry pan sat waiting. A small square table and two benches nestled in one corner. The cabin was not unlike the one Otto built—the place Tuck was born in. Memories had rushed back.

"I set this plank floor 'bout ten years ago," Peg Leg boasted, drumming on it with his silver tipped stump. "Was nothin but bare dirt, before." Missy Ann was excited just having a real roof over their heads, though it took them all day to shovel out pack rat nests, sweep and clean away years of cobwebs and dust. Greased paper windows were torn and rotted. Peg Leg hauled in an armful of wood and got the stone fireplace putting out much welcomed heat. Missy Ann scrubbed the blackened pots clean.

"She ain't much, but back in the eighteen thirties I built her with my own hands. First cabin built here...yer welcome to stay long as ya please."

Peg Leg took off hippity-hoppin' toward the Inn. Soon he'd returned carrying a bundle. "Fresh victuals," he sang through his toothless grin.

As the day wore on no one had approached the cabin. All Peg Leg said was, "They all cut me a wide birth. An don't none of you don't go wanderin off without me."

A tin lined, varmint safe, storage box held several colorful quilts and old gray army-issue blankets. They stretched a couple of cords from the log rafters and hug the blankets just so, dividing the cabin into three sections. Two, for sleeping, one, for cooking and sitting. Deer's Foot and Gray Owl would sleep in one, Tuck and Missy Ann in the other. On the floor, in the kitchen next to the fireplace, hacking with consumption, Peg Leg bedded down.

This first night in the cabin with the place scrubbed clean Tuck and Missy Ann finally lay together on their buffalo robe pallet. Tuck's thoughts were miles away—back at the cabin, where Otto didn't care. Whenever Otto wanted to bed Tuck's mother he did. Day or night, drunk or sober, no matter if Tuck was asleep or awake. Those old feelings and impressions always vex and anger him.

Sometimes Missy Ann's strong opinions and outspokenness crowded him. Back at the village in their lodge it was different. He could just walk out and there was always a place of silence within a few paces. Not now. Not here inside this cabin.

Missy Ann pulled him close. As usual, she sensed his uneasiness and said, "It's okay darling, just hold me."

And like a warm breeze on a winter day her words helped calm his troubled thoughts. Relaxed and at peace, he wrapped his long arms around her tiny waist and pulled her over on top of him.

Next morning Peg Leg rattled around the cook fire before the sun was up. Soon the aroma of coffee, fried eggs and smoked bacon filled the cabin. Then came Gray Owl's chatter and Peg Leg making even more ruckus trying to shush him.

"Eggs and bacon?" Missy Ann waking from her sleep, happily called out.

"In this fort we got plenty of hen's eggs. And they's more than plenty enough roosters in these parts," Peg Leg chuckled, "but for my tastes, they ain't nearly enough purty pullets."

Tuck roared with laughter...Missy Ann poked him with her elbow.

Outside after breakfast, Tuck and Peg Leg sat alone talking.

"You can grow one can't ya?"

"Always shaved...in our village no one had much face hair to speak of but me. I reckon I'd have felt out of place."

"Not here. This be white folk's quarters. I were you, I'd let'er grow." Thoughtfully, Peg Leg stroked his own chest length gray beard.

Tuck saw, that was true. Men at the fort sported all manner of chin whiskers. Long hair and braids were a matter of convenience and warmth. The women there dressed in long lindsey-woolsey frontier skirts and men's Mackinaw or Hudson Bay coats and sunbonnets that protected their white skin from the intense high mountain sun.

Peg Leg noted, "There still be a few of us early mountain men left who've gone Injun. Most dress Cheyenne—fringed buckskins, moccasins and all. But old buckskinners always have the longest whiskers, reckon for to show our white manhood." Now and then smooth faced Indians did come to the fort to trade, Blackfoot, Crow, Snake and others. Tuck hadn't paid much attention before but now he noticed the contrast between them and the whites living at the fort.

From the store Tuck bought Missy Ann enough wool and flannel and white ribbon to make at least two dresses, one for her and one for Deer's Foot. Like most young ladies trained in sewing skills Missy Ann soon created proper attire for them both. The bonnets, well, she would think about that. Deer's Foot declined wearing the new dress still preferring her old doeskins. He'd kept his decision to himself but in a week Tuck's beard sprouted dark and full. Red cheeked, Missy Ann complained but soon got used to its abrasiveness.

In time some folks at the fort began speaking to them. Gray Owl tanned brown but obviously of white heritage drew whispers. Mostly Gray Owl jabbered in Ute and ran around the fort with the uninhibited freedom given to Indian children. But it was murmured, "Who's the father? Whiskers and blue eyes—he's obviously a half-breed."

Peg Leg shrugged off the gossip, "Ain't one thing it's a tuther. We done em a favor—give em something to gab about." And they had. Questions and all manner of gossip, like where did their gold coin come from? Was the old squaw really Walkara' s mother...maybe Peg Leg's woman? Tuck his son? And who was sleeping with whom? When they got around to snubbing Missy Ann, Tuck started wondering if doing what Peg Leg advised was worth it.

"Papa," as Gray Owl now called Tuck, "why do the other children call me a buzzard? I'm Gray Owl, not buzzard."

Peg Leg muttered to Tuck, "Ain't buzzard they's callin him. T'is bastard."

Tuck's face glowed red with rage. Missy Ann encouraged Tuck that with time the gossip and name-calling would stop. But receiving insults was not the Ute way. Tuck had learned to believe insults were something he had to deal with. But it was children not the adults who were careless enough to let themselves be caught speaking openly about Peg Leg's new family. What could he do? Winter was upon them and leaving now would not be wise.

Missy Ann found a certain comfort living at the fort. Insults and gossip were not unfamiliar. "Like water off a wee duck's back." And she took each day as it came, trusting for better times come spring.

Oblivious to cold, Deer's Foot had her daily rituals. Gathering herbs, roots and berries despite Peg Leg's cautioning that none of them to go off alone. Sometimes at night, especially when the moon was full, she would trek the half-mile down to the river and bathe alone. At those times she went stone deaf and all the complaining did not slow her down one bit.

Tonight she'd gone off alone to bathe despite a light dusting of new snow just beginning to fall.

Until Missy Ann called them to bed, Tuck and Nip sat next to their outside campfire listing to a distant pack of wolves howling. Before he went in the thought crossed his mind—Deer's Foot knows how to look after herself. But by morning Deer's Foot had not returned. Without waking the others at first light Tuck went looking.

There on the riverbank, face down and covered thinly with fresh snow, was the naked, Deer's Foot. Tuck knew she would not be lying that way unless she was dead or unconscious. He walked slowly toward her, old age he figured...she'd lived a long life. Nip whined, raised his snout, sniffed at the frosty air and growled.

Reaching her side, Tuck saw blood. Not much, just a small knife wound under her left rib in her back. Deer's Foot's face was not just lying on the earth but jammed into it. Her long thin legs were spread wide and there in soiled mud were two round depressions of someone's heavy knees between her legs filling with new snow. Someone had knelt there and done their demented dastardly deed.

Tuck cursed himself for not coming to check on her sooner. But he knew how independent she was. What sort of vermin could do something like this? Also filling with snow was a single set of store-bought boot prints around her body. Her clothes were nowhere to be seen. Whoever did it had done it sometime in the middle of the night before much snow had fallen.

Tuck did not have much time before the tracks would be completely buried. Quickly tracking down river, about fifty yards, he soon discovered shod hoof prints. It had been a white man. He heard a shriek and turned back to see Missy Ann running toward Deer's Foot, and throw herself on the body weeping—until she too noticed signs. Lifting her head, with wild and panicked eyes, she searched for Tuck. She screamed, and kept screaming, "*Oh Dear God*!," again and again. Nip, excited and confused, raised his head in a mournful echo.

Tuck ran to Missy Ann's side and pulled her to her feet. He growled, "Go back to the cabin. I'm going to take care of this." He turned her and shoved her toward the fort.

Missy Ann kept looking back and crying in protest, "No...no...No." Tuck pushed her on ahead of him back to the cabin.

His mind was cold and calculating. He'd figured what needed to be done. Carry his rifle, yes, he might need that. But it was his skinning knife he intended to use. To be on the safe side he stuffed two loaded pistols into his waistband.

Peg Leg came trotting back to the cabin from the outhouse, "What's all the caterwaulin—" and stopped in mid-sentence.

"Some white bastard raped and killed Deer's Foot." Tuck swung his leg over Desert Winds back. He hissed, "I don't reckon this will take too long."

Before Peg Leg could argue, Tuck galloped out through the fort, Nip bounding on ahead of him. He called back over his shoulder, "Go fetch Deer's Foot's body."

Heads poked out of their doors and some heard Tuck say, body. All wondered about the commotion. Peg Leg stood there, one arm around Missy and his other hand clutching the sleepy-eyed Gray Owl, watching Tuck disappear into the timber. Returning to the hoof prints, a light snow was still falling. He and Nip followed the tracks down river. In less than a mile he saw the wispy white curl of a smoldering campfire. He dismounted, ground hitched Desert Wind and went ahead on foot. The man was asleep under his canvas covered bedroll. His horse was still saddled and bridled, covered with ice and frost, it lifted its head and snorted. The sleeping man did not stir nor pay any heed to the warning. Tuck and Nip approached. There on the ground scattered next to the fire were Deer's Foot's clothes. No other questions needed to be asked.

With an inch of new snow on soft ground, their steps were silent. Tuck considered sicing Nip on him, then stand back and watch the wolf tear him in pieces. No, he wanted to see the man's eyes first. Then he and Nip would finish it.

"Hey mister," Tuck nudged him with his toe. The man didn't budge. "Hey, son of a bitch" Tuck shouted and kicked the sleeping rapist in his whiskered face. Before the man could lunge for his pistol in his bedroll, Tuck's knife sliced off the only part of the man's face not covered with hair—his big, red veined, bulbous nose. The man screamed and threw up both hands to cover his face. And Tuck's razor sharp skinning knife ripped open both armpits up to the man's elbows. With the blade still embedded, Tuck drug him kicking and slobbering out from under his blanket.

The man was maybe fifty, fat and dressed in filthy back-flap faded long johns. His long red hair matted—now likened more to the color of fresh blood.

Nip, snarling and lunging, waited for an opening. Then leaped on the man's expose backside and began to rip at his rank white pimply flesh. The man's arms, he kicked, struggled and pleaded for his life. Tuck placed his foot on the man's throat, strangling his cries. Then as slowly as possible he began to carve a circle around the man's head. With one powerful sudden jerk, and at the same time taking his foot from the man's throat, Tuck lifted the bloody scalp to the sky.

The man's blubbering screams reverberated through the forest clear to the fort. Still alive and bleeding like a stuck hog, he kicked and flailed until Tuck dropped all his weight onto the man's fat belly. One thrust with his skinning knife and he mercifully cut out his heart. Then all was still. Only Tuck's heavy breathing and Nips panting, cut the stillness.

The dead man's broken-down piebald mustang stood spraddled legged, ears flat back, bug-eyed and trembling with fear, staring at Nip. It screamed once, spun stumbling and lashed out with both back legs. Its ironclad hooves flashed just past Tuck's face. Yanking out one of his pistols, his rage yet boiling, he shot the horse dead.

Cutting off the tattered worn saddle and bridle from the dead animal, he hurled it angrily into the smoldering campfire sending sparks and embers flying. Rubbing some of the blood from the palms of his hands in the snow he carefully rolled up Deer's Foot beaded doeskin dress and picked up her moccasins and stowed them in his saddlebag.

Bloody scalp in hand and the still warm heart twitched in his other saddlebag, Tuck slowly rode back into the fort covered with blood. Looking straight ahead he made an undeviating line toward the cabin. Several pairs of snooping eyes watched his return. He sensed their critical presence and hoped one of them would just say one wrong word.

Missy Ann insisted, but Tuck refused to wash off the blood saying, "Walkara would be proud of me. But first I must dance, see flames of Fire Spirit reach to the heavens and cry out my vengeance for all to hear."

"*No*, not now—not here," and Missy Ann yanked and tugged him inside. She had never seen Tuck so crazy daft. She trembled, trying to calm him.

Finally she pulled him down onto their bed. He lay there in his bloody clothes. She lay next to him listening to his heart pound and feeling strength surging and tremoring through his body. Surprisingly, within the hour, he fell asleep—like a man just satisfied. She slipped out of bed and prepared a pot of hot water.

When he woke, there was no conversation. Peg Leg and Travis

watched him silently. Tuck washed. Missy Ann dried his hands, arms and face. Then he slipped his still bloody knife from its sheath and with the same blood stained edge began to shave his face smooth and clean. Now he knew who he was.

22

"DIVIDING ASUNDER"

None of Deer's Foot's own came to Cry. Peg Leg long ago accepted graves were where you made them. But over the years not far from the fort a small cemetery had evolved with its hard wood and limestone markers and the pretense of a white picket fence. Nobody had ever come right out with it, however when Peg Leg's Blackfoot wife passed on some years before he almost put a musket ball through the fort commander's heart for reminding him which kind of folks belonged there. White folks only...of course.

"So I buried my wife in a nice spot down in the meadow yonder," said Peg Leg.

And today Deer's Foot became his wife's earth companion. Missy Ann and Gray Owl stayed behind at the funeral site gathering wild flowers for the unmarked graves. Tuck and Peg Leg moseyed toward the fort as Desert Wind dragged the empty burial travois behind.

Tuck asked, "Who did you say that fella was I skinned?"

"Called himself, Bear-grease Caliente, Cal for short, though I doubt he ever set foot in Californee," Peg Leg answered.

"Caliente? That's a Mexican name ain't it?"

"Yep means hot. Swore Mexico was where he hailed from. Funny though that hombre never spoke nothing but American and a smattering of Crow."

"Crow?"

"Yep he had a hankering for young Crow squaws. Thing is—" Peg Leg stopped talking.

"Thing is what?" asked Tuck.

"Well, by skinning him, ya may have bumped yourself a hornet's nest. He has two growed Crow sons just as ornery and shiftless as he was." Peg Leg tugged at his own scalp, "sort of like to keep this but they's a passel o' Crow living just north in them mountains. Been sometime since I done business with them."

"So Bear-grease had family then?"

"Family maybe...friends, I doubt? Never mentioned it, but the fact is a long time back your old partner Beckwourth was his sidekick. If lies was mouth-suckin' flies, the two of them woulda choked to death. Once," Peg Leg chuckled, "Bear-grease convinced poor old blind Crow Chief Red Drum that Beckwourth was his long lost son. Red Drum darn near made him chief. Both of 'em took so dang many young wives Crow, Blackfoot, Snake and Ute there might still be more n' one ol' Injun pappy looking for Cal's scalp. Well they needn't bother now," he heehawed.

"Beckwourth, his friend?" said Tuck, "I can't imagine that."

"Tuck, in this life, friends are mighty few. I just done my best to keep on good terms with all men, but there are some—" he paused. "Back in Santa Fe did ya'll see any of us passing the pipe with Beckwourth?"

"But Chief Walkara and him seemed—"

"Purely for business. Before ya'll come along nobody saddled up with him."

"Yes, but he said it was because—"

"T'was because of his blood, right?" said Peg Leg.

"Sort of. I guess I was feeling the same way about myself back then," said Tuck.

"Well lad, its said, misery loves company." Tuck glanced sideways at him, drooped his head and nodded in agreement.

Peg Leg said, "Out here—least the way it were—men got judged by what they were doin, not what they mighta did and not the shade of their hide."

"Don't seem that way now," Tuck said.

"Things change."

Out of earshot from Missy Ann, Tuck said, "Speaking of Beckwourth, what about, Christina?"

"Want my honest opines? Daresay he's kept all the gold and more than likely sold her to go work—"

Tuck finished the sentence, "A whorin'?"

"More en likely."

"Damn."

Still some distance from the fort there wasn't a sound other than wind rustling through the pines and the clop-clop of Desert Wind's hooves. But suddenly Nip spun, growling and looked back the way they came, ears flat and neck hairs bristling. Tuck cried, "Never should have left them alone!" In a heartbeat he tore the travois from Desert Wind. "Damn," he hadn't brought his Hawken only his knife.

Glancing around he grabbed the digging spade from Peg Leg's hand and in one motion leaped on her back and spurred hard. Desert Wind, sensing his urgency, was at a dead run in two strides leaving Peg Leg sputtering and hollering, "Wait for me." And as best he could hop-sprinted after them.

On the meadow's far edge two mounted and painted young Indians were laughing and slapping each other's backs. Just as they disappeared into the forest Tuck drew near. Gray Owl and Missy Ann kicking and protesting, both hog-tied and gagged, were slung over the pommel of an Indian's saddle.

In great leaps and bounds the meadow disappeared under Desert Wind's hooves.

Bows across their backs and arrows still in their quivers there was little time to react before Tuck and Nip were on them, spade swinging, knife slashing and Nip's fangs flashing. Instantly both Crow were bloodied and knocked from their saddles but still very much alive. Tuck wheeled Desert Wind and trampled the nearest. Nip already had the other by the nape of his neck and on his knees before Desert Wind's slashing hooves sent the Indian sprawling. Tuck took a flying dive through the air and slammed head first into the staggering Indian's back. One smooth arc of Tuck's powerful right arm and the brave's cry became a strangling gurgle of spurting blood. Tuck's Green River skinning knife had had a busy couple of days. With the help of Tuck's slashing spade, yet pretty much on his own, Nip finished off the second kidnapper.

Peg Leg came across the meadow cursing, his stump digging in the soft earth, gasping for breath, "Wait for me, dag nab it!"

It was all over before those words reached Tuck's ears.

Back in the trees Missy Ann and Gray Owl were still tied and draped over the saddles. The two Indian ponies had stopped in their tracks trembling and sprattle legged, eyeballing Nip fearfully.

"Stay," Tuck commanded Nip. He rode slowly and talking softly until he held both pony's reins.

Missy Ann squealed and kicked until Tuck untied and lowered her to the ground and took off her gag. "Never-never-Never will I be without me own gun," she blurted.

Gray Owl's eyes were wide with excitement, "I wasn't...scared, Pa," he stammered as soon as his gag was removed.

Tuck left the bodies intact and said, "Seems word travels fast enough around here. If their people don't come fetch them, there's always the wolves and buzzards to clean up this mess." And they all hurried back to the fort.

"I've got to buy me a good big caliber rifle," said Tuck back at the cabin.

Peg Leg said, "Tuck, that Inn Keeper won't sell ya a gun. Don't fret yourself askin'."

"Why, Damn it? My gold is as good as—"

"There ya go boy. Ya got to learn," Peg Leg scolded, "things is the way they is. Most whites hate Injuns. Far as they be concerned, you're Injun. Work around 'em, not through. I'll go buy what ya want. That Inn Keeper won't dare open his yap to me."

Tuck said, "Okay but after today Missy Ann is going to get my Hawken .33. And hanging on the wall in the store there is a Hawken .52—it's about time I get me a decent buffalo gun. Fetch a bullet mold while you're at it. Cartridges loads, if he's got them."

"Cost a heap," Peg Leg said.

"What's gold for? While you are at it try and trade those two new Indian ponies for something," Tuck said.

Shortly Peg Leg came trotting back grinning like a bear in a honey tree. He had Tuck's new Hawken but what he was waving wasn't any bigger than his paw...fact, smaller. "Derringer, he calls 'em. They's bran spanking new. Double barrel, with one over, the other under. Thirty-two caliber. Big enough to change any fool's mind. Your Misses kin pack it most anywhere—leggings, pouch or pocket. Lookee here, Missie," as Peg Leg had taken to call her. "Brung ya a dandy pocket pistola."

She came out on the front porch drying her hands. Peg Leg grinning proudly held the small Derringer out to her.

Noo. T"is a toy ya brung me?"

"Toy, me arse. Cost two ponies. That palm size tornado will knock a sizable hole in any screachin Comanche," said Peg Leg."

She took the pistol in her small hand and examined it. Its weight was impressive and she had to admit the caliber was sizable.

Peg Leg reached into his britches and pulled out a hand full of brass saying, "And lookee here—no need for ball and powder—brass cartridges too." And Missy Ann also got her rifle. Never again was she without one or both.

Heavy storm clouds rolled in from the north. The month of Falling Leaves Moon was over. Winter in the cabin would be spent mostly chopping wood and cooking. With a great deal of complaining from the men folk, Missy Ann began to teach all three to learn their letters and numbers. "Can't be havin' no dummies in this family." Even Peg Leg learned to write his name and do something with numbers besides count on his fingers.

"How did ya ever do yer trading without numbers?" she scolded.

Cabin fever was finally getting to all of them. Once the heavy snows let up Missy Ann spent a lot of time practicing with her Derringer. The first time she fired it, not keeping a good tight grip, the little weapon leaped right out of her hand. She already knew how to load and fire her Hawken—aiming and shooting straight still needed work.

Peg Leg got to talking everybody's ears off until he was so ignored the only conversation he enjoyed was with himself, which was considerable.

Weather permitting Tuck began to spend more and more time riding off on Desert Wind hunting. Then in early spring the day arrived when Tuck came plodding through mud and snow back into the fort his lariat tied to Desert Wind and dragging the largest Grizzly any of them, including those in the fort, had ever seen.

Desert Wind didn't like being hitched to that monster bear. Big eyes rolling white trying to keep a watch on the grizzly she was pulling and at the same time keep a straight line toward the cabin.

Tuck dismounted looking satisfied. He whispered to Peg Leg, "There was a couple of Crow Indians watching me when I drilled this grizzly with one shot. They followed me for a ways. Couldn't say for sure if they was friendly or what? Stayed back some distance."

Tuck saved the giant grizzly's hide, claws and fangs and there was enough bear meat for the whole fort. Some joined in, some not.

As far as Bear-grease and his two dead sons was concerned nobody ever came to fetch the bodies. By spring they were just piles of scattered bones.

Early yellow crocus were pushing up through warm soil the first time the storekeeper came banging on their cabin door. Not to visit but in near panic to deliver an urgent message. "Chief Butte of the Crow wants to see you. There's a slew of 'em waiting outside the fort and they are all dressed up like Astor's plush horse."

Peg Leg stepped forward.

"Not you, Peg Leg," the store keeper snapped. "That tall Inj...ah, what's his name, Tucker?"

Tuck stepped out onto the porch. "Name's Tuck. What do they want?"

"Talk...just talk, their chief promised," the man said his voice shaking. "Please come. We don't need no more Indian wars, ah...Mister Tuck."

Tuck hadn't worn his two eagle feathers since they left Fish Lake. But now he got all gussied-up, feathers, tomahawk, rifle, the beaded sash Walkara had given him and all Tuck's medicine and totems.

"Mighty impressive," said Peg Leg.

"And mighty cocksure to be goin off by his self alone," Missy Ann snapped.

"Got no choice." Tuck rode out alone to talk.

Gray Owl bawling, "My Pa-my Pa."

Missy Ann, slamming pot and pans and crying, "Two times a widow." She stomped around the cabin carrying on despite Peg Leg's reassuring words.

"They said talk, an talk it'll be Missie. Stop your frettin lass. Chief Butte's a man of his word."

Near sundown an orange glow streamed in the open door and Missy Ann and Gray Owl were still sniffing back tears. Tuck finally reappeared.

"Ooooh," she gasped and raced out the cabin door to meet him.

The expression on Tuck's face seemed peculiar, him sort of smiling and just sitting there ramrod straight on his horse saying nothing. He still wore his feathers but darned if didn't look like he was now wearing three. Cradled in his arms was a long beaded buckskin pouch. When she extended her arms to greet him, he just handed her the pouch a bigger grin spreading across his face. Expecting an embrace, "What's this?" Missy Ann frowned.

Not answering he swung down from the saddle. His first step was unsteady...the second he fell flat on his face.

Missy Ann let out a scream and fell on her knees next to him, "I knew it—I knew it. They've poisoned him." Tuck's face landed in the mud. She rolled him over on to his back.

"Howdy Darlin'," Tuck mumbled the big grin still spread across his face.

"Peweee, yer stinkin drunk. Ba goom! All the long day I had the glooms and you be out gallivantin'." She left him lying there in the mud with his white teeth grinning and she stomped back into the cabin carrying the beaded pouch.

Peg Leg watched it all and though he wasn't certain he had an idea what had taken place. Remembering the two bodies were never claimed, gave him the best clue. Then the Crow seeing Tuck kill that massive grizzly with one shot. Chief Butte waited for spring before he came to talk—winter not being a time for such ceremonies.

"What ya got there, Missie?" As Peg Leg, reached for the pouch, she almost threw it at him.

"Look at that big bum flopped out there!" she shouted.

Tuck just rolled over, got to his hands and knees and crawled slowly toward the cabin door.

Peg Leg slid out the contents of the pouch. "Well, lookee here, a Chief's Pipe. By golly, I reckon Butte done made our Tuck a Crow chief." He figured something like that must have taken place seeing three eagle feathers in his hair.

Missy Ann cried, "But he's rotten drunk...Injuns ain't allowed ta drink hard liquor."

"Allowed? I allow they do whatever they want," Peg Leg laughed. "Any who, that's a dang white man's lie. Some of em can drink me under the tradin table. Enough Kickapoo lightin an a Chief makin ceremony, can set a man, any man, way back on his haunches. Tuck just ain't used to hard firewater." And Peg Leg headed outside to help Tuck into the house.

Gray Owl cheered, "Wow, my pa is a real Crow Chief too!"

Just in time Peg Leg steered Tuck off the porch and out behind the cabin. There he chucked up quite a bit of his ceremony.

Missy Ann stood there perplexed with her hand on her hips listening to Tuck puke, out back of the cabin. "A Crow Chief? So what's that supposed to mean to us now?"

24

"HEALED"

Black's Fork of the Green River was still running high but most of spring's runoff found its way down to the muddy Colorado by early June. The crossing was uneventful and Tuck led them high into the Unita Mountains following the direction Chief Butte gave him; a summer camp up through majestic blue spruce, fir and pine—a large meadow of Indian Rice grass located on the north side of Kings Peak—a clear stream lined with Quaking Aspen and River Birch running just below the sacred Buffalo Hump Rock—there they would find the Crow.

Tuck was a little uneasy heading in the general direction of Salt Lake but there would still be plenty of rugged mountain country between them and those who drove him and his people from their village at Spanish Fork.

Blue-crested Stellar Jays screeched at them and tree squirrels chattered in the treetops as they wove their way through the ancient forests. The higher they climbed the cooler air tasted sweet and crisp. Missy Ann and Gray Owl's cheeks glowed ruddy pink in the forest's shadowy canopy. Yes, it was a good day to travel.

That night they made camp under a moonless, star matted sky. No sounds, but wind voices in the high tree tops, their campfire warm and food and blankets a plenty. That night in bed, for the first time in along awhile, they came together. Rest and sleep followed as was intended.

They didn't find the Crow—early morning breakfast was cooking when the Crow found them and escorted them to their secluded summer camp. An understandable suspiciousness and caution accompanied the first greeting but as soon as Chief Butte appeared and embraced Tuck all was well and they were treated as privileged guests, by most.

"Chief Butte, my Father was Chief Walkara," said Gray Owl.

Tuck reminded Gray Owl it was not their way to speak of the dead.

It seemed everyone already heard of Walkara's light skinned only son. Missy Ann had never told anyone otherwise, whose son Gray Owl was. Those who knew the facts were dead or far away. Tuck had his doubts...he knew it took a least eleven moons for a colt to be born and nine moons for a man child but he never questioned Missy Ann.

Chief Butte knew Tuck's true status as Walkara's only Grandson. And nothing more was said. Before nightfall Tuck and Missy Ann had their own lodge and Gray Owl was running and playing with the other children. Regardless of Chief Butte's welcome there were those who were jealous of Tuck and his chief status. Others just referred to him as, Tall Tree for his size and strength. Some wondered if he was really so important, or if he had actually killed the giant grizzly and the terrorist Bear - grease and his sons? And why, if Chief, did he only own ten horse and two mules?

It didn't take long and Tuck's prowess as hunter and provider brought further respect from most.

Under warm summer skies and four easy Moons living with the Crow, Missy Ann had mixed freely with the other women of the camp. She learned a few new medicines and new ways to cook using Crow methods. Tuck never complained about the results either.

Gray Owl, once he put aside the need to boast, became one with the other youth emulating the deeds of respected leaders and braves.

Most of the meadow grass was eaten down and turning brown. Success in the buffalo hunt, food gathering and their winter supplies were heavy with a promise of a winter of wellbeing. As often happens, several babies were born at almost the same time—Missy Ann gained favor with her doctoring skills. There was even time for games: horse racing, foot racing and wrestling which occupied the men during the pleasant Indian summer.

Sixteen hands tall, Desert Wind towered over shorter Indian ponies. In races she fared well on straight-away, flying ahead of the short-legged rivals but on sharp turns they gained ground on her. Where the obsession to win came from, Tuck couldn't say, but he had to force himself to not press Desert Wind to her fullest to win every time. A similar discernment arose during wrestling matches; Tuck's size and strength acceded to his smaller rival's quickness and skills. Everyone laughed, screaming with delight occasionally seeing the giant Tuck flat on his back.

Chief Butte saw and respected Tuck's wisdom.

That year the two men became close friends.

In the darkness of their lodge Tuck and Missy Ann spoke softly with each other. Gray Owl slept on the far side of the lodge. This night Tuck wiped tears from Missy Ann's cheeks...this was unusual...he could not remember when he last saw her cry without knowing why?

"I don't know...I don't know why." She buried her face in his naked chest.

At the first quarter of Resting Moon they and the tribe left the Crow summer camp by heading back down Black's Fork and skirting the fort to where the Big Sandy merged with the Green River. Winter camp was many miles to the east in a protected valley in the heart of the Great Divide Basin. Under a full moon before the first snow they reached their destination.

Inside their lodge, next to a keep-warm fire, Tuck's hand rested lightly on Missy Ann's smooth but flat stomach. "It will be all right, Missy... some day we will have our child."

For weeks now she moped during the day and now, in this moment, after so many disappointments, as each Moon passed, she wept.

With Chief Butte's blessing, Walkara being dead and the time for mourning long past, he told Tuck and Missy Ann it would be an honor to marry them in the way of the Crow. Missy Ann secretly hoped—wanted to believe—that would be the thing that would bring God's favor on her womb. Thus far nothing had changed.

Privately Tuck pondered the fact, Spring Willow was Walkara's only child and she too had but one child. And like Missy Ann—still one child— and not from his own loins. Still he had no great feelings of urgency.

The time came when Missy Ann's sorrows metamorphosed to anger. "Ya think it's me, don't ya?" she snapped, "Well just maybe not." Hands on her hips and fire in her eyes, "Well mister chief, I've heard tell sometimes it be the fella's fault. Him shootin' blanks."

Tuck stomped out of their lodge feeling insulted and embarrassed. Maybe it was time he asked Butte's advice? After all Butte was old, maybe fifty moons, twenty years his senior. If he wasn't too old maybe he still made babies with his wife?

Butte caught off guard with the question looked flustered and said, "I do not know of such things. Perhaps we should ask my wife?"

And Tuck saw no harm in that. Except she didn't know, either. So she asked one of the very old women who, as it were, was almost deaf. Butte's wife shouted her question not once but twice and soon everybody in camp was discussing the possibility of such truth, sometimes white man's guns did shoot blanks...Indian arrows never did. Much laughter and gesturing followed.

Outside his lodge, in the presence of others, Tuck could not raise his eyes. And when he finally did venture out it was quickly to fetch Desert Wind then he and Nip trotted off through the snow for a three-day hunt. When he returned no one mentioned the mysterious question but he was sure the younger women of the tribe giggled whenever he passed. In the future he would keep his mouth shut about such matters.

During the long winter Tuck heard many tales of strange and wondrous places, both east and north where endless herds of buffalo still covered the prairies. Especially interesting were those tales of the place of yellow stones, where Mother Earth's breath burned hot. Missy Ann's wanderlust and curiosity paralleled Tuck's.

Come spring, Tuck thanked Butte for his hospitality and Missy Ann and Gray Owl bid farewell to new friends. They hugged and shook hands when it was time to leave. The three of them rode northeast across the Sweetwater looking for the South Pass. There, they'd been told, good trails were many, but also many white men.

What they were told was true. They skirted several wagon trains and hunting parties of white men on horseback dressed in all manner of store bought attire. Usually, one of their group wore the dress of mountain men. But all carried long barrel, large caliber rifles. And behind them followed wagons stacked with what at a distance appeared to be buffalo hides.

One morning early just as the sun spread its warmth across the frost tipped prairie grasses they came upon a plateau littered with mounds of slaughtered carcasses of bulls, cows and calves, still steaming. Ravens and buzzards were already circling overhead. There would be plenty for scavengers. Tuck wondered of such waste, though many Indians and whites still believed there were as many buffalo as blades of prairie grass.

Tuck and Missy Ann spoke little to each other these last few months. Both appeared to take a step back. Their manner toward each other cordial, on occasion even affectionate, but the thing heavy on both of their minds went unspoken. Even Gray Owl noticed. It was like they waited for something to happen that didn't. He stayed close to Missy Ann but his eyes were on Tuck, watching and trying to understand. Something was missing, maybe it was Uncle Peg Leg or his kindly old Great-grandmother?

There was no need to hurry on their journey. The country bountiful, weather held friendly and up the Wind River they moseyed. In Peg Leg's old bag of possibles, Tuck found steel fish hooks. Keeping their eyes peeled for grizzlies, Tuck and Gray Owl spent days casting their lines, setting their hooks in native cutthroat trout in clean clear streams.

Gray Owl munched away on both smoked and dried fish, saying they were his favorite food, especially seeing he did most of the catching.

They camped close to a small tributary near where the Shoshone joins the Wind River. Most days Gray Owl went alone to fish but with grizzlies around he kept within sprinting distance of camp.

Missy Ann sat by Tuck's side, even more quiet than usual. Then for no apparent reason she blurted, "Ya know Travis is not Walkara's son." And she jumped up, dashed down to the creek and sat next to Travis's side and gave him a big hug.

A bit surprised, Tuck stayed put just watching Gray Owl try to teach his mother to put a grasshopper on the hook. But Missy Ann kept glancing back toward Tuck, a look of defiance on her face he did not understand. What- ever it was going on in her mind, she seemed mighty uncomfortable. He wondered why she would say something like she did and then run off? Heck it wasn't like he hadn't figured that out a long time ago. Yes, he knew the truth but it did not matter to him. He loved the boy as his own. Perhaps Walkara too had known?

What matter? Sometimes it was right to speak things that were not, as though they were. Particularly, if they were good things. Travis Gray Owl was certainly a good thing...a gift from Great Spirit to many. Tuck lay back on his elbows watching the two of them. She was as pretty as the day they met...maybe even prettier. And Travis was beginning to grow out of his buckskins about as fast as Missy Ann could cut him new ones. From a shaky start health wise, now even his eyes were almost normal.

Both the boy and his mother were growing trail hardy, complexion's tanned, a balanced quickness in their steps and Travis learning to ride his own horse almost as well as him. Far as Tuck figured, life was good. So why is she acting so darn persnickety?

He stood and stretched. From his private reverie he suddenly realized Missy Ann, pulling Travis by the arm, was standing directly in front of him. The smile he intended didn't have time to show itself before she postured defensively with an expression on her face he had never seen before... corners of her tight-lipped mouth trembled, lines of anguish contorted her usual almost childlike visage into a mask of fear. Yet her green eyes flashed desperate ire. Tuck thought, don't know why, but now she's gone and let her stewpot boil over. He started to speak, "What is—?" And before he could ask his question she began screeching at him.

With a great lung full of air she bellowed, "Quiet now." She shoved her face up toward him her eyes bulging, "Before you run us off..." her choked voice was almost unrecognizable, "I'm gonna speak me peace." Fingers curled like talons, tears began to well in her eyes. Words like bitter tastes spit out from between her pursed lips, "Mister Chief Tuck, for yer information, yer old grandfather wasn't the only man I bedded with. Fact is some called me a hopeless tramp. Fact, Brigham Young promised to put me in front of a firing squad for getting knocked up by one of his big shot Bishops, til he traded me to Walkara for Diablo."

Taken completely by surprise Tuck stood there with his mouth hanging open. He'd listened to her angry words but heard a louder voice of desperation.

"An one last thing," she gasped. "Then me an Travis...will be leavin." And her voice turned to a broken stream of tears and woeful mewing sounds, "Never to any man before did I say, I love ya, till I said it to you." And she collapsed to her knees by his feet. Travis, wide eyed and scared, still held tight to her hand.

Tuck reached out his long muscular arms and pulled the two of them to his chest.

"Nay...Na—" briefly she resisted. Scarcely could she breathe—his right arm grasped her so tightly. For several moments they stood there together saying nothing.

Tuck's heart pounded, his thoughts left hapless and his eyes brimming with tears, able only to scan the silent landscape until the right words might find him. All he knew to do was hold the two of them, heads buried tightly against his body. Finally Missy Ann, her body tight a bowstring began to relax, her silent sobs muffled in Tucks chest.

Travis was first to look up at Tuck. "Papa?"

Travis' question was met by the smile Tuck intended earlier and Tuck kissed him lightly on the forehead. He smiled back. The look they exchanged said: all the fearful, confused words don't make any difference. Travis's small hand patted his mother's back.

At the moment the only thing Tuck could think to say seemed out of place, but he lowered his head next to Missy Ann's ear and whispered it anyway, "How's fishin, my loving sweetheart?"

Sounds like a kitten mewing slipped from Missy Ann's throat, followed by a shuddering sigh and, "Ya be my best catch...Big Chief."

Tuck lowered himself to the ground. A head resting on each of his shoulders the three of them lay there on a carpet of tender grass listening to stream songs sounds, and watching white sailing ships drift in a pale turquoise sky, a warm breeze caressed. Spoken words, unimportant.

That night as they lay together Missy Ann couldn't resist saying, "Seems I was once married to yer grandfather. Sooo, Mitakoye Tokehe, how do ya like beddin down with yer grandmother?"

25

"WHO I AM"

Chief Butte had confirmed what Peg Leg once told Tuck, "James Beckwourth deceived many. From the Blackfoot and Snake tribes he took more than his share of young wives and beaver pelts, never paying for wives or pelts. After he left, his name among many tribes was, Weetah (buffalo) Skunk." It was fairly obvious now why few had a good word for him.

But to Tuck, Beckwourth was teacher and friend when he felt no one else cared. Yet concerns for Christina still crossed his mind, maybe Beckwourth mended his ways? He wanted to believe Christina and Beckwourth were living somewhere in California on a big white fenced rancho and owning lots of top grade horses...the gold used by both for enjoying many good times. He mused, I've still got most of my gold...maybe me and Missy Ann should go to California and buy horses?

Tuck gazed west, laying prone on Desert Wind's back his head resting comfortably on her round rump and his arms and legs dangled loose along her sides. He whispered, "Wonder what really happened to them?"

Peg Leg's earlier speculation hadn't been far from the truth figuring Beckwourth would grab all the gold for himself, and he had. But only after Christina ran off and married a young Spanish vaquero whose wealthy father just happened to own the biggest ranchero in San Bernardino.

Christina had laughed at Beckwourth, flaunting what her new husband, Don Jose De La Cruz owned. By comparison, making the paqueno pouches de oro, no importante mas. She tried convincing her eager but naive Spanish lover, there was still hope of Revolucion—taking back the lands 'gringos' stole from the people.

In a sense, that made Beckwourth almost one of the enemy. So he drifted north to San Francisco trying his hand at gold prospecting, not with pan, pick or shovel but hiring others to do the dirty work. Bad rumors followed, of high-grading ore and cheating with rigged gold scales. Then he finally found himself an honest niche, investing his take in building roads through parts of the Sierras. Toll charges and a hotel of sorts kept the projects solvent for a time but his dreams of prosperity never came to pass.

Using the last of his gold he tried ranching for a few years but in a no-limit poker game he finally went broke loosing lock, stock and barrel, including Concho, and all his silver trappings.

Beckwourth reckoned it was time to return to more familiar country. So he headed for Taos and Santa Fe, arriving on a borrowed mule. The only livelihood he found was tending bar until, in '58, the gold rush at Pikes Peak lured him. Less than one in a thousand even made expenses. He cursed himself for not being one that did.

Busted, he skulked into Pueblo Colorado, nothing left but his last pair of britches, a red flannel shirt and the old lop-eared mule. So Beckwourth decided to offer his services to the army as guide, interpreter and scout. Always the opportunist, he knew the Civil War's end was at hand and the army would refocus its attention on the Indian problem. Because of his language skills and knowledge of tribes and their camp sights he was hired on the spot as scout with The Third Colorado Volunteers to serve under the command of the fighting parson, Colonel, John Chivington.

It annoyed Beckwourth to hear the derogatory title the troop had earned: "The bloodless troop" as yet never actually fighting or killing anybody. I'll fix that, he promised himself.

Beckwourth saw nothing wrong with leading the army soldiers against those his government deemed unruly or a menace to decent folks. And that included Indians that resisted relocation to reservations.

Chivington loaned—Beckwourth later claimed gave—him a string of five good army horses. In Beckwourth's financial straights he would have done anything for those horses. That's just who he was.

The war was almost over and there would be plenty of drifters, deserters and ne'er-do-wells, who, for the promise of a horse, three hots and a cot, would do anything for employment. And killing savages for the army paid better than most jobs.

As Tuck and his family traveled, "Ah-hi-e," the exclamation of friendly greeting was exchanged often with most Indians of that region. But the trio preferred keeping to themselves enjoying the long warm days and private personal nights together.

They crested the Continental Divide and a tableau of geological wonders met their gaze as they entered the mysterious, enchanted land of the Yellow Stone's burning waters. They stood watching as twilight stole down on their campsite there on the shores of a mirrored lake that reflected nearby granite peaks. The following morning the gates of dawn opened to a bountiful specter. Tuck thinking, enough to feed dreams of any hunter, as herds of elk and buffalo greeted his eyes. Here also, black bear were as common as jackrabbits and 'Oso Grande' the giant grizzly roamed as king.

Everyone and everything folded back out of the grizzly's way as the ruling beasts plodded and rambled, fishing and foraging in almost every meadow and stream. Tuck cautioned Gray Owl about that fact.

There Tuck saw roving bands of Sioux and Cheyenne hunters. Surprisingly, some knew and uttered the name, Tall Tree, given by the Crow tribe, who in turn told northern Crow Chief Plenty Coups, who mentioned it to friendly Lakota Sioux. Others, Tuck recently met, Oglala Sioux, acknowledged the honor of Chief toward him and called him, Wichasa Tonga—Chief Big Man. Tuck glowed with pride, perhaps for the first time fully believing, I am Ute, grandson of Walkara, Hawk of the Mountains, I too am Chief.

Though the Lakota saw Tuck as warrior, hunter and Chief they were equally fascinated by Missy Ann and Gray Owl, how except for light colored eyes and skin, spoke and behaved as Ute. Many Lakota had never seen a white person up close. And, to Tuck's relief, most hunting parties were no longer as interested in striking coup with strangers. They now pursued peace among 'cousins' and holding parleys to speak of the invading whites and dwindling hunting grounds. All recognized the increasing need to unite for mutual protection.

Weeks later under leaded skies, Tuck, leading Missy Ann and Gray Owl, followed a narrow deer trail along a precarious descent. Below, in the steep and deep canyon, the Yellowstone River growled like muted thunder, plunging and cascading over craggy yellow and crimson cliffs. Even with hot springs and thermal geysers, the Absaroka Mountains were no place to spend the winter. They must come down out of the high country and find a protected winter camp...by themselves if necessary.

Caravanning out of the great Yellowstone valley, Tuck's mind turned back to the easy days journeying up through Wind River country many miles south of the place of Burning Waters. There, in those grassy foothills while visiting other villages, for the first time he observed the Arapaho Sun Dance Ceremony and caught glimpses of the cautious and private Shoshone Tribes.

It was only a week's ride, down from threatening skies that now hung on snow tipped peaks, to the Yellowstone River, where it turned, slid and twisted eastward through rolling hills and bluffs of the Sioux and Northern Cheyenne Nations. So east, toward the rising sun they went, following the meandering Yellowstone.

Endless grassy hills cushioned the eastern horizon when suddenly they crested a long knoll—before them, an undulating sea of frost nipped golden green—they were standing on the western edge of the Great Plains—nothing but grasslands as far as they could see. Their eyes searched the eastern horizon, but even in the brightness of daylight, in crystal clear air, nothing stood out except the meandering river and a few willows and cottonwood trees to compass their journey in this unfamiliar terrain.

They rode as far as the Powder River and received no invitation to share a camp for the winter. The few Assiniboine, who dared to hunt south across the Yellowstone, galloped away laughing, after Tuck saluted them with a friendly greeting and introduced himself as Chief Wichasa Tonga of the Ute. His face reddened in spite of his dark summer skin. Apparently not everyone had heard of him. He should always wear his three feathers, and then, they would have recognized him.

Perhaps he'd waited too long to find a winter camp? All too soon, north winds came lashing like whips, stinging their faces, bending, flattening and spinning prairie grasses into mysterious patterns like giant footprints. Drab clouds scuttled above them in advance of early snows. Whistling sheets of sleet fell, piercing and foreboding. In haste, turning their horse's tails into the wind, they headed back south.

In the evening, a pale lemon sun hung on the glazed horizon. Tuck used the eastern most tip of the Bighorn Mountains, just a silver and mauve silhouette, as their reference point. Back to, and up the Tongue River, across to the Rosebud they raced the first blue northern of winter into the foothills of the Bighorns.

Great Spirit smiled on them, a protected place, a broad south-facing overhang of granite, near the headwaters of the Rosebud. For lodge poles and fire wood, a grove of cottonwood trees on three sides near the stream. There close to the overhang, they erected their lodge.

Little more than twenty miles west, on the Little Bighorn, a large encampment of Unkpapa Sioux made their winter camp. Freezing crystal days...star flecked nights watched over both campsites.

Since Tuck was a young man, rumors of Indian and white wars

circulated through Ute country, back then he had no idea of its ongoing bloody, two hundred year history here, this side of the Rocky Mountains. These wars, compared to Walkara's War with the Mormons, made that battle look like a family squabble.

Sometimes at night when the air was damp and heavy, when the west wind blew across the bluffs, Tuck thought he heard war drums. On those moonlit nights Nip stepped gingerly through the snow to the top of the granite overhang, howling into the wind. The sounds troubled his sleep—Missy Ann pressed her body close.

"Papa...Papa," Gray Owl cried.

Tuck rose to his elbows looking across the lodge.

In flickering firelight Gray Owl's eye, as big as silver dollars, whispered. "I too, hear the drums, Papa."

For the rest of that night Tuck laid with his arms folded behind his head and gazed into the fire, heart pounding, awake and wondering?

Missy Ann too, laid quietly, her hands resting on her womb feeling the new heartbeat within. Thinking, I am a good wife and mother.

Then the lone wolf came. Maybe the smell of their food or the presence of the horses or Nip's howling? Whichever, the wolf became more and more bold.

Its tracks circled the camp and each night drew closer. One stormy night Nip did not come back into the lodge to rest by the fire. Maybe he'd gone off to die? Tuck knew he was no longer young, in fact he was old, by dog standards, but not that old.

Gone for the better part of a week when Nip did drag himself back into camp, his thick winter fur was wet and matted. Exhausted, it was obvious he was glad to be back, curling up by the fire and sleeping for almost two full days. Wolf tracks never again came close to their lodge. Nip's howling ceased, but the drums continued.

Tuck hadn't heard a thing that quiet morning as he returned from chopping a hole in the ice-locked stream for his horses to drink. And yet there they were, most mounted on pinto or appaloosa ponies. Their bodies caped in blankets and furs, with frosty breath and with dark eyes staring. Braids twisted and wrapped in painted buckskin, a rifle across each saddle blanket, they watched silently from the top of the rocky ridge.

There was no chance at all for Tuck to defend his lodge. In the moments of panicked fury he hadn't any way of knowing, there was no need.

"Ah-hi-e," the lead brave raised his right hand in friendly salutation.

"Ah-hi—" and before Tuck could finish his greeting they stormed down the ridge and into their camp. Missy Ann and Gray Owl poked their heads out of the teepee hearing voices and the stomping of many hooves, not knowing what to expect.

Guttural sounds of mixed words, "Wichasa Tonga." The brave thumped his own breast. "I, Crowfoot...Sitting Bull...want see you." He leaned forward in the saddle and grasped Tuck's forearm in the traditional arm-hand shake. Crowfoot pointed west in the direction of the drums. "Chief want see." He pointed at Tuck. "Oso Big Ute With Sky Eyes."

"Oso Big Ute With Sky Eyes?" Tuck wondered how many names he'd been given? He answered Crowfoot with hand talk pointing to the sun halfway through its arc, made a double cut with his open left hand and said, "Tomorrow...this time."

"Plenty good," Crowfoot grinned, "Woman and boy too."

Tuck frowned and balked, "No, I cannot do that!"

The group of Sioux stepped their horses into a tight half circle around Tuck. Crowfoot's face lost its friendliness, he scowled, "You will!"

Missy Ann cried out from the lodge doorway, "Yes, Tuck, we will go," her cooler head prevailing.

Masterfully pirouetting their ponies, in unison they rode to the top of the ridge. Pausing, Crowfoot turned and pointed to the sun, cutting the air twice with his left hand and shouted, "Mar-'ro. Honka hey!" West, in powered snow, they left as silently as they came.

Missy Ann said, "Darlin, if I be a judge of any man they come in peace. Be not doubtful."

Doubtful? No. But all 6'5", 260 muscular pounds of him had considerable concern. Who had not heard of Sitting Bull and him not well known for hospitality? Except, toward pretty women.

26

"PASSING THE PIPE"

Just in case they might have to leave in a hurry Tuck would try and imprint the surrounding landscape, an almost flawless talent he'd developed years before. Why be at a disadvantage? The Unkpapa Sioux knew every inch of this land and so did Sitting Bull. Steep sided bluffs between the Rosebud and Little Bighorn were almost flat, only few hilly places with sloping sides for access. Wier Point, some miles away, small and treeless, was the only change breaking the horizon. No place of concealment, no natural barriers from which to shoot and in winter snow deep enough horses had to walk slowly.

At a distance, looking like a cluster of dark steaming rocks, two dozen mounted braves waited. Midday and overcast the sun just a dull orb. Reluctantly Tuck had agreed to go. He, Missy Ann and Gray Owl rode slowly in the direction pointed out to them the day before.

If Missy had understood them right, she concluded, if the three of us hadn't come willing they might have been bound hand and foot and brought anyway.

Nip growled and Tuck glanced back. Bounding along in the horse tracks he glared back over his shoulder.

Three more braves, those who secretly watched their camp that night, followed just in case they changed their minds. Sitting Bull knew what he was doing.

Tuck had prepared himself. Not sure what was appropriate attire, but wanting to honor the great Sitting Bull, he chose to not wear a blanket or robe, but to dress in his southern Ute finest buckskins, long hair streaming down his back carefully brushed, crowned with his three bald eagle feathers.

Missy said he looked grand but warned him, by the time they were half way there he'd be almost frozen stiff. Missy Ann and Gray Owl were wrapped snugly in blankets and fur with only their red noses showing.

Between his legs the warmth from Desert Wind's back was the only thing keeping his teeth from chattering and his body from shivering. He gave the mare her head. For more warmth he tried keeping his thin Ute moccasins tucked behind Desert Wind's forelegs and sat on his numb hands. The rifle slung across his back felt like a rod of ice. It was doubtful he could hold the weapon even if he had to. He wished now he'd listened to Missy Ann and wrapped himself in a buffalo robe.

With steaming breath and frost covered muzzles the Indian ponies pawed the earth restlessly, midday temperatures hovering near zero. Only dark eyes of the greeting party shown from beneath their blankets. They whispered amongst themselves...see how he dresses, Wichasa Tonga makes war with winter. The two groups exchanged greetings. The many formed a circle around the three, no weapons showing they led the way.

Nearby the Sioux camp hundreds of grazing horses dotted the slopes, pawing through crusty snow to reach dry grasses beneath. Leafless cottonwoods and willows lined the icy banks of the Little Bighorn. A flat blanket of gray smoke cloud drifted over each soot stained smoke-flap, their tall pointed lodge poles etched the sky above every smoky tan and gray teepee. More teepees than Tuck had ever seen—a hundred or more. And this was only a portion of Sitting Bull's tribe.

As with Chief Walkara, the central and largest lodge was made of perhaps fifty stitched buffalo hides and was the hub of activity. Outside the snow had been cleared to bare earth and a large fire pit was being filled with logs. Robes of black, fur up buffalo hides were spread in a circle around the fire ring.

Their escorting party reined up at a distance, "We wait here," Crowfoot commanded, Tuck. Adding, "When, Tatanka Yotanka (Sitting Bull) sits...we walk up. Your wolf stays here."

It was several frigid minutes before the fire roared to life. Slowly, deliberately Sitting Bull emerged from his lodge and seated himself in the place of most importance next to the central lodge's door.

Muted, the welcoming drum began. In amongst lodges shrill cries of eagle-bone whistles merged with wailing chants from inside the lodge. The second person to emerge, Sitting Bull's Medicine Man, was naked except for a small loincloth. His body painted ocher red, face divided red and yellow and a headpiece of raven black feather with bull buffalo horns. In his right hand, a painted turtle shell, decorated medicine stick and in the other a buffalo scrotum rattle.

Around and around the fire pit the Holy Man stomped and at the same instant his voice filled with growling guttural roars and yodeling shrieks of proclamation.

Following in his steps, painted head to toe with white dots, long hair wagging covering his face, Keeper of The Fire dusted the blaze with a fine powder creating blue/green bursts of flames. Tuck thought he'd never seen such Power.

Milling groups of onlookers drew close chanting in low tones. Four times around the fire, and the Medicine Man stopped in front of Sitting Bull, thrusting both arms to the sky. All sound, except for the fire's crackle, ceased. Every face turned toward Tuck.

"Now, we go," said Crowfoot. He dismounted and strode toward the circle.

Tuck, Missy Ann and Gray Owl followed suit and slid off their mounts. "Mmmmuuh," Tuck grunted struggling to stand. From his knees on down, felt like frozen stumps. Missy Ann, pretending to cling dependently to his arm, actually kept him from stumbling. For the next fifty feet, his benumbed, pigeon-toed pace appeared to the on lookers like the shuffling grizzly's stiff-backed, leg-swinging swagger. Together they eased slowly toward the circle. Children pointed and whispered—mother's scolded.

Crowfoot stopped, waited and stepped behind letting them go first.

Wild eyed, the Medicine Man glared at Tuck. Approaching in a crouch he held the medicine stick like a saber pointed at Tuck's heart all the while he trembled the rattle toward Tuck' s feet—warmth began to flood into his legs—their eyes joined, unspoken instruction guided Tuck from that point on. Suddenly, he realized he now sat at Sitting Bull's left hand. Missy Ann and Gray Owl sat directly across the fire pit. Tuck's entire body suddenly thawed. He realized it was more than heat from the fire.

"Keeper of The Pipe," Sitting Bull called, in almost perfect Ute. A fourth person emerged from the lodge cradling the long, white tanned, fringed buckskin, pipe-pouch. His head bowed, he handed The Pipe to Sitting Bull.

With a dramatic gesture, Sitting Bull slid the ancient Ceremonial Pipe from its sheath. The Most Sacred, red catlinite pipestone bowl with its marvelously carved head of a buffalo, he carefully adjusted onto the long beaded hardwood stem. From a small red pouch he removed a pinch of kinnikinnik, using a small bone pestle he packed it carefully.

Seemed everyone's eyes were on The Pipe. A length of sage branch stripped of its bark was plucked from the fire's edge. Sitting Bull blew its tip until it glowed bright. Placing it to The Pipe's mouth in one motion he lifted the stem to his full cut lips and drew heartily on the eagle-bone mouthpiece.

Tuck thought, this man has the body of a buffalo, the eyes of a wolf and the beak of an eagle.

Sitting Bull exhaled slowly, dense white smoke settled into a cloud on his breast. Cupping his hand into the smoke slowly, like lifting unseen water, he poured the Smoke Offering first to his heart then to his mouth and head and then into the sky.

Sitting Bull prayed, "Oh Powerful One, Maker of Day, hear our cries." A subdued murmur then a hauntingly pleasant tone of confirmation rose from those around the circle. He passed The Pipe, stem first, to Tuck.

Tuck did exactly as he'd just heard and seen...ending with the same spoken words as Sitting Bull. Other faces in the circle radiated pleasure some smiling openly. He returned The Pipe, stem first, to Sitting Bull. Only the two of them smoked. Then, The Pipe, was picked cleaned with a carved bear's tooth and handed back to The Keeper.

A torrent of words from Sitting Bull and the majority around the circle rose and scurried toward their lodges. Twelve men stayed seated. Missy Ann looked uncertain, but started to rise while holding Gray Owl by the hand and not knowing which way to go.

Sitting Bull's voice soothing and gentle, not at all like the earlier voice, crooned at Missy Ann, "Raven Flower...you, are welcome to stay."

Tuck and Missy's eyes met for an instant.

Another woman stepped forward and took Gray Owl by the arm leading the reluctant but obedient boy toward a group of children standing down by the creek. Missy Ann reseated herself. Again her eyes glanced toward Tuck but she nodded compliance toward Sitting Bull.

The Medicine Man reentered the lodge then returned with a rolled up scroll of elk hide and passed it to Sitting Bull. He then moved to his position directly behind the Chief.

Sitting Bull spoke in his loudest baritone, "Wichasa Tonga...Big Man of our Ute brothers." And Sitting Bull began to unroll the elk skin. "You, Wichasa Tonga, are well known by many. From the lands of the Paiute, Mojave, Shoshone and Arapaho to the Yellowstone and lands of the Cheyenne and Lakota Sioux, your brave deeds *inspire* our people."

Tuck was mystified and lines furrowed his brow...what could these far away people know of me? And what brave deeds of mine are worthy of mention?"

"Oso Big Ute With Sky Eyes," you have many names among your cousins. All of them names of Honor and Courage." He pointed to the elk skin. "In our lands, from great waters to great waters, traditions of our people are passed on from mouth to mouth. We do not have books or writing pages of the white man. Our history, your history, is kept around lodge fires...father to son for thousands of moons." He paused. "But... sometimes—for what reason only Great Spirit knows—some keep story-paintings on..." and he pointed again to the elk skin. "And times long ago, even before "Real People" were born, those before us made pictures-stories on rocks. Back when animals talked with men."

Tuck nodded. "Yes Chief, I have seen but do not understand the picture stories."

"Some say they do...but I do not believe they can...because I do not."

He turned and faced Tuck. And Tuck did likewise. The elk skin was paced between them.

Immediately Tuck' recognized something he'd seen his Mother drawing pictures of long ago. And after she died, Deer's Foot did the same. However, since Deer's Foot was murdered, he hadn't seen it again.

"This, Tuck Mitakoye Tokehe, is your life since you were a boy and became the only hunter for your family. Spring Willow tells of your hunting skills and wisdom. Tells of your bravery even against the white man, Otto. Even how you spoke strong words to great Chief Walkara and how he listened to you."

Tuck was dumfounded. He looked closely at the drawings trying to decipher their meanings.

Sitting Bull chuckled, "Even as a boy you were willing to fight anyone... Peg Leg and even Ouray who is now biggest Chief of the Ute. It is said, he still fears you. You became a fine horseman without anyone's help. You killed many Mexican soldiers and American soldiers and took their gold and horses, saving Buffalo Head Beckwourth." And reverently he spoke, "...and you hunt with wolves. Tuck shook his head in amazement.

Often when Sitting Bull spoke several of the men sitting close by uttered, "Howah," meaning, Yes, we agree.

"See here," he touched a line of fallen horsemen. "With one shot you killed many of a hundred Mormons and saved your people."

Tuck wanted to object and set the exaggerated stories straight, but would not dishonor Sitting Bull's words.

"You refuse to go to the government lands like so many of your people and you defied Ouray and his braves. Your people would have followed you but in wisdom of Everywhere Spirit, you knew you had not yet been prepared to lead a people."

"And now?" Tuck asked.

"Wait, there is more," Sitting Bull placed his fingers on three scalped figures. "See here, the man Bear Grease and his sons most feared by the southern Crow. You killed all three with only your knife."

Tuck wondered how that incident could be painted on the hide as Deer's Foot was already dead at that time?

"Great bear, who killed many Crow, you killed with one shot and took him to your fort...and how you were made Chief Tall Tree in parlay with the Crow and your marriage too." He smiled and glanced at Missy Ann, "And stealing Brigham Young's favorite horse. You see, we know many other tales of your wisdom and bravery not written here. Crow Chief Butte had this story-painting when he...well, gave it up to my son, Jumping Bull."

"But how did Butte get—?"

"No one still alive knows," a cunning look flashed across his face, "it is here to welcome you to our people. Your feats of courage have gone before you—Wichasa Tonga we have been waiting for you."

Tuck and Missy Ann exchanged bewildered glances.

Sitting Bull rose and addressed those other seated, "You my Elders know of my Vision. Many times this day you have spoken, Howah, at my words." He rose and stepped behind Tuck placing his open right hand over Tuck's head, "Do you say, Howah, now?"

In unison their cry, "Howah!" echoed off the hillsides.

He turned and stepped in front of Tuck, saying, "First," placing both hands on Tuck's shoulders, "Chief Wichasa Tonga, you will hear my Vision. We will pray together, and then you will decide what this Vision has for my people."

Shocked, Tuck thought, *me* decide? He needed to hear more, but found himself compelled to utter, "Howah."

Sitting Bull commanded, "Bring the gift for Chief Wichasa Tonga!"

27

"VISION"

Black as midnight, sideways he came prancing. Two struggling braves held him back on taught rawhide leads. Head tossing, nostrils flared, eyes cut of obsidian rolled and flashed. Thick, wavy mane and tail floating and swirling at a length greater than Tuck had ever seen. Feather-like shaggy fetlocks covered drum size hooves, a shrill rumbling tremolo pulsated from his gaping mouth like the steaming breath of dragons. And he was not yet three years old.

Everyone stood and cried out, "hye-hye-hye, oooh and aaahh."

Sitting Bull spoke, "I traded fifty of my best ponies for his mother, from those on the Yellowstone River who drive the floating steam-wagon." Laughing, "They did not know he was growing inside her belly." Mouth turned down he said, "His mother gave herself in birth for this noble, club-headed and great-hoofed colt."

"He was a gift from the Spirit so that I, Seeda Boo," as Sitting Bull called himself, "might honor you, Wichasa Tonga." Sitting Bull ushered Tuck to the young stallion's side.

He stood almost twenty hands tall and his withers as high as Tuck's head. Its back, neck, chest and rump, as broad and muscular as any two horses. Tuck had never seen anything like him.

"Big horse, for Big Man!" Sitting Bull exclaimed, slapping Tuck on the back. Eyes narrowed a glint of challenge teased his face, "No one here dares to ride him. Some say, devil spirit horse."

"No one's ridden him yet, you say?" Tuck eyeballed the stud.

Missy Ann gasped, seeing the colt's huge and perfect conformation.

Seeda Boo shrugged, smirked and shouted at the bystanders, "Is there none to tame Tonga Sapa Tasunke? (Big Black Horse)." No one answered the challenge.

Missy Ann stepped to Tuck's side, "He's a beauty—like the Knights of old, rode."

Sitting Bull seemed to understand, saying, "Man on boat tell Seeda Boo, Mother was of kind Cru-say-dor iron men rode to fight in God land."

"Oh my, the Crusaders," said Missy Ann.

Tuck wasn't listening. He focused only on the amazing tremoring statue of black horseflesh standing before him. "Nobody's ridden him, huh?"

His eyes met Sitting Bull's. Both men smiled, but Tuck emitted a haughty, jocular, "Humph, we'll see."

Seeda Boo, responded with a cautions doubtful wide-eyed grin.

The young stud, head aloft suspiciously, stared sideways as Tuck drew near.

Tuck, taking both lead ropes from the nervous Sioux, lifted his mouth close to the skittish charger's ear. Whispering something, he moved stealth fully and deliberately. In a flash he fashioned a crisscrossed hackamore from the lead ropes. Loose ends he grasp tight in one hand, twisting a handful of thick mane in the other, with one powerful lunge he swung onto the surprised animal's back.

The stud spread his legs and crouched, appearing to shrink several inches. With his eyes bulging and ears laid flat, he lowered his head, lips curled, he bared his teeth and froze. A few anxious moments passed. Tuck continued to speak in whispers. The stud just stood there quivering. Tuck pulled on the right rein, trying to turn his head just a bit. His forearm muscles bulged. It was like tugging on a rooted stump. Tail thrust down, the stud took a few short jerky steps backward, flexed his brawn and froze again. Tuck nudged him with his heals, not spurring kicks, but with quick firm pressure.

The young stud was almost too heavy to buck much. But when he did get moving it was like being on the back of a runaway locomotive. His back was plump, round and slippery as a rolling barrel. Tuck's legs spread wide, yet clasped tight as a catamount on a moose's back—away they went—Tuck pretty much just along for the ride. Pull him back, and he'd charge ahead. Nudge him to move forward, and he'd roar back a dozen paces. Try to turn him, and he plowed in the opposite direction.

Women and children, young, old or infirm, scattered. The other humans, horses and dogs be damned. Quickly the area was vacated by anything that could run—nearby lodges were stomped flat.

Nothing was sacred. First things to go, the Chiefs Circle, buffalo robes trampled and kicked into the fire pit, lodge poles snapped and hides torn asunder. The Medicine Man and his apprentice, the pipe and paraphernalia pouches clutched tightly, headed for the creek.

Sitting Bull's, quick hop-stepping, managed to keep him from under the pounding hooves. All the while he roared with laughter.

"Ride em', Darlin!" Missy Ann shouted back over her shoulder, as she and Gray Owl scooted for higher ground.

It could never be a contest of pure strength. Tuck wouldn't stand a chance. This struggle was going to be about force of will. This rider had no doubt about the final outcome and the irate young stallion was indignant beyond exasperation.

Sitting Bull had offered the challenge, and Tuck didn't know quit. First he tried to head the colt out of camp, but it seemed determined to take down the entire village. The struggle went on for the better part of an hour before a glint of fatigue showed itself—the horse not Tuck. It slowed. Tuck egged him on, all the more.

Finally, as if to say, okay...okay, let's think about this, the big black youngster came to a shuddering stop. His handsome head hung low, sides heaving. But Tuck still held his grip—hands and legs as tight as in the beginning.

Tuck allowed the subdue animal, now dripping sweat and steaming like a dowsed campfire, a few minutes to cool off and catch its breath.

The stud's head lifted slightly. Whispering continuously, Tuck let his heels lightly tap its ribs. Amazingly, it began to walk slowly around in a wide circle, ears up but pointed back toward Tuck, listening. Tonga Sapa Tasunke, for the first time in his young life was listening to the soft talking intruder affixed on heretofore-untouchable territory.

Nip sprinted in, taking a few protective swipes at those awesome shaggy fetlocks only to hear Tuck's voice saying, Get. Now he lay by Missy's side, tail between his legs, muzzle hidden behind his paws and eyes just yellow jealous slits, looking like a polecat had just sprayed him.

Suddenly, Tonga Sapa Tasunke's game of being a devil spirit aberration was over. He seemed more than pleased with himself. Neck bowed, tail arched and prancing hooves lifted to the point of bravado. The fear he sensed from other men was not in this man. At last, someone who knew for what he'd been bred.

Many miles away down on the Big Muddy, his sire, bred for power and strength, hauled beer wagons in Saint Louis. He too had been considered the best of his line. Powerful and intelligent, gentleness and obedience also were in his blood.

However, Tonga Sapa Tasunke growing up, always had his own way. Spoiled rotten, he realized why not get away with whatever he could? The Sioux gave him the name, so he played the game and once he grew large enough, he pretty much buffaloed anybody who got near him.

Today, this strong but calm man knew him better than he knew himself, and it felt just fine. His bloodlines and breeding said, "There's work to be done."

When the dust settled, Sitting Bull exclaimed, "Tonight we make great Pow-Wow!"

A large rock-lined fire pit and a much bigger fire—roasted buffalo calf—the whole village came to dance and offer gifts. Small groups whispered and pointed, smiled and bowed. Tuck and Missy Ann, as guests of honor did not yet fully understand the reason.

Tuck smiled and bowed back, whispering to Missy Ann, "I reckon, riding that big black sure must have meant something dang special."

"Me love, its more about them wantin' to hear of your coups an victories, me thinks."

It was, more than that. Sitting Bull's Vision was on everyone's mind, if not their lips. Tuck's role in it was yet to be spoken. That would come tomorrow.

A sliver of a moon sat low in the western horizon—the rest of the tribe slept. Sitting Bull, with Tuck following, rode toward the top of the highest bluff. This day would be fair and soon the sun would warm them. There on a sacred place all would be spoken.

The two of them rode to the lookout point on the bluff and reined up. Remaining in his saddle, Sitting Bull began, "My brother, let me tell you of Sun Dance." His eyes taking on a distant stare—hand gestures demonstrating his spoken words, "Many peoples come to make reverence with Great Spirit, Wakan Tanka. Days of Sun Dance, and Tribal lodges had formed a great half circle, all facing east. It was time for purified men to Dance, those who dared to display feats of Spiritual Power and strength."

Sitting Bull turned his eyes directly toward Tuck. "Remember these words: To prepare for Sun Dance, first we choose tall cottonwood tree. Braves strike tree with coup sticks and call out names of enemy. Then chop down tree, paint tree-pole blue, green, yellow, red—four directions, north-east-south-west. We plant tree-pole in center place of dance. Call it, enemy pole. Many offerings tied to top of pole, tobacco, robes, two piece buffalo hide—one cut like animal, one like man.

"Top of pole, we hang rawhide and buffalo hair lariats. Strong Heart warriors pierce sharp wood and bone spikes through muscles of chest, dance and hang from those lariats. Harder he pulls, more he dance and louder he blows his eagle-bone whistle. Only most brave can dance all day. Saada Boo dance for two days and two nights." His gazed shifted toward the descending tip of the setting moon, "Time of Dry Grass Moon...days hot. Sharp bone spikes tug flesh of my chest. Two days Saada Boo only one left dancing. Sun-fire talked to my eyes. Then for my people...a Vision."

He stared back at Tuck, eyes like fire he urged, "Carefully listen with your heart and spirit to these Vision words I will now speak." Trance like, he began. "It is so: Saada Boo, on winged stallion, enter loop into circle of past...back when dogs talked with men and all were one. Once inside circle we race toward many tomorrows. We galloped forward through a blood sky trailing crimson tears to shattered skulls of great Tatanka (buffalo) and many, many moons of butchered souls. From our red flesh life poured out but our land soon turned pale. Up from Rosebud Creek came a second sun. Four blinding rays became man's limbs. From its center emerge, The Man."

Sitting Bull stopped and again looked deep into Tuck's transfixed face. Beginning again his words spoken precisely, "The Man is Wearer of Sash and of Strong Heart Warrior riding a mighty Tonga Sapa Tasunke. One side of Man painted white with red dots. Other side red, with white dots. His one eye dark, other, as summer sky."

"Whirlwinds lift bones of my people, dancing and dancing, they cried, the circle is broken, the circle is broken, the circle is broken."

"Like thunder the Man answered them, Return, return, return. Live again, live again, live again. Good south wind, come from his mouth and blow away whirlwinds.

"North wind, then come swiftly. I see many yellow stripe buzzards with dark blue wings. They cried words of honor, 'As long as sun is in heavens and prairie winds blow, grass is green and mighty waters flow. We promise, we promise, we promise.' But their message smelled like vomit."

Sitting Bull's voice became excited, "Behind Saada Boo, bursting from Big Horn River, came red war eagles—two, three, four, maybe eight more. Painted Man, call up to red eagles circling overhead, his voice, like morning breeze lifted their wings. Painted Man say, This my Brothers, is what you must do when that day comes—" Sitting Bull's voice dropped, "My vision end before Painted Man could finish."

His face now pressed close to Tuck's, his voice speaking gravely, "I, Saada Boo and our people believe, Painted Man, is you—Wichasa Tonga. Great Spirit bring you to my people to complete vision. We wait for answer."

So this was what Tuck needed to understand. Sitting Bull held himself to be a patient man but Tuck could see the Chief yearned to know if Wichasa Tonga could finish the vision.

Tuck wanted to, but there were no words. He too hoped for something, but no utterance of wisdom or vision came.

Sitting Bull waited, what to Tuck seemed an uncomfortably long time, finally saying, "We go." Was it just the cold? His face seemed to turn to stone.

Tuck felt he should say, something. They rode in silence. Then unexpected words formed in Tuck's mouth, he blurted, "Saada Boo, I too will seek Wakan Tanka." The thought flashed through Tuck's mind, why did I say that?

Sitting Bull's head turned toward Tuck. He did not speak, but he thought, I wonder if Wichasa Tonga knows what that will mean?

28

"RAIDERS"

Upon his return, Missy Ann smiled hopefully when she greeted and said, "They've asked us to stay."

Tuck sensed Missy's eagerness to accept the hospitality, but instead he replied to Sitting Bull, "We thank our new Brothers...but we left horses and supplies at our camp. Wolves and bears might reckon that's an invite. Best we head back today."

"Yes, Wichasa Tonga, winter many kinds of wolves come out of mountains." The concerned look on Sitting Bull's face a clear warning.

They said their good-byes vowing to return in early spring.

On the trail back to their camp the weather had warmed a bit. Tuck said, "Missy, Sitting Bull told me if we cut right straight across the bluffs yonder just below that rise we can stay out of the wind and save about an hour's time."

Tonga Sapa (Big Black), as Tuck had taken to call him, was tethered closely between their two horses. Gray Owl brought up the rear, a long fresh cut willow stick whip in his hand.

"Boy," Tuck said to Gray Owl, "if he lags just pop his rump with your willow stick." Astride his own spotted pony, Gray Owl rode drag.

But today, Desert Wind chomping and snapping at Tonga Sapa's shoulders and Nip at his heels, gave the young stallion little opportunity to lag. Hemmed in on all three sides he behaved like he'd been tethered and led all his life.

It pleased Tuck to see Gray Owl riding his own horse. The little fella was eager to take responsibility—lips pursed looking serious, he was itching to keep his willow working. Tuck recalled his own first herding job, but that was riding behind a drove of a thousand dusty hooves. And trailing on snow wasn't much like eating grit, flies and horse-gas for hundreds of hot miles.

By the time the horses worked up a little sweat the sun was burning off the gray overcast. Tuck said, "We drop over that ridge about a mile north, then it's only a few minutes or so to camp."

Missy Ann held her belly most of the way and wasn't saying much.

"Be glad to get back to our own lodge," was about all. She'd missed her last two periods and to be certain, she hadn't as yet told Tuck.

They reached the Rosebud just north of camp and turned right weaving their way through the leafless cottonwoods and headed up stream.

Tuck said, "You look a little green around the gills, girl. Feeling all right?"

She kept swallowing trying to keep down her breakfast of pine-nut mush and dried plums. Just before they left the Unkpapa Village, with Sitting Bull's giggling wives fussing over her, going to the trouble of preparing clabbered milk taken from the butchered and still warm stomach of a fresh killed buffalo calf. Insisting she needed it to be strong. They knew right off, she was with child.

"Who, be green around the gills?" she fired back at Tuck.

Still wanting to be absolutely sure, and wait for the right time, she would have denied it anyway. But at this moment she would not have an opportunity. Reining to a quick stop, she pointed up stream.

Tuck reined up. A curl of white smoke hung in the air near to their camp. Hair on the back of his neck bristled. They had been gone three days and he knew he'd smothered their campfire.

Nip's ears peaked, his nose to the ground, he started to charge ahead in the direction of camp. A short whistle from Tuck and he jammed to a halt.

No one had heard the approach of their horse's snow cushioned footfalls, but the whistle—that was heard.

Directly ahead, where the Rosebud curved sharply, was the clearing where he'd hobbled their other horses. Good grass was still poking up through the snow only a few feet up from the creek. Would the horses have wandered far? Tracks should be everywhere? He handed Tonga Sapa's lead to Missy and told Nip to stay. He fresh primed the Hawken and alone moved ahead cautiously. Rounding the bend he'd expected to see some of their stock. None of their horses or mules were there. Where were they?

Silent shadows turned into moving forms. Through the trees advanced a group of long-haired, mounted warriors. Friend, or foe? He wasn't sure yet. But they were not Sioux.

They spotted him. Rifles and bows pointed right at him they howled and kicked their ponies to the attack.

Instincts attuned, ducking flat on Desert Wind's back, Tuck headed for the creek and plunged in. Though knee-deep water and ice he plowed to the far bank. There he turned and leveled his rifle at the lead rider. His first clear look at his pursuers came and it was pretty obvious, with their pointed buffalo skin caps and long unbraided hair clear to their waist, they were Northern Crow. And they acted like a swarm of angry hornets, as if he wasn't at all welcome at his own camp. Did they know him? He reckoned not.

He recalled Deer's Foot saying, "Northern Crow, the ones always at war with Sioux and Cheyenne." And when Chief Butte had mentioned his northern cousins he'd spit on the ground. He too, steered clear of them. Horse thieves, even from their own brothers, and worst of all, they worked for the U S Army as scouts and sellers of scalps—Indian or white. Butte considered them traitors.

Tuck knew his 52 caliber would throw a sizable hunk of lead better than a mile. At this close range it would stop a grizzly dead in its tracks. Tuck squeezed...black powder smoke and flaming lead erupted. Lifted completely off his horse, the lead rider's lifeless form plowed into the snow. As Tuck hoped, the others kept following—away from Missy Ann and Gray Owl—single file they too swung toward the creek directly at him.

Perfect. Tuck raced to reload. This time, with scatter-shot and a bit of extra powder. The raiders were half way across the creek when the scatter-shot loaded Hawken roared, stinging death into the first four of the Crow war party. Tuck aimed high. Their bursting, bleeding heads, reared back, bodies flopped backwards off their ponies and splashed into the frigid Rosebud.

On the far bank the snow and now the creek had changed color. Rosebud-red, crossed Tuck's mind, Four dead—three left.

In mid-stream they pulled up, spun their ponies and turned back west, their hair whipping in the breeze, they pounded frantically at their horse's ribs. Up the ridge they scattered. Tuck smiled, if they keep on running in that direction Sitting Bull will have them for dinner.

He reckoned, at least Crows left mighty good spoils, two rifles and five ponies. He smiled again.

Returning across the creek, he hurried back around the bend. Tuck found Gray Owl holding tight to Tonga Sapa. But Missy Ann was on the ground on her knees. All over the white snow it was pretty obvious...her stomach was giving up breakfast. Was she just scared? He doubted that.

Her pitiful watering eyes looked up questioningly at Tuck. Still retching she tried to speak, "Shots? Arraaghp. I heard shots? Arraaghp." Dribbling chin and gagging, and not much use trying to talk until the heaves were done.

She finished her heaves, got up and walked toward Tuck. "Desert Wind is soppin' wet...been in the creek have ya?" He nodded, yes.

"Chasing wolves across—" and she clasped her hands to her mouth seeing two of the dead Crow, hair floating, come drifting down the creek. "Ba goom, did ya shoot them fella's?"

"Was me or them. If I'd missed, maybe you and Travis too."

"Two shots...two dead. Ye be a deadeye me love."

Another body came drifting. "Oh my, a tuther." She squeezed his arm.

"Let's get to getting, girl," Tuck said.

Fifty yards up river they passed the other dead warrior lying face down in blood splattered snow.

"Four?"

"Five, but who's countin'?" He didn't feel like boasting. He'd had about enough killing. And he did not need any more enemies.

He and Gray Owl rounded up the Indian ponies and two rifles. One Indian's rifle, still in the creek, Gray Owl waded in. Missy Ann led Tonga Sapa, peacefully trotting along by her side, they got back to camp first. Their belongings had been gone through pretty thoroughly, but it looked like the Crow, unfortunately for them, had decided to rest and eat some of their larder before loading up and helping themselves to everything.

"Biting off more than ya can chew sometimes makes ya deathly sick," She laughed. "Only us three, fer dinner. Thank goodness."

No doubt, the northeastern Rocky Mountain wilderness and the grassy expanses of the Great Plains had their appeal. Tuck knew they hadn't seen it all and probably no man could in one lifetime. But, Home? That was a place that evaded him. The longest he ever stayed in one place was back in the cabin when he was a boy.

Without intent, he often found his thoughts back in the warmer climates of the western High Plateau and the stream filled valleys of the eastern Sierras. Yes, there were also cold winters and some snows, but for the last two confining winters in this northern country, when he daydreamed

of hunting and just living, the cabin...the canyon...days with his Mother...
even Otto, something inside yearned and pulled at him. Maybe this will be
our last winter so far north? Come spring he would speak with Sitting Bull.
Seek his council about dreams and longings. Maybe Missy Ann dreamed of
where she came from? He would ask her, too.

When he did ask she happily replied, "Your people are my people...
where you go, I will go." And she returned to her work.

Why then he wondered, is she always humming or singing old Irish
songs? Her favorite she'd told him, "Gary Owen." An Irish quickstep her
Pa taught her: "Instead o' Spa we'll drink doon ale, n' pay the reck'ning on
the nail. No man fer debt shall go ta gaol. From Gary Owen in glory...."

Sometimes, when Missy Ann sang, Nip howled joining in and Gray
Owl marched around the lodge keeping time.

Tuck could still recall the only songs Otto ever uttered, stomping his
boot and tootin on his mouth organ, were dirty mocking ditties, debasing
Spring Willow: "Wimmin' n' injuns, thar ain't nothin' lower, fightin n'
screwin's be wha livin is fer. Whisky's me darlin', poon-tang's me passion,
what me rifle kain't shoot, me pecker kin fashion."

"Uuummph," Tuck uttered, "Imagine me remembering that, after all
this time."

Shaking his head, "Why in the heck did my Pa have to act like that?"

A dumb song, or cleaning Otto's old Hawken, or just a particular whiff
of something Missy Ann might be cooking, sent his memories soaring? And
the time he got stinking drunk with Chief Butte and darn near heaved up his
guts. That too brought back those tugging images.

He reckoned, drinking whisky every day, no, that's not for me. But,
by golly, that day with Chief Butte I sure do remember, having myself a
mighty jollifying good time. He'd never told Missy Ann but every once in a
while he got the hankering to wet his whistle again. Maybe his father Otto
just couldn't help fancying whiskey a heap more than him?

And well, the few times when Otto wasn't mean drunk, he did teach
me a heap of things. Things even now I use most every day. Maybe he
wasn't so bad after all? Checking himself, the reverie vanished. "Hell no!
He was no good, through and through."

But words are not as durable as feelings. He would think more about
that another time.

"What are you mutterin about, Darlin?"

"Oh nothing," Tuck replied.

Missy Ann went back to her cooking.

Deep snows fell. Winter was long, too long to suit Tuck.

She finally told Tuck the good news. But by late winter she still had a few of months to go and was anything but bored. Sayin, "Some sounds send me heart to racin. Been a decade since I heard *those* sounds...baby sounds." Soon, she and her true love, would be hearing another.

She scolded Tuck, "Quit your moonin around here. Git out from under me feet, Darlin. I got a heap of fixin to be doin...baby's comin before long ya know."

Next to the warm fire on a comfortable bed of buffalo robes, thinking deep thoughts, Tuck protested, "Its miserable cold outside."

"Go git on that big lazy moose of a horse an work some blubber off him. He's bustin Desert Wind's back, and drivin her daft, tryin to mount her. That young stud already knows a bit about courtin."

"What," Tuck sat up startled, "Why I—"

"Me love, your handsome colt, be bustin out of his foreskin. He's all spoony over that ol mare."

"How come, I ain't see him trying to—"

"Ya never see nothing, snoozing an day dreamin all the time." She opened wide her big green eyes and grinned, "Me love, ya might be takin a lesson or two from that naughty boy," she giggled and licked her lips. "Ya know what's said about a healthy young woman with child?" and tossed back her hair and cupped her hands under her full breasts.

He sat up quickly. "No, what?"

"Desert Wind might be objectin, but I—" Belly bulging, puckered up lips, she came sashaying toward him.

"I best go check on them." Now on his feet, he grabbed his buffalo robe and sprinted out the door. Her laughter, following after him.

Tuck muttering, "Woman with child ought to know better."

29

"PROPHECY"

Striking coup, and killing the five Northern Crow, had barely aroused Tuck's passions, though he did think the battle should have deserved a dance of victory but he did not dance or celebrate. Keeping his family safe and the killing of so many Crow seemed in its self, enough. He wondered why? Come spring that would be another reason to seek Sitting Bull's wisdom.

Tuck counted the days until New Leaf Moon. It was then he planned on visiting Sitting Bull. The days finally warmed and snows vanished almost overnight. It changed from winter to mild spring to blazing summer in less than three weeks. Greening prairie grasses sprung up almost knee-deep. West winds tickled the full leafed Cottonwoods quaking in the midmorning sun. River, stream and creek tumbled brim full and endless blue skies were filled with cries of migrating fowl.

The day was hot and dry when Sitting Bull, mounted on his spot-speckled strawberry appaloosa, suddenly appeared on the ridge above their lodge. He was naked to the waist with one large white, black tipped eagle feather standing erect in his double braided hair. A beaded buckskin rifle strap slung tight across his bronze, massive chest, his long barrel Plains rifle held snug to the rippling muscles of his short but sturdy back. Surprisingly, he rode alone.

"Wichasa Tonga," he called down to Tuck, "My Brother, it is good to see you."

Seeking shade down by the creek, Tuck and Missy Ann also stood bare-chested watching Gray Owl tug on his fishing pole, struggling with a big catfish. Three weeks in the sun both mother and son were already turning from winter pink to summer tan. Modestly, Missy Ann with her belly round like a bear's cub and her ample bosoms swaying, hurried and ducked into the teepee, but not before she returned Sitting Bull's wave. His eyes glowed with pleasure.

"Hye," he cried out leaned back and jammed both heels into his horse's ribs. The Appaloosa sprung forward its front legs thrust stiff—sliding, head down, rear hooves digging in, its rump almost dragging. Sitting Bull, ignoring the trail, slapped his horse and in his usually flamboyant manner slid right down the steep face of the granite ridge. Dismounting he cried, "Honka hey," his right hand grasping Tuck's left shoulders.

Tuck responded in kind, adding, "Chief, welcome to our camp,"

They searched out a private place to talk. A large fallen log next to the creek met the requirements. Sitting Bull slipped off his moccasins squatted and cupped cold creek water in to his mouth. "Aahh, sweet like honey." He wiped his face, girded the back of his breechclout forward and straddled the log next to Tuck.

"Big Snows. Were you successful hunting?" Sitting Bull asked.

"You were right about wolves from the mountains."

"Wolves?"

Tuck told him of the eight-man Northern Crow raiding party and what happened the day he and Missy Ann returned to camp. Tuck tossed a stone downstream, "Four of them, fish-bait, drifted yonder to the Yellowstone. The other's bones, left creek side, picked clean by four legged wolves."

"Eight you say...aaah yes, Red Cloud's band captured three Crow that very night. Before they died they spoke of their leader, Yellow Dog and four others killed by a thunder-stick spirit man. Was that you?"

Tuck said, "I reckon they were the ones that high-tailed it outta here."

"Aaawooo, good, my Brother!" Sitting Bull howled slapping his thighs. Silent admiration fixed his gaze on Tuck.

Tuck cleared his throat feeling uncomfortable getting attention. He sighed and scratched his head. Maybe change the subject and ask Sitting Bull about those other things?

Before he could, Sitting Bull's voice low, and petitioning began, "Wichasa Tonga, we last spoke when I told of my vision." He sat silent again.

Suddenly Tuck realized what he was about to be asked.

Sitting Bull continued, "In your seeking of Wakan Tanka what has he revealed to you?"

How could Tuck tell him, since the battle with the Northern Crow, his thoughts were on other things. He'd not kept his all too casual promise to seek the Great Mystery, Wanka Tanka.

How could he lie? But to speak the truth would make him as a covenant breaker.

Sitting Bull's unwavering conviction was that Tuck held the key to his vision.

However, at this moment he could not help but see the painful truth in Tuck's eyes. Wisdom in times like this is what made Sitting Bull a respected Lakota Chiefs: What good would come from allowing pride or anger to separate their parts to this spirit puzzle? Not to mention respect and friendship.

Diplomatic wisdom for which Sitting Bull would someday become famous as Chief of the all the Sioux Nation, he spoke, "You need not speak, Wichasa Tonga. Each man seeks in his own way and in his own time."

Tuck's cheeks flushed and his eyes looked down, "Yes. In a man's own time."

"But perhaps you do know if you are called to join Strong Heart's in Sun Dance?"

"Oh yes," Tuck replied, perhaps a little too quickly, "That much, I do know. When will that be?"

Sitting Bull's piercing black eyes searched Tuck's face knowing all men question their own bravery. Some put it to the test and some don't want to know. Only a very few, Sun Dance.

He answered Tuck, "First day, after the first night, of the fullness of Buffalo Calf Moon."

"In number of days, how many is that?"

Sitting Bull flashed both hands open and closed three times.

"Thirty days then. What must I do to prepare?"

"Come to our camp seven days before. You first need to find purification in the sacred Sweat Lodge. Better yet I will send for you and your family. There will be many peoples there. Some may not know of Wichasa Tonga. If you wish, you may share my lodge." He added, "And your son and lovely green-eyed wife."

Weeks followed with long rides alone on Tonga Sapa. Tuck's seeking of Great Mystery had produced only silence. But the quiet, that seems to come right down from heaven, was always good.

Still Sitting Bull's visit pricked Tuck's conscience—he should have kept his word. The day before they were to leave for the village Tuck made one more quest alone. Only a day's ride. Tonga Sapa, learning quickly to obey, was behaving himself.

He planned a half-day's ride out, then a half-day home. Up from the banks of the Yellowstone they climbed. A gusting east wind at their backs bent and whipped the drying prairie grass and kicked up dust from deeply carved buffalo trails. He paused on a ridge above the river. For no particular reason he turned Tonga Sapa east into the fullness of the sun. Hand hooding his eyes in the glare of midmorning sun drying prairie grasses shimmered and the river glistened. He sat and gazed without thought.

It was then a still small voice whispered across the yellowing plains, "Do you see the golden hair of Mother Earth?"

"What?" Tuck exclaimed. He looked around for the source of the voice.

Louder, came the voice, "Do you hear the flowing waters, voice and tears of the people?"

There it was again. Not the wind. On the back of his neck, hairs tingled. From the east up the Yellowstone, bending and dancing it came. The form and roar of a towering whirlwind embraced him. He threw both arms around Tonga Sapa's massive neck and clung tightly.

Its voice surrounded them in a circle of thunder. "Who is it, you please? Man? Your own spirit?" The thunder ceased. For a moment only silence—the world as in slow motion. From all Four Directions came, "From your heart, you will seek me, only!" Then as quickly as the whirlwind had come it lifted high into the blue sky and became no more.

Under Tuck, Tonga Sapa trembled. His ears had swiveled into the wind listening. Tuck also trembled his heart pounding. Spinning Tonga Sapa around, a west wind now at his back, he raced toward camp. He thought, I must tell Missy Ann as soon as I get back. But by the time he returned to camp he understood; what he had experienced was for his wisdom only.

Slowing to a walk, oblivious to anything, he rode into camp. Missy Ann saw the change. She watched him pause before dismounting, his face almost glowing, as he gazed eastward. Like in a dream, he walked Tonga Sapa slowly down to the creek where he pulled handfuls of dry grass and ceremoniously wiped him dry. All the while they whispered to each other.

Across the creek grazing peacefully, Desert Wind, her stomach rounding out ignored the two of them. In her womb she carried another task.

Belongs were stowed carefully inside their lodge and the horse packs made ready. Much to Missy Ann's chagrin, for the last week, Tuck and Gray Owl had taken to urinating around the outside perimeter of their lodge.

"Keeps the critters away. Marks our territory," Tuck believed.

At dawn they were ready. Their horse herd gathered together pawed impatiently. Being gone over a week the other horses would come along too. They saddled their mounts.

Tonga Sapa whinnied and looked up atop the bluff. A solitary rider stood silently. Tuck wondered if the man was on horseback or standing alongside his pony. The man raised an arm in greeting. From that distance Tuck thought, maybe he could be holding a small lance, but no, it was only his long skinny arm and hand reaching skyward in greeting.

The man waited. Tuck took one last look around their camp. He and Gray Owl sprinkled the ground one more time. Only then did the three of them mount up, Missy Ann riding Desert Wind who pulled a small travois, Tuck on Tonga Sapa, and Gray Owl on his paint.

A longer but easier ride, they drove the herd weaving their way up the narrow trail to the top of the ridge. There to come face to face with the waiting escort.

"I am Makhpiya," he said, head bowed humbly.

They could not help but stare. He was mounted and on a short-legged pony but his legs nearly reached the ground. Thin as a willow, his narrow shoulders slouched. His face, long jawed, bucktoothed and ears like lodge door flaps. He was a good half a foot taller than Tuck and not more than a teenager.

"Sitting Bull sent me to bring you, cousin." Tuck arched an eyebrow but did not reply. Makhpiya continued, "My Great grandmother was Deer's Foot sister. Tsistsistas, Southern Cheyenne, like me."

"Cousin?" said Tuck.

"It is so." He turned without further comment and the four of them, the young man leading, headed toward the Little Bighorn. From behind the toes of his moccasins appeared to drag in the dust. Tuck thought it looked like Makhpiya was carrying the pony between his long legs.

Tuck smiled when Sitting Bull told him, Makhpiya's complete name, "He Who Touches The Sky." (Makhpiya means sky or cloud) "You, Wichasa Tonga have Mitacoye, or as you say, Kin, among the Southern Cheyenne."

"Kin?" That word intrigued Tuck.

30

"BATTLE PLAN"

"Wichasa Tonga, you see our seven council fires? We are all Dah-kota, Alliance of Friends," spoke Sitting Bull. He walked with Tuck through the Sioux encampment. Tuck was amazed. Row after row of painted, smoke blended buffalo hide teepees with their traditionally tall lodge poles stretched for almost a mile. The half circle crescent of lodges opened to the east. In the center a flat open field was cleared of brush and grass. Totems, feathered lances, flapping painted standards and banners encircled the clearing.

"Place of Sun Dance." Sitting Bull nodded toward the clearing. "Tomorrow we cut Enemy Tree. To be carried to the center and planted... you will see."

"I have never seen so many lodges in one place, Chief. Your people are many."

"Teton Sioux are many, maybe fifteen thousand. Our name, Ocheti Sakowin, seven great clans of Teton Sioux: Ukpapa, Two-Kettle, Sans-Arc, Blackfoot, Miniconjou, and the two strongest...Ogalala and Brule," he sneered. "And two other Sioux nations...Santee and Yankton—they farm and make marriage with white lies."

"Will they all come for the dance?"

"No, only Teton, this time. But one day, Sioux, Cheyenne and Arapaho, must fight as one. Our lands, our ways and customs are sacred and ancient, but white men respect nothing...their armies are in our homelands. War will come."

"Can there not be peace? Must there be war?"

"You know my vision...it is War Vision. That is why we come together to Wiwanyag Wachipi, Sun Dance."

Tuck said, "The Ute, my people, know little of big wars. We fought Mormons, but now it seems like so much foolishness. Very few coups and even less died from that war. Their spotted sickness killed most of our people not white man's wars.

"So you see. We can never live as brothers with whites. The ways of war are strange. Coup means nothing to them, only killing. They are without honor or bravery. And no Indian can war with spotted sickness. We must live apart or we will all die."

Next Tuck was led to a cleared area not far from the main lodge. He saw the silhouette of the domed hide-covered Sweat Lodge. Outside, a smoldering conical pile of large stones.

Sitting Bull explained, "Unipi ceremony, Spirit stones hold the fire's searing heat are carried into the lodge, there sprinkled with Spirit water, bringing cleansing heat, purging those inside from sickness and evil. The pipe passed...smoke lifted prayers rise to Wankan Tanka."

Tuck asked, "Who will be in Unipi Sweat? Who can be purified?"

"Two from each clan, seven Chiefs and seven select Strong Heart warriors.

"Only fourteen from all these many people?"

"Fourteen, and you." Sitting Bull smiled, tilted his head and said, "My Brother." He chose his words carefully. "It is no small thing for a man to be called to Wewang Waci (Sun Dance) for his clan. A man can gain much power for his people...or much shame for himself. You will dance last. And you will dance for Wakan Tanka's vision." He gave no command, but a spirit discerned confirmation.

Breathing easier, Tuck thought, good I can watch others go first, him not ever actually seeing the Dakota Sun Dance Ceremony. His eyes went from the sacred Sweat Lodge to numerous offering placed around the barren exposed earth in the center of all those many lodges. The Enemy Pole will rise there. Thousands of eyes will watch me dance.

The gravity of the commitment settled on his broad shoulders His moccasins seemed to press heavily on the earth...again came the words, "From your heart you will seek me only."

So the eyes of others—praise or scorn—was not important. They alone would not be sufficient to sustain him in those personal moments of trial.

"One man...one Great Spirit," uttered Sitting Bull.

Tuck glanced at him. How did he know what I was thinkin'?

Four days of Sweat Lodge. The fifth day and the fourteen rose early. Enemy Tree had already been selected.

Sitting Bull explained, "Bring only your hatchet and coup stick, moccasins and breach clout. Paint your hands and face white. The days of Dance you will paint your entire body white."

With much ritual and ceremony, along with animated fury, the dance pole was cut, trimmed and carried to the clearing. There younger braves painted it. To its top, Medicine Men from each clan tied offerings, tribal power bundles and animal and enemy effigies. Lastly, they attached the rawhide cords that would hold the Dancers. Tuck and the fourteen would fast the next day and then no water until the dance was over.

Tuck had lain awake most of the night. The fullness of Buffalo Calf Moon lit the crescent village giving an eerie luminescence to the place of dance. It was time for the dancers to make ready. Body painting began. There would be no more talking. Few slept. Throughout the village, outside and inside, lodge fires burned until the morning hours. Children were fed and shushed. Filtered by a feathery haze covering the plains, mercifully cool, the sun eased itself above the eastern horizon. The Little Bighorn, slick as glass, appeared to cease flowing. Prairie sunflowers lifted their faces east. Except for the thudding beat of the morning Welcome Drum, everything was silent...waiting.

A slap of leather. The central lodge door flap flung opened. And the wail of fifteen eagle-bone whistles spilt the silence.

A great "Aaahheee!" rose from the waiting crowd.

Single file, the chalk-white dancers came forth...feet shuffling in unison to the drum's heartbeat. Muscular legs springing without actually jumping, skipped from flatfoot to toe-tip. Barefoot, bedecked with wristlets, anklets and head wreaths of sage and rabbit fur they came toward Enemy Pole. Some stared at the morning sun—some at the four-colored pole and its sacred objects. Tuck gazed at an eagle's form almost invisible, low on the blue birthing eastern horizon.

Inside the Sweat Lodge it been explained to Tuck and each dancer—when they exited they would be accompanied by a Medicine Man. Four of the chosen, chest's muscle smeared with minted pine oil stepped forward. Pointed bone or wood spike dipped in a crushed nettle and bee's wax potion, the first to momentarily numb the entry wound with stinging pain—the other to allow the puncture to enter without excessive bleeding.

Tuck watched each preceding dancer carefully. During the piercing the dancer's legs never ceased keeping pace with the drum beat. Nor did they flinch or blink...eyes fixed on the rising sun or intently toward the pole's top.

Several more drums joined in. Three of the warriors leaned back slowly until the ever-tightening leather leads began to lift and stretch the muscles of their breasts. But one of the four reared back instantly, thrusting his chest skyward, yanking his restraint taut in one mighty heave...his eagle-bone whistle screamed. As did the voices of the onlookers.

The dancers, picking up the increasing rhythmic throb of the drums, began dancing clock wise, around and around...more and more taut became the cords binding them to the pole's top. Within the hour, two fainted, a third staggered and stopped, but his eyes remained fixed on the sun now degrees higher. All but one's whistle went silent.

Tuck waited. The day's heat accelerated. The forth danced on, his chest covered with blood. Skin and muscles distended several inches from his upper ribs. Like ripping cloth...finally his bone skewer tore loose. Stumbling backwards, struggling for balance...he kept dancing. Kept blowing his eagle-bone whistle.

Three more joined in. Some fell in pain within the hour. More were added, and by late afternoon most of the Sioux dancers were either carried or crawled off. Three still danced.

All eyes turned toward Tuck. His eyes, though open, were already as one in the midst of deep vision—unaware of anything, but sky – sun – drum – whistle – dance.

As Lead Warrior Chief, Sitting Bull would not Sun Dance this day. But stripped to his breach clout, himself trance like, wildly danced alone beyond the perimeter of the Sun Dance clearing.

After the first few dancers Missy Ann had seen enough. Although women were not allowed to participate they could stand at the far edge of the clearing and watch. But soon, Missy Ann made her exit taking Gray Owl down to the river where, at that distance, she listened to the onlookers, the chanting and drums. A messenger was sent to her. The message: "Wichasa Tonga dances."

Somehow she knew beforehand...first the momentary silence, then a loud murmuring filled the village. Her body tingled and she knew.

The messenger left. She took Gray Owl by the hand. As in the manner of her Mother's childhood faith, the two of them crossed themselves. Kneeling side by side, they prayed for Tuck's safety and pain. There was no need—his courage and strength were beyond concern...he would dance like no other.

The second day's sun rose through a crystal clear sky. Its first rays, hot...dry...testing the dancers. Tuck still danced. Also, another that had danced from the beginning.

Tuck did not know Red Cloud personally but soon, around the council fires, everyone would speak of Red Cloud's courage. Tongue swollen, lips split and parched, chest wounds scabbing over, he now stood, his face still lifted...finally the whistle fell from his gaping mouth. Before he collapsed attendants rushed to his side and guided his ridged, stumbling form back to the central lodge.

Wichasa Tonga now danced alone. No longer the graceful sole to tip toe steps, the muscles in his massive legs felt like leaded weights. Pierced but powerful chest muscles held. From the center of his back lines of stretching muscles reached around his Herculean torso. Blood ran, and then dried. A dusty circular path now grooved into the earth around the Enemy Pole. He danced with great pounding steps.

Third night of Buffalo Calf Moon and still Tuck danced. Sitting Bull watched. His eyes now on his friend. Refusing water or rest, his only thoughts—over and over—a prayer of petition for the Victory Vision which his people must have.

Third day and Tuck continued to dance—in many ways a day rare on the Great Plains in midsummer. At dawn, from the south, towering spires of dark clouds advanced rapidly. From their core flashed blinding arrows of lightening. A few large raindrops splattered the dry and dusty clearing before the storm actually arrived. By high noon the thundering rains came.

"The Dance is over!" Sitting Bull threw his arms skyward. Drums stopped. He ran to Tuck's side and cut him down. It took two men to carry him back to the central lodge.

When the drums stopped Missy Ann and Gray Owl ran back to the village. Taking nothing other than water, throughout the afternoon Tuck rested. Late that day, as lingering rainstorms pounded the lodge, Tuck requested a hairless elk calf hide and paints. He said nothing else. Not even to Missy Ann, who stood in the shadows with Gray Owl at the back of the lodge.

Others there by Tuck's side watched silently. Sitting Bull, the recovering Red Cloud and a young warrior named Crazy Horse also watched.

Tuck knew he must hurry before any of the Vision's details were lost. For the remainder of that evening and late into the cool night, the vision flowed through his spirit eyes to his fingertips, never taking them from his task as he painted the battle plan. Was this the last part of Sitting Bull's vision?

31

"YEARS TO COME"

Montana Territory, Little Bighorn River, summer 1864

Though exhausted and in pain, Tuck forced himself to record every nuance of his vision. On the elk hide's outer edge he painted twelve white buffalo, their backs rounded and humped like mounds of winter snow. Legs of the first buffalo its hooves crimson. Clockwise each buffalo grew smaller and legs more crimson. The twelfth, larger than the others, legs pure white, horns crimson and sacred Sun symbol on his forehead.

In the middle of the hide, a large triangle of three rattlesnakes; to the north the largest snake was painted yellow. Rose red, the smallest snake to the east, mouth gripping the yellow one, the dark crimson snake to the west, mouth also gripping the yellow one.

From the west, across the dark crimson snake, two pairs of black eagles flew arcing west to east. Heads facing each other their red beaks met at the heart of the triangle.

Centered in the triangle many white tipped blue feathers and one yellow. All broken and crushed. Streams of flying arrows covered the entire painting.

"It is finished," Tuck said, leaning back and looking into the faces of those watching. It was then stabbing pain and nausea hit him. Missy Ann, sitting in the background, rushed to his side.

Colorado Territory, Denver, summer 1864

"Damn it, Beckwourth, if I hear them call us, Chivington's bloodless, again I'm going—" Frowning up his dark browed, thick bearded face, he pounded his desk, "and-quit-calling-me, Parson."

Colonel John M. Chivington, former Methodist Episcopal Elder, commanded a volunteer militia of cavalry, Colorado's 1st. and 3rd. Though numbering a thousand, carbine equipped and having four Howitzers at his command, up to that time they had less than a half dozen scalps to their credit.

Sometimes referred to as the mad preacher, the coal-eyed, intense, massive man, was quoted as saying, "I have come to kill Indians and believe it right and honorable to use any means under God's heaven to kill them."

"Beckwourth, I didn't take this command to be held in contempt by the white people of this territory." Clenching his teeth, hands trembling he added, "Scalps are what we are after...I long to be wading in gore!"

"Aahh, Colonel Chivington, Sir," mockery in Beckwourth's voice. "I know where a big bunch of them will be making winter camp. But right now they're in the mountains hunting and too spread out for us to attack. Patience Colonel."

His eyes blazed. "You're scouting for me, Beckwourth...you find them and for every Indian scalp I'll see you get a bonus of a dollar." Adding, "Any scalp."

Back on the Little Bighorn River: Tuck's body healed rapidly. After much prognosticating he gave the elk hide pictograph to Sitting Bull. The only thing Tuck added to the painting—a spoken explanation, "The war vision is for some time in the distant future."

Sitting Bull insisted knowing, "When?"

Tuck could only tell him, "How distant? I can't say."

Privately he wondered if hearing Sitting Bull's original war vision first had caused him to conjure up...agree with it? But when I danced what I saw...I saw, and there isn't any denying that. Well maybe in time its meaning will be shown? Seems revelation as a rule is figured out in hindsight.

Sitting Bull didn't get exactly what he'd hoped for. But among the seven other chiefs' consensus their opinion found the vision favorable. Other dancers told of Visions of Plenty in times ahead. Although none spoke of their mutual qualm, in the remaining free and boundless homelands of the Sioux, this might be their last Sun Dance.

Over the next few days Tuck took the opportunity to seek Sitting Bull's council. Answers to most of his wonderings were satisfied but not the ones about daydreams—about returning to the land of his youth—they still hung on.

Sitting Bull's reply. "It does not seem so for woman. They go where their men lead. But for a man, he always a powerful hunger for lands of his youth." He paused, and his hand did a complete circle around his head. "Sometimes, for that, a man will be willing to die."

During Tuck's time of healing, He Who Touches The Sky, clumsy and awkward, did everything he could to be by his side. Including eagerly offering to herd Tuck's horses back to their lodge on the Rosebud. Shy at first his conversation soon opened to his own yearning—no longer considered a Sioux captive—he wanted to again see his family. Ride south, back to Cheyenne country in Colorado Territory.

Motives fairly obvious, he chattered endlessly, "There are others of our tribe who are tall, Cousin. You will see your face among them. You are Ute raised but, like Deer's Foot, you look Southern Cheyenne." And so on.

In bed that night Tuck whispered to Missy Ann, "There's no getting shed of him." She just sighed.

"Missy, Indian ponies sleep standing up. But did ya see that? Why Sky most near picked up that scraggly pony and laid him flat down. For warmth we sleep together, he told me. Sure enough, that long necked goose coiled up himself and fit snug up between its legs and shaggy belly."

She giggled, "He walks like a stork too." Then patting Tuck's back, she snuggled up to his bare behind, "A pushy lad, but just a little lonely like me," she purred.

"Yeah, but a man and his horse—ouch!"

Missy Ann had forgotten and squeezed his still tender chest. "Sorry Darlin'," she touched her lips to his the back of his shoulder, "Roll over Big Horse an I'll be makin it feel better." She did.

"Mmmm, girl yer belly is warm."

"See me love, the young beanpole lad ain't so daft...is he?" She swung her thigh over his middle.

"Ooow," he howled, "careful of my chest."

"Oh ya poor puny fella. Actin like a wee poltroon...maybe I should be tellin yer dancing stouthearted friends about—"

Bare bosomed, he yanked her on to his chest, mumbling, "Shud-up," pressing his mouth to hers.

The night too short, morning came too early. The sounds of branches snapping, then fire crackling. Outside Mahkpiya built up the breakfast coals. No one joined him, and before anyone did, he had lifted his leg across the pony's back, smacked her into a trot, high-tailing it back to the Sioux village.

"Don't suppose he heard us talkin?" As the clip-clop of Mahkpiya's pony faded over the west ridge. "Finally, a day of peace and quiet," Tuck sighed.

At sunset he was back, his big ears back-lit by the sunset and glowing red, silhouetted atop the bluff at the same spot where he disappeared just that morning.

"Can you beat that?" But Tuck gave him the high-sign anyway.

Next thing, he moseyed down the long-way trail in their direction.

"Lucky he din na do the grand slide like the Chief. We'd a been fishing him and his horse outta the creek. Best heave another chunk of elk in the pot."

"A big chunk," Tuck chided.

"Out of house an home, that bottomless lad." She called, "Travis, ya got company." In the same breath, "Come sit, Mahkpiya, you be always welcome."

Tuck opened his mouth—Forgetting his sore ribs, she deftly elbowed him, whispering, "Opps, sorry me love...be nice." The jab bringing a sharp gasp from Tuck.

Mahkpiya, somewhat out of breath, said, "Tomorrow Dah-kota Chiefs want to see Wichasa Tonga." Doing his best to puff out his chest, "They sent me, a Cheyenne, to bring you."

Before Tuck left—Missy Ann and Gray Owl left alone for the first—he loaded every rifle and pistol they owned.

"There, across the creek," he pointed, "yonder, behind those rocks and the thicket of rose bushes. I'm gonna put these extra guns and loads there. Anybody come snooping, you two hotfoot it across the creek and hole-up."

Back again, he followed Mahkpiya to the village, to the central lodge and to the Chiefs Fire. Before, when preparing for the dance, the headmen had dressed like the others. But today the spectacle of dress and finery was beyond anything Tuck had ever seen. Full eagle feathered war bonnets hanging to the ground. Complete array of weaponry, but no trade items—no white man's iron weapons, only bows, stone tipped, multicolored feathered arrows, polished stone ax and tomahawks, sheathed obsidian and flint knives. Dyed porcupine quill, shell and bone beadwork covered their buckskins like he'd never seen before. Each face painted to represent their tribe.

As Tuck approached, Sitting Bull stood and offered him a place at his left hand, the place of honor. It was then Tuck noticed the elk skin sash he wore. Perhaps three hands wide and elaborately decorated in crimson war symbols. It also hung to the ground and beyond. In the Circle of Chiefs, no one else wore such a sash.

Tuck also couldn't help notice the red painted, head-tall, war lance. Why was its slender, finely honed white quartz blade sticking through the tail end of Sitting Bull's sash, deep into the earth?

"Welcome Chief Wichasa Tonga." It was the first time Tuck had been referred to publicly by that full title. Though he wondered, chief of what?

Sitting Bull spoke, "This will be a year of war. Already American armies prepare. But you know that." He turned his head and commanded, "Bring the Pipe. We smoke." He seated himself, Tuck by his side. They smoked.

"Eyes of Wichasa Tonga see Lance of the Sash Wearer?"

"Yes Chief...it is a fine war lance."

"And you see, Sash?"

"That too."

"Wichasa Tonga do your eyes question?"

"Is it for me to know?" asked Tuck.

"Oh yes." And Sitting Bull looked for agreement from the others.

"Aye," seven times, came from those seated.

"Lodge Keeper." Sitting Bull called. And out from the central lodge came the Unkpapa Medicine Man. In his arms he carried a folded white elk skin sash. It too decorated with crimson war symbols.

Sitting Bull stood again. He placed his hand on Tuck's shoulder, saying, "Rise Chief," then took the sash from the Medicine Man and began to wrap it around Tuck's middle, leaving the end trailing, saying, "Only for most brave of Strong Hearts. Those with many coup and Sun Dancer of valor and Vision."

Confirmation shouted by all, "Aye-aye-aye-aye-aye-aye!" and finally Sitting Bull's, "Aye."

Sitting Bull pulled his red war lance from the earth. Handed it to Tuck and instructed him to stab it through the trailing end of his sash and into the ground. "Now listen carefully, our Brother, in battle when your people need to see bravery you will bind yourself to Mother Earth this way and there you shall stand and fight—fight to the death if necessary."

Tuck was dumbfounded. What did all this mean? And who were his people? But he stabbed, and the circle cheered, hye-hye.

The ceremony over, Tuck and Sitting Bull walked and talked by the Little Bighorn.

"Chasa, (abbr. Wichasa Tonga) your cousin Makhpiya tells us you have much caring to go see kin in Colorado Territory."

He saw Makhpiya had told it his own way. Tuck replied, "Here your people treat my family well." Tuck could never say he was not pleased with Sioux hospitality and friendship.

"But...is it land of your people?" asked Sitting Bull.

"Cheyenne blood flows in my veins, but Ute also." Unexpectedly he added, "And the blood of my white father." He watched for some reaction from Sitting Bull. There was none.

"No man chooses what flows in his veins. Rather he can only choose what lives in his heart." Sitting Bull smiled, "Like apples, some have red on outside...white on inside."

Quiet for a while, Tuck asked, "Can a man have two hearts?"

Sitting Bull thought for several minutes before he answered, "I have many hearts, one for my people and our ways, one for my wife and children, one for my friends," he looked at Tuck. "One for this land and one for Great Spirit." He lifted his chin, a thoughtful frown on his forehead but a look of satisfaction with his answer. "Chasa, your words make me look deep."

"And what of your home, Sitting Bull?"

"My home is here. I was born not far from this very spot."

"But Sitting Bull, I was born and lived my youth many days ride west from here. I wonder, is that where one of my hearts live?"

"Chasa, you speak of things," he stopped in mid-sentence and pondered the question. "Yes, among the older ones, sometimes in their eyes I see a heart wanting to return to land of their fathers. It is a sadness, as loss of a friend...no...loss of heart."

"Can it be healed?"

Sitting Bull shook his head and shrugged, "Perhaps." He took a few more strides, turned and stepped in front of Tuck. "We have a request of you, Chasa. With so many army soldiers in the hills the time has come for a parlay. A big tribal parlay. We are many, if we stop fighting among ourselves—bring all Indian people together before it too late. South, the Cheyenne are many. We must speak with all their chiefs. We need a messenger, a man who all respect, to go and tell of this great parlay." He paused. "A man of courage. A man who is not just Sioux or Cheyenne or Ute...or white."

"Do you speak of me?"

"Maybe when you go, besides danger, you will find home of your heart?"

32

"HEADING SOUTH"

Tuck reminded Sitting Bull, "It will be two maybe three moons and Missy Ann will have her youngin."

"Mar-is-ha and Gray Owl boy welcome to stay with Unkpapa until you return."

"About how long will it take for me to bring the message to the Cheyenne?"

"Southern Cheyenne on buffalo hunts now. If you and Makhpiya ride alone you will return by..." Sitting Bull thought a moment, then held up one open hand, "Five, yes five Southern Cheyenne chiefs you must find: Tall Bull and Roman Nose. More south, Little Robe, White Antelope and Black Kettle."

Tuck asked again, "How long?"

"A fast ride...you return before snows come."

"When will you parlay, early spring?"

"Before...if snows not too deep."

"But when?"

Sitting Bull pondered the question for a moment, "Before buffalo come to Yellowstone. Yes...four moons after Falling Leaf Moon (October) the buffalo start moving."

Tuck was still not certain about the answer and he hesitated, saying, "First, I must ask my wife."

"Must ask?" Sitting bull blurted, eyes wide mouth open. Sioux did not ask women anything...least ways not in public...they told them.

"Great Chief," Tuck fumbled for words, "You see...my wife—"

Sitting Bull held up his hand for silence, head nodding, "I know, Chasa," then in an apologetic tone, "Seeda Boo knows. My friend...these days even Sioux young girls grow stiff necked and stubborn." He sighed, "From where do these evil ways come?"

"Chief, I believe she will want...insist to go. Though with child she still rides like the wind."

"And boy, Gray Owl?"

Tuck looked chagrined, "Don't even have to ask that. She won't leave him behind for nothing." They walked back to the lodge in silence.

"Seeda Boo will tell," he grinned, "ask, my youngest wife, Many Robes, to travel with you. On journey when child comes, Many Robes will be plenty help. Chasa and Makhpiya will then be free to ride swiftly."

So it was settled. Discussion between Tuck and Missy Ann about the journey was short. "Missy, I'm telling you—this is something I must do."

"So, Sittin Bull's sendin his wife, aye? Is a simple thing for me then. But not too much gallopin if ya please. Me bladder, ya know."

It took the entire day to pack. By sunset the three of them were in the Sioux village receiving instructions from Sitting Bull. On a deerskin he had painted a map plotting their route and possible locations to find the Cheyenne Chiefs. The deerskin would also serve as safe passport and introduction if their journey happened to be challenged by hostile Shoshone, Arapaho or Cheyenne.

Unrolling the map in front of Tuck and Mahkpiya, he pointed, "See here? First, go toward morning sun to Tongue River. Up to Big Horn Mountains. Long way south across Powder River Valley. From there you must watch for army soldier and also be on guard for Comanche who kill as quick as U.S. soldiers—both take scalp. On North Platt River you will be at Laramie Mountains. Ride toward setting sun and Medicine Bow Mountains. Look for Elk Mountain, here," jabbing his finger at the map. Tuck focused, imprinting the instruction firmly in his mind.

Makhpiya never stopped grinning, his head bobbing up and down like he remembered the way. Only a young boy when he was first captured, but all those years since he never stopped asking questions about his people... and dreaming of today.

Sitting Bull leaned back looking serious. Placing his finger on another location he said, "Fort Laramie, many soldiers camp here. Wagon trains and white people pass each day. It is here you must avoid everyone. Between the two mountain ranges, below Elk Mountain, find Rock Creek and then Chief Roman Nose and maybe Tall Bull, too. Do not worry, they will see you first. His scouts are everywhere, watching. Speak our Parlay Message only to those chiefs. They will tell you where to find Little Robe, White Antelope and then Black Kettle. On your return, if snows come early or if too many soldiers, wait until Popping Tree Moon (late December) before you start back."

"Why Popping Tree Moon?"

"Army soldiers won't fight in frozen snow," he sneered.

"Who will come to the parlay? Can all Southern Cheyenne people travel in times of deep snows?"

"Leaders of clans and warriors will move north first and chiefs will follow. Old men, youngest braves, women and children will stay in camp. New Grass Moon, all may come here. Cheyenne are not as many as Sioux—maybe now, only three thousand.

Tuck wouldn't need the map except to use as an introduction. Every word Sitting Bull spoke he'd remember. Moonlit and silent their last night in the Sioux village passed quickly. Early the next morning everything was ready. Many Robes was packed and waiting. Her lower lip pushed out with fire in her eyes and it was obvious she was not very happy. She was younger than Missy Ann and right off Tuck noticed Makhpiya peeking sideways at her. Tuck wished Sitting Bull was sending his homely older wife.

At the lodge door the older wife stood with chin raised and a superior smirk on her face. Sitting Bull ignored them both. The decision was made, and now he figured it wise to keep his eyes on other things.

However, even before they all mounted up, Missy Ann had the sour faced Many Robes laughing, and that was a good sign. The older wife with a flip of her hair disappeared back inside the lodge. Tuck breathed a little easier.

Sitting Bull approached, his voice low, almost somber, "Chasa, you see Teton people break camp today. We go hunt. Each to tribal hunting grounds. Sioux ready to fight if wasichu's soldiers on our lands."

Pensive, but anxious to be on his way, Tuck wondered...would he ever see his friend again? Then all were mounted. Sensing the long journey, Tonga Sapa under tight rein, nostrils flared and snorting, nervously stomped one massive hoof and then the other.

Sitting Bull reached up and rested his hand on Tuck's thigh—it was time to bid them good-bye, "Chasa, my Brother, it was good Sun Dance... may Wakan Tanka mark your trail." That was it. Head bowed, he turned and disappeared into his lodge.

Tuck had no way of knowing. One month later Sitting Bull's Unkpapa had their first notable skirmish with the U.S. Army.

Tuck allowed Makhpiya to lead the caravan. Alongside Tonga Sapa his stubby legged roan pony, head hanging barely a foot off the trail, ears flopping with each step, looked like an overgrown shaggy dog. Yet a tough and durable one, and he kept a plodding stiff legged but steady pace. Bringing up the rear, Gray Owl duties increased. The larger caravan, five people, twelve horses, and three pack mules and the now gray muzzled Nip, kept him occupied.

It would take longer—they would stay off established trails. No dust to give themselves away. Across hard-cap rocky buttes, down narrow gravely gullies, hugging damp shadow canyon sides, fording rapids, up chest deep creeks and across boulder strewn arroyos. Some days they slipped and slid over clay bottom alkali flat lands and the next day squeezed through branch busting stands of close growing willow trees. Winter's heavy snows were fully thawed and dry creek beds and gullies were tumbling full with runoff.

Not since the Mormon War had Tuck felt like the hunted. Every time he thought about it his throat rumbled a silent growl. Why in just a short period of time had things seemed to change? Trouble was in the wind...nature herself seemed to be waiting.

Without conscious effort, his eyes trained by years of hunting, Tuck never stopped scanning...horizon, groves, hillsides, shadows and the slightest movement. Anything, anything alive, no matter how obscure instantly imprinted his mind. He focused, analyzed and once identified he decided one of three things: Ignore it, was it fresh meat or an enemy. Should it live or die?

An uneventful month on the trail passed. After leaving the protection of the Big Horn Mountains they crossed the wide but shallow Powder River then rode west to its upper tributaries. In the mostly flat land between the Powder and North Platte summer skies hung heavy. Days were long, hot and sticky.

For Missy Ann, without mountain peaks as reference points, the trail seemed long and without end. Cool streams were mostly behind them and now only a few shade trees grew where she could lie comfortably and rest her head. The end of her nine months was swiftly approaching. But from what she'd heard she reckoned there was enough time to locate the Cheyenne.

Smells of horse sweat were usually pleasing to Missy Ann but lately they almost made her gag. So she rode point, with Makhpiya trying to stay upwind. Nothing worked and the farther south they rode the more uncomfortable she became. Finally, though reluctantly, she asked if they could stop and make camp for a day or two. Tuck readily agreed. And between the clear flowing Belle Fourche and the Powder River they made camp.

Tuck got his bearings. "Missy, just west of here about a hundred miles lays the Sweet Water and South Pass." You know that's close to where we left the Green River...Peg Leg and Deer's Foot back a Fort Bridger?"

Her eyes moist, how could she ever forget.

That evening Tuck rode alone to a high place with the aging Nip chugging along at his heals. Tonga Sapa strode along easily in his rolling and surprisingly light-footed gate. Slowly they climbed to the top of a low treeless mountain. The sun was dim and hung lazy like on the far distant Central Rockies. He sat and stared west, breathing deeply. Were those smells and scents familiar...beyond...from way out there? And could his hunter's eyes reach as far as his memories?

Sixteen years he figured, since he left the cabin. That day his life changed—the day he and his Father Otto fought. Walkara, his own Grandfather scalped Otto...well, had ordered him scalped. He grimaced. Maybe Otto isn't dead after all?

"Sixteen years," he muttered again. Dismounting, he called to Nip, "Come here old boy." Nip, a little foot sore and stiff, walked to his side and nuzzled him. "Way back then you weren't much bigger than a cottontail." He smoothed his short summer fur—a lot of gray now mixed with silver. Lifting Nip's head he looked into his face, Nip giving him a quick lick. "Your eyes are a little cloudy too." Then rubbed his hand across his sides feeling his ribs, "Kinda scrawny now ain't you, fella."

Twisting off hunks of antelope jerky and each sharing a piece they sat close—Tuck's arm draped over Nip's back until the Rocky's silhouette dissolved into night. But in one of his hearts he imagined the sun might just now be setting on the far distant Eastern Sierras. At dark they headed back to camp.

Next morning early on, to the south, he spied a yellow dust cloud and figured it must be a large herd of buffalo moving fast. Trouble was they might just be heading directly toward them. He thought, don't want to get us trampled, let alone eat their dust.

He warned the others, then said, "From up yonder," he pointed to a low knoll, "I'll go get a fix on them." From that vantage point he'd never seen such a sight. "Those are cattle, not buffalo." Tuck galloped back to camp.

Hollering, "Roll it up there's a sight to behold and we're right in their way...a gang of white fellas and a mile of longhorn cows...maybe a couple thousand? Those cowboy fellas are kii-yiing the whole dang herd. And if I don't miss my guess, it looks like they're packing plenty of iron too."

Missy said, "What are they doin way out here?"

"Herding them somewhere? They're shouting and trying to head-off the lead cows to keep them from stampeding to water. Unlike buffalo, cattle are just stupid enough to trample their own calves."

Concern in her voice, Missy said, "They must be getting close didn't we just cross the Bella Fourche?"

"Yep, we did, and they're all bawling and moving along right pronto. My guess, directly toward our camp."

Tuck's little group didn't give them a chance. What might take a couple of hours packing was done in minutes. There was no other cover so they hurried back to the Bella Fourche where they dropped down the creek's steep sides with hardly a splash. They dragged their travois in the shallow water and herded their stock upstream away from the approaching cowboy outfit and thousands of thirsty longhorns.

Their own tracks wouldn't be noticed with the long line of longhorns racing for the creek—leaving nothing in their path but cow-pies and steer tracks a quarter mile wide. In a few weeks the herd would cross the Yellowstone in Montana and a new passage would forever be pounded into Mother Earth.

33

"FACES FIVE"

Tuck said, "Might as well relax. We'll just wait em out. More than likely once their herd gets watered, they'll be moving on."

High in the afternoon's turquoise sky golden edged clouds chase each other east as Tuck checked over their mounts and gear carefully. Travis played quietly down by the stream. On her knees down next to the stream Missy Ann had an audience, "Look, it be round," she whispered, drawing circles in the sand. "what's called Earth, round like a ball, an the sun," she jabbed, "right here, it's a big round fiery ball."

"Flat," Many Robes looked up in to the sun shaking her head no, and in a that's final gesture, slapped the palms of her hands flat together. In agreement, Makhpiya nodded his head adamantly.

For the umpteenth time Missy Ann smoothed the sand and started to draw more circles determined to explain how planets, the moon and such, work together to cause the seasons and stars to change—that there was no danger in falling off the edge if anybody traveled too far.

Tuck stood back listening, recalling a similar argument between Spring Willow and Otto. Something had told him Otto was more than likely right but out of loyalty to his Mother he sided with her, which best he could recollect got him smacked upside his head.

Frustrated, Missy Ann turned, her eyes appealing for Tuck to help with the explanation.

"Gotta go check on the horses again." He left them to wrangle what might or might be round or flat, near or far.

They'd been sitting cross-legged in a circle hiding out in a step-down cut aside the banks of the Bella Fourche. Horses tethered in close and no cook fire. Tuck was right, by the time it took the first yellow dust cloud to settle, midday the kii-yiing and hoo-rawing commenced again. Within a couple of hours another dust cloud marked their way moving north. Little by little the bawling and bellowing died out...it looked safe to continue south.

"Let's mount up," Tuck said.

Back to where the herd passed across the creek its banks were caved in and water still ran muddy. Standing spraddle legged ankle deep there in the creek was a red-eyed, dun-brindle longhorn cow and her newborn, tiger-dun calf. Its nose jammed up under Mama's flank suckling and trembling, bug eyed and lop-eared. Half floating alongside the creek, a crimson heap of afterbirth still trailed blood. Overhead and waiting for a meal, circled a dozen redheaded, yellow beady-eyed, soot-black buzzards.

Quick as a wink Makhpiya aimed his rifle and drew a bead on the newborn calf. Cow calf or buffalo calf he'd never pass up a newborn delicacy like that.

"Stop! don't ya dare shoot that little baby," the heavy pouched-belly Missy Ann screamed and splashed Desert Wind in-between the two.

"Looks like the cowboys missed this one," Tuck barely had time to speak before, in a heartbeat, the mother longhorn lowered her pointy horned head and charged toward Missy Ann. Tuck crying, "Look out, here she comes!" But in one explosive lunge Tuck spurred Tonga Sapa's broad chest into the longhorn's side sending the vexed cow sprawlin and bawlin.

Nip made his usual swipe at the irate cows heals and trotted back satisfied.

The calf stood there mouth dripping milk wondering where dinner went? Then it made a bleating hungry bee-line toward the side-stepping Tonga Sapa who was sucking up his belly almost tripping over his own big feet trying to escape the calf's puckered lips and rough tongue. The mother bawled, the calf changed course and it all got sorted out. They all had a good laugh. Mother and calf trotted off north. And the buzzards circled a little lower.

Sitting Bull had warned Tuck, the next hundred miles or so, would be filled with hazards of bluecoat cavalry soldiers and hostile Comanche. And not long after the big cattle drive almost daily they sighted curls of camp smokes, a few cowboys drifting with bunched up cattle droves and lines of white top wagons plodding west and even the occasional sod roof settler.

To remain unseen, required pushing their trail along a defensive zigzag path toward the North Platte, to the foot of the Laramie Mountains. And one morning, there it was and flowing east. A mile wide, a thousand miles long and six inches deep...the Platte River and on the southern horizon, gradually rising above the Platte valley, the Laramie Mountains.

"Look-look-look," Missy Ann cried excitedly, "Was here we crossed with Brigham and the wagon train to Salt Lake." And sure enough there alongside the river carved into the prairie grasses bare dirt wagon wheel tracks maybe a foot deep headed West.

"Here's the place we swung the wagon train, west," she cried.

Tuck added, "Things have changed Missy Ann. There's a big fort down river where the Platte joins the Laramie and Sitting Bull says they're a bad bunch."

They still had another hundred miles to go—Rock Creek, and there he hoped he'd find Roman Nose and Tall Bull.

Single file, Tuck now leading on a trail less defined, the valley floor rose sharply. The Platte narrowed, twisting its course upward and now running swift and clear. The ascent brought cooler climes and fewer signs of whites. Then where the Sweetwater joined with the Platte and the river bottom was firm ...they crossed, but not without event. Tuck and Tonga Sapa went first and were almost swept away in the swift current. On the south side, using lariats, Tuck used the massive Tonga Sapa as an anchor. Missy Ann first, they ferried everyone else across safely.

Don't worry...they will find you, Sitting Bull had said. Tuck was not too comfortable with that and his eyes never stopped searching. "Sooner we find them, sooner we get headed south to Black Kettle and the rest. All total, it's still a good four hundred miles." With that thought, their little caravan tightened up, heels dug in and resolve on each face. Late that evening next to a clear running spring they made camp. After their labors, sleep would be sweet. This morning for the first time a frosty bite was in the air. They took the day to dry out their things and rest. Now the cooking fire was a comfort as well, and they all sat close. No one asked but Tucked offered, "Elk Mountain and Rock Creek can't be too far."

Wispy almost cloudless skies—sunset dripped scarlet trails through shafts of sunlight. A different kind of sky and the echoing noise they heard might have been thunder. Rapid fire, thud-thud-thud! Soon following, the sky rumbled and the earth trembled. Buffalo hunt! Tuck and Makhpiya knew the sounds which faded toward the south.

"Tsistsistas-Tsistsistas!" Makhpiya shouted, "My people-my people." He grabbed his rifle and aimed skyward.

"Hold on now, don't shoot!" Tuck shouted. "It could be whites or even Comanche."

Sky, lowered his rifle and glared in Tuck's direction. He was not Teton Sioux but even Cheyenne don't like to be shouted at or told what to do. And he and Many Robes walked out of camp muttering between themselves. Gray Owl chased after. "Not my chief" was all Tuck heard Sky say.

"Seems, Touches the Sky, is a bit touchy," Tuck grumbled.

Missy Ann said, "Specially young folk. When I was their age, nobody told me nothin."

"Differences," he sighed, recalling their clashes in the last few days. "I reckon there sure is more than one way to skin a cat. But I got a job to do... right now message given is more important than kin." He suddenly realized they'd been on the trail for almost two moons...he'd done all the hunting, Makhpiya had yet to fire off a single round.

Before he could speak again, Missy Ann chirped, "Try lettin Sky do the huntin, Chief Tuck Hunter." She watched his eyes. It always amazed him how she could read his mind. He considered for a minute and nodded, yes. How did she know what he was thinking?

"Yer a bonny wise darlin'," she whispered. Tuck got up and followed the three youngsters out of camp. Approaching them, they stopped talking and stared at the ground their moccasins shifting nervously.

Like nothing happened, Tuck said, "Makhpiya, we're low on fresh meat. Would you mind doing a little hunting? Use my Hawkin if it suits you."

Their faces lit up. Gray Owl's pubescent voice cracking, deep as he could make it, said, "I'm going with Makhpiya." He didn't ask, he told.

Tuck opened his mouth, then shut up, smiled, nodded and walked back to camp.

"Now Gray Owl's doing it," he grumbled.

"That fur he's growin is ticklin more than his arm pits...Papa." She rose to her tiptoes and kissed him on the cheek.

Makhpiya eagerly took him up on his offer. Gray Owl did as stated, and Many Robes joined them. In minutes they were ready. Night comes on quickly in the mountains and this night was going to be no exception.

"Some hunting party," Tuck muttered out of earshot. But then loud enough to be heard, he added, "Getting dark."

"Leave em be." And she and Tuck enjoyed dinner alone, "First time since, can't remember when."

Dark came on solid and the hunting party didn't come back. Tuck got busy and for the first time since they left the Rosebud he put up the big white canvas teepee. He didn't say why but they both knew why. Clearly visible there on the ridge where they camped it shown like a beacon when the rising moon finally got above the trees

Dinner alone was fine. With just the two of them in the lodge there was plenty of bed but little sleeping. Laying quietly in each other's arms their eyes traced moon shadows sliding across the outsides of the teepee. Awake, they listened for the sound of returning hooves. Dawn was mighty slow in coming. The horizon barely blushed in the east as he rose to fetch Tonga Sapa and began making ready to try and track them.

"A resounding POW electrified the stillness—time enough passed for two more reloads. POW. POW. Tuck froze trying to figure the direction of the shots from the echoes. Gray Owl's high-pitched wail came down thru the trees. "Ayee - ayee - ayee" and Makhpiya's bass voice following, "Tsistsisitas—Tsistsistas, we come, Chief Wichasa Tonga!"

He stood listening. One thing Tuck could tell right off...more than three horses were coming their way. Horses and Cheyenne. A party of five, big boned, angular faced, and stoic.

Tuck raised his open right hand in friendly greeting, "Ah-hi-e," he saluted each man. Laying his rifle on the ground he walked toward the advancing warriors.

Suspicious of Tuck's every move, all they had to say was, "Tell us your message from Tatanka Tyotake (Sitting Bull)."

"Only for Roman Nose and Tall Bull," Tuck stated flatly.

"That's what we told em too, Papa," Gray Owl whispered.

Tuck's refusal and explanation, courteous as he could be, was finally agreed to. They would follow. He glanced at Missy Ann, eyebrows raised he grinned, humorously his lips formed the question, My Kin?

With a little smile on his face, Tuck looked back and forth at Makhpiya and then his horse, both palms up and empty, in a questioning gesture.

Makhpiya got the message, "No meat," he shrugged sheepishly.

The trip to Elk Mountain to the hidden camp of Roman Nose and Tall Bull took about three hours. There the greeting, even for Makhpiya, was not much warmer. At the council fire Tuck, officially wearing his Sash and his three feathers, searched the faces of his hosts.

Roman Nose, Chief of the Lance Soldier Society, was belligerent and obviously suspicious of the blue-eyed Tuck. His name fitting his narrow squint-eyed glare was pinched behind an arched turtle like nose. Tall Bull, pleasant faced, soft spoken but not tall, compared to Makhpiya and Tuck. He was Chief of the Dog Soldier Warrior Society and he seemed more reasonable—even enthusiastic about combining the fighting power of Cheyenne and Sioux. He suggested, Lone Wolf of the Arapaho should also join the parlay.

Tuck offered no opinion about that. He continued with Sitting Bull's message.

And the two war chiefs listened intently, eventually agreeing to parlay at the designated time and in the place of smoking waters.

Only one night they camped with the Cheyenne. Except at the council fire when the Pipe was passed, somewhat to Tuck's disappointment, the majority of the tribe, and there were many lodges, stayed aloof, dark eyes probing, but keeping their distance.

In the morning, Tuck was presented with a buckskin map where to find the rest of the Southern Cheyenne and the chiefs they had yet to meet. Words of caution were spoken and warnings about their journey to find Black Kettle. A gift of buffalo hindquarter and then farewells were offered.

Tuck knew the way—up between the Medicine Bows and the Laramies, they headed. The plan, next stop, a few days rest near Long's Peak. Head east and drop over the continental divide along the tumbling upper reaches of the South Platte. Out of the mountains they would travel ten suns down to the slow flowing Platte carefully staying clear of Denver. Then cross the South Platte and travel southwest toward Sand Creek, and locate Black Kettle. Tuck hoped they'd arrive during the waning of Yellow Leaf Moon.

The travel plan was fine, but perhaps Missy Ann miscounted. Late September, under what she called a Harvest Moon, she asked Tuck to make camp and lift their lodge into position. Her labor pains began. That night with difficult straining labor, she gave birth to a beautiful chestnut skinned, green eyed, raven haired baby girl.

The birth was long and exhausting but the baby was plump and full term. Afterwards Missy Ann bled till the morning hours. Many Robes never left her side, making medicine and singing all the nightlong. Full and white, the moon hung on the western mountains. Missy Ann and the baby rested, leaning back on Tuck's chest in between his legs.

"Little Moon Song, would be a grand name," Missy Ann whispered, and the name fit.

Missy Ann appeared pale and weak for the first time since having the spotted sickness long ago. Finally the bleeding ceased, the baby nursed herself to sleep, and Missy Ann rested.

Half asleep Missy Ann muttered, "Tomorrow I'll be fine...we can be on our way."

"We'll see." But Tuck refused to travel until he was sure she'd gotten back her strength.

They camped there five days, and then the first cold snow storm of the season came whistling down off Long's Peak. Like it or not it was time. In haste they began packing for their journey down the Platte and into a warmer climate.

Makhpiya decided he would ride fast and go on alone. "Chief Tuck, our aunt lodges with Black Kettle," he persuaded, "and I will go first and tell them all of your arrival and message."

Gray Owl announced, "I'm going too."

This time Tuck spoke an emphatic, "No!"

By convincing Makhpiya he needed his help hunting, Tuck persuaded him to wait until they were well across the Platte. Then maybe Gray Owl and Many Robes could make the last leg of the journey together, adding, "Under your leadership."

Those were the perfect words to Makhpiya's young ears. In a most serious voice he said. "It is so, Chief Wichasa Tonga."

34

"SAND CREEK"

Tuck led them down out of blue spruce forests to where they slipped unseen through east sloping gaps in the canyons. Up and over, nothing level for days on end until they again reached the Great Plain and crossed the trickling headwaters of the Republican River.

Moon Song's first long ride and she took to her cradleboard without a whimper. Tuck, filled with quiet pride, watched Gray Owl push to be lead rider. Missy Ann's long black hair spilled off her shoulders and over plump breasts, her eyes now as keen as any hunter. A man could have no greater blessing in this life.

On occasion Tuck heard Missy Ann sigh and saw her shoulders slump slightly. Ahead, another five suns, they turned south into an undulating valley with waves of yellowing prairie grass rolling out before them. The journey was long and endless. Vistas seemed to mesmerize—days of silence—each to their own thoughts.

Eventually Tuck said, "Darling, we can make camp for a day or two if you're so inclined?"

"Inclined?" She laughed. "I'd rather be reclined. No, I'm fine. I'd forgotten how much givin birth takes it out of a lass."

According to the map Roman Nose gave Tuck, maybe two days ride there between the Republican in the south east corner of Colorado Territory and the Arkansas, they would locate the centuries old Southern Cheyenne camp on the banks of Sand Creek.

For Missy Ann the journey's end would be welcome. "Tuck darlin, I stink like a barnyard billy goat and the baby's bottom is a bit crusty too. First good bathin place, I want to stop and scrub up before we meet your people."

He pondered those two words. That was the first time Tuck ever heard Missy Ann refer to the Southern Cheyenne as, Your People.

It was settled they would stop for a day. No need to hurry now. As agreed, Makhpiya, Gray Owl and Many Robes went on before them to announce their arrival and its purpose. That way there should be no unwelcome surprises.

Missy Ann had long since gotten used to bathing in cold streams. For what seemed like years they were at last alone. She and Tuck preened, combed and washed each other from head to toe. Secluded in a wonderfully private willow shrouded pool—though the water was cold—there was no need for additional body warmth amidst their passionate grasping, and holding tight moments. That day passed all too quickly.

Tall Bull said Black Kettle's would be returning by the beginning of Falling Leaf Moon. Now, along the banks of every stream and river, Tuck noticed leaves quaking golden in Fall's gusting winds. A secure friendly winter camp for his family sounded mighty good to him.

Moving slow and easy for the next few days they had nothing but clear and kindly skies with gentle winds at their back and warm sunshine resting on their shoulders. Now and then, far to the west above Denver, slanted sheets of ominous squally clouds hung speared atop the snow-streaked tips of the Rockies. Those days were as close to stormy weather as it ever got, but the frosty breath and the slowing heartbeat of winter could come calling anytime.

At night, Moon Song had her own voice, yodeling like a coyote. Nip sometimes joined in keeping everyone awake. Then she'd sleep all day tied to Missy Ann's back, bound tight and cozy in the willow cradleboard Many Robes wove during the days at Long's Peak. Desert Wind's easy swaying stride rocked her back and forth.

From his youth Makhpiya recalled the old trail and told Tuck what to look for, "Sand Creek lined with cottonwood and willows, where many gullies funnel into a single, wider, sometimes wet sandy bed." Sure enough, before they'd ridden a half day, Tuck and Missy Ann's horses hooves soon started sinking and their tugging travois poles dug deep wet grooves. Water tables from distant mountain storms raised and sands became soggy...then slurry...as rivulets of muddy water seeped to the surface.

"When creek wet, leave the creek bed and ride onto tree-lined bank. You go single file and follow an old overgrown buffalo trail." Sky had instructed.

"Good name, Sand Creek," Tuck said.

He and Missy Ann first smelled smoke. A half mile away on a broad sweeping bend in the creek, and above in a spacious bowl shaded opening in a forest of cottonwoods trees, campfire smoke rose to the heavens.

The first thing to catch Tuck's eye, besides the hundred or so lodges, flapping in the breeze and tied off on the tallest lodge pole was a tattered, thirty star, red and white striped American flag. He yanked Tonga Sapa to a halt. Nothing in the village moved. Turning to Missy Ann he asked, "Reckon something is wrong?"

"Ba Goom, I wonder where Gray Owl and Makhpiya be?" They waited, looked and listened. Was it an ambush? In just moments, Missy and Tuck heard them before they saw them.

"Papa...Mama," Gray Owl cried out.

From behind the camp rising over the hilltop and pouring down its grassy slope came a colorful scurrying mass of Cheyenne. Many were on horseback but all singing and cheering. Travois' heaped high with buffalo hides and meat. Others with hind or front quarters slung on the backs of their mounts, while women and children walked along carrying large baskets heaped with bloody innards.

Buffalo hunters, just returning. The entire village had run to meet them and help carry winters meat. There, riding to the rear of the festivities and waving his rifle over his head, was Makhpiya with Gray Owl by his side.

"Hope he didn't forget to tell them we're coming and why," said Tuck.

Makhpiya hadn't forgotten. The Cheyenne swarmed down the hill— Tuck and Missy Ann and the pack animals came up the creek bank and arrived at the village edge at nearly the same moment. The five hundred or more men, women and children, like a tree full of spooked owls in mid-hoot, they all stopped and every eye shifted to the new arrivals. A murmur spread, then hands began to clap and en masse voices broke into a cry of, *welcome.*

"Yep, looks like Makhpiya's done what he said. Must have told one heck of a tall-tale," Tuck chuckled.

"To say the least. Musta been somethin grand." Missy smiled at him and poked his ribs, "Yer 'ihness."

The crowd stopped, opened and split in two. Out from their center a powerfully built man came striding erect and adorned in full eagle feather headdress. Walking at his left arm was a tall willowy weathered woman, the spitting image of Deer's Foot.

Directly behind them trotted Makhpiya waving and calling out a loud greeting: "Ituwan (look), Mitakuye Oyasin (all my relatives), Wichasa Tonga. Wichasa Wankan (big man—Holy man)!"

"Wichasa Wankan...Holy man? What does he mean?" Tuck gasped

Chief Black Kettle escorted Makinpan Wapiyapi (Call me doctoring), Tuck's Great Aunt and Deer's Foot's youngest sister, to his side. Here was Kin, Tuck's heart soared.

Evening's celebration fires roared welcoming Wichasa Tonga and the first successful buffalo hunt in years. Throughout the village each breath of buffalo roasting aroma was a feast. Buffalo grease dripped from every finger and chin.

Tuck offered Sitting Bull's message for the people and it was accepted without dissent. Makhpiya's tales of Wichasa Tonga's Sun Dance courage, his many coups and victories were repeated time and time again. The drums beat loud and hard—beginning ritual chants cried into the darkness.

And close to the fire, men's high-step dancing erupted spontaneously. An outer ring of young women danced, their vivacious hips swaying and breast quivering, hand in hand, snuffle-stepped delicately around the whooping, grunting and perspiring warriors.

Wearing his best, sash included, Tuck sat side by side with Black Kettle.

For the first time, even Missy Ann got caught up in the dancing. And Little Moon Song's usually pampered wails were ignored as the Pow-Wow reached a clamorous crest.

Satisfied bellies bulged and through the night smiling wives, and eager giggling young women whose men were absent for weeks on the buffalo hunt, without complaint, were tugged inside lodges or simply to places of partial concealment. As in times past, the circle of life would continue. Nine moons hence many babies would be born into the warm easy days of, Summer.

Drums continued until the beats and chants turned to dawn's welcoming sun. Then, except for a few armed sentries, the gratified village slept.

The next morning, seated around the breakfast fire, Black Kettle explained to Tuck, "Treaty of Fort Wise in sixty-one, Father of Indian Affairs gave me that," referring to the American flag flapping over his lodge. "And this," he took from inside his buckskin shirt a large round silver medal. "Peace medal." And Father of Indian Affairs promised, "As long as Black Kettle wore the medal and flew the flag, the army would not only never bother him, but also protect his people from those who would drive them from their lands."

Black Kettle boasted, "So you see, Peace medal is big medicine for me and the American flag, big medicine for all my people."

"I hope you are right, Chief," Tuck replied.

"My friend, the Wasichus, (white men) wars and lies will end someday. Remember, hand that throws fiery stone of anger is burned first. You see, it was Chief Little Robe and Chief White Antelope who urged me to accept Sitting Bull's request for war parlay. The people look to them for council and so, I must. But nothing should be done to anger or bring fear to wasichus. Today, they are our friends."

"Friends?" Tuck muttered."

That evening the tribal council would follow Sitting Bull's message and agreed the Cheyenne would leave Sand Creek at the end of Falling Leaf Moon. Clan leaders and most of the warriors would leave first. Next sun, Tall Bull and the other chiefs would join those of Roman Nose and Tall Elk. Together they would journey to the land of smoking waters and the *great parley.* Youngest braves, old men, women and children, would remain at camp. That move was, as yet, three weeks away.

Black Kettle asked, "Wichasa Tonga, you are neither full blood Cheyenne or Sioux, but will you ride with us? Or do you have others who must hear the messages?"

"Others, no. Ride with you?" His eyes shifted toward Missy Ann but there was no answer in her eyes. He looked back to Black Kettle and answered, "We shall see."

Black Kettle invited them to erect their lodge next to his. But Tuck elected a spot just outside the main village near the edge of a rising slope, where morning's sunlight would touch their lodge first. Already morning, grasses silver with morning's frost crunched under their moccasins. But the days were warm and good and filled with happy preparation for coming snows.

No one spoke much of Sitting Bull's war parlay. It was easy to believe these quiet, pleasant days would always be. Missy Ann, her face tanned dark, Little Moon Song always at her side, glowed with health and happiness. Gray Owl spent his time with the other young boys practicing warrior's ways of hunting and battle.

It seemed, Tuck's mind never rested. Responsibility constantly kept his senses honed. It was not that he actually heard voices—in his mind, thoughts and images of war burst like lightning strikes—but he knew that understanding came from beyond his own. It weighed heavily on his mind.

But there were refreshing times, when Tuck's thoughts took him to those places of long ago in Western Nevada and California into canyons of the eastern Sierra where streams and sweet-water springs poured down from year around icy glaciers. The cabin no doubt was still standing. Was it his imagination, or there did the sage, willow and aspen have their own special aroma? We're not trails sandy and softer and easier on moccasins?

He longed to see those high and lofty peaks of the majestic Sierras and the clear tumbling creeks and azure blue lakes so deep no man could find their bottoms. In those moments of reflection he knew a deep and abiding peace, remembering the special power always felt there.

Inside their lodge that night, from off in the darkening distances, slowly approaching directly overhead, the deep mournful hoot of a great horned owl throbbed through starless skies.

Missy Ann rolled over close to him, "Me love, yer thoughts be a million miles away of late."

He sighed, "Messenger of death some say."

"What, just that Great horned owl a hootin over our lodge? I don't put much stock in it." She grasped his hand, "C'mon me love, tell me where yer thoughts be."

He sighed again, rolled onto his back his arms folded under his head, "Can't seem to get home—. I mean I've been thinking about showing you where I grew up way yonder west."

"Though I never saw it, sometimes I think about Ireland...just what me Mum told me," she yawned.

Quickly he rose up on his elbows, "Does something deep in your gut ever say 'go see—go back—go see?'"

In the middle of another yawn, she stopped, sensing the intensity in his words. Sleep for a moment no longer seemed important. She too rose up on her elbows and by the glow of their lodge fire looked close into his glistening eyes.

"No, I only wonder, what were those growin up years in Ireland was like, fer me Mum."

"Not, going there?"

"No." She felt his breath close to her face, warm, almost panting. She said, "And you?"

He plopped back thrusting his arms under his head. "Missy, seems heading west is always troubling my mind," he said almost apologetically.

The owl hooted again and faded into the night. It was silent for a while.

Her breathing came slow and even.

"You going to sleep?"

"Wha...sleep? Somethin wrong with that?"

"Wrong...hell no. You get me all stirred and then you go to sleep."

She sat up and turned toward him, legs akimbo under her furs she said, "Hello now? What's behind them frowny words?"

"Excuse me Missy," changing his tone. "You know I never told Sitting Bull we'd return with the Cheyenne."

"So?"

"So," he took her by the hand. "So, what if we don't go back? What if we head toward Utah, the old village and—," he paused and wrapped his arms around her, "I'd like to show you where I spent my growing up years."

She didn't answer just then, but from Gray Owl's side of the lodge, "Yeah Papa, that's a grand idea."

She clung to Tuck, "Travis speaks fer me too, me love." And their lips met. Sometimes it was hard for him to tell where she began and the smooth furs let off. And then, as they rested, he put into words the plans he'd been heedful of for quite a spell.

35

"GARY OWEN"

For the next few weeks Tuck stayed close to camp. Seemed he couldn't get enough of Missy Ann. He thought, nothing like it when a man can be honest and have his women listen. It was agreed, when the time was right, they would journey west together.

The last week, each day, small eager clans of men left early to join up with Roman Nose and Tall Bull. Then the long trek to the agreed meeting place far across the Power River to the creek at the base of Owl Creek Mountains. North, up the Big Horn to the Shoshone to the lakes above, and the place of parlay with the Sioux.

The day came when the last clan leader departed. Three Head chiefs planned to make the trip the next day; White Elk, Many Robes and Black Kettle. Black Kettle made sure those remaining behind were prepared to face winter with only a few men to help. The village was quiet. About 300 would stay and face the next winter months alone. That night the Pipe was passed. Prayers for wisdom were lifted up. Songs of sadness and songs for safety were sung. No one even considered singing death songs.

Tuck said to Missy Ann, "In the spring we'll head over the Rockies, visit Fish Lake and Walkara's grave then the old village at Spanish Fork then west."

Those were the pleasantries they fell asleep with, that night in the Cheyenne winter camp.

Missy Ann thought she was dreaming. Through clouds of slumber came that unmistakable tune, the one she sang to Gray Owl and to Little Moon Song, "Gary Owens."

Tuck was already up and dressed by the time she realized it was no dream. *Bugles, drums and fifes.* The hair on Tuck's neck bristled. Nip rose to face the lodge door, his chest rumbling and hair from head to tail, erect and trembling.

Tuck's first thought, no reason to fret the army is looking after Black Kettles people. But still he ordered, "Get dressed." Tuck lifted the lodge flap and poked out his head. Below in front of his own lodge, Black Kettle stood smiling and pointing toward the American Flag hanging limp in the ground-mist surrounding the village.

Abruptly the Gary Owen stopped. Bugles screamed, "Charge," cutting the peaceful morning. The earth began to tremble with the pounding thunder of many hundreds of horse's hooves and the first volley of shots rang out.

Tuck watched Black Kettle, holding out his peace medal, a pleading expression etched on his face. He was the first to drop.

"Get out!" Tuck yelled at Missy Ann and Little Owl, "Get down to the creek, find cover—find your horses and git."

Missy Ann scooped up Moon Song in her cradleboard, grabbed her rifle and shoved Gray Owl out the door. "Get your Papa's horse and bring it here!"

"When the people must see bravery." Sitting Bull's words thundered in Tuck's head. He turned and quickly wrapped the Brave Heart Sash around his middle. Slinging the Hawkin on his back and the Sharps in his hands he turned to Missy Ann and ordered her to flee.

Not like rapid shots but a continuous deafening roar erupted and sunlight began streaming through bullet holes appearing in the sides of their teepee.

"Go on," he yelled.

"I'll not," she screamed above the din.

Now they were both outside, chunks of deadly lead whistling and buzzing past their heads.

"Then at least get to those trees, find cover and fire from there if you must."

With Moon Song in her cradleboard bouncing on her back Missy Ann hunched over with her rifle in hand and scurried for the protection of the big cottonwoods.

The crazed blue wave enveloped the village. Mounted cavalry raced, screaming and yelling, firing at anything that moved and trampling everything in sight.

Tuck had no choice. He began to fire, reload and fire again as quickly as he could. Down the hill below his lodge he could see the old men, women and children being shot and hacked to pieces—saber and club—no one being spared.

From the cottonwoods a shot erupted, and a blue coat galloping close by fell head first, the front of his face gone.

For Tuck there was no time to be afraid. No time to consider the possibility of defeat. Keep firing, keep firing, keep firing. It seemed to Tuck, he and Missy Ann were the only ones shooting. The others frozen in disbelief, simply ran, trying to find concealment anywhere. And there was no, anywhere.

Missy Ann screamed. Two mounted blue coats had flushed her out, yanking the baby from her back and then without mercy slammed Moon Song to the ground. Quickly, even before Tuck could reload, the blue coats aimed their pistols.

"Don't ya dare shoot my little baby," Missy Ann screamed.

And in that instant of bloodlust decision, though clearly hearing her speak English, one of the army shooters turned his weapon toward Missy Ann firing spontaneously at point blank range.

Missy Ann's last thought, back on the Bella Fourche, the longhorn mother cow charging and doing anything to save her baby.

In two shots, and Tuck avenged his sweetheart and their child. It was all he could do. War Spirit commanded his heart—kill as many as you can.

The main charge of cavalry swept passed, as Tuck fired from in front of his lodge. But, above on the hillside, just rolled into position, two howitzers rained death down into the camp and surrounding trees. Furious, almost hysterical at the overkill, "You bastards," Tuck cried.

The cavalry was easily doing what they set out to do. Tuck turned, leveled his Sharps and, one by one, silenced the small cannons.

Almost knocking Tuck off his feet the black horse slammed into him. Tonga Sapa with Gray Owl on his back. He had done what his Mother asked of him.

No doubt what to do. Tuck reached up and handed his son Peg Leg's old rifle and tenderly squeezed the boy's shoulder. He turned Tonga Sapa's head and slapped him with full force on his rump shouting, "And don't look back until you reach the Yellowstone!"

Between the trees, up the old buffalo trail with Gray Owl's light weight, hooves churning, ears flat back, Tonga Sapa galloped as never before. In an instant he was out of sight, army bullets whizzing after him.

Tuck felt defeat slipping across him like a death shroud. He charged to the crest of the hill. There he stood for all to see. Turning, he stabbed his knife through the end of his sash, firmly into the earth...raising his arms... screaming at the top of his lungs. "Fight my brothers, FIGHT."

And for an instant those below paused, turned, and cried out, "Fight Brothers!" Hopelessly out numbered, they rushed toward the enemy and—with bare hands—attempted to resist their slaughter.

In the same instant, behind the hill where Tuck stood, in a protected gully, the hired scout who brought Colonel Chivington's troops to Black Kettle's winter camp, took careful aim at the back of the tall one wearing the sash.

The scout figured it was an Indian of importance—more than likely a maverick chief of the Cheyenne. But in a glance he saw the big Indian's dress was not that of the Cheyenne with the long Brave Heart sash of a Sioux Chief. The scout fired. After all...a dollar was a dollar...maybe two for a real big chief's scalp. His rifle was also a Sharps .50.

Before Tuck's arms lowered from his cry to fight, the heavy ounce of roaring lead tore through his back literally blowing his heart from its place inside his powerful chest. The Brave Heart Sash held fast where it was stabbed into the earth. The sash unraveled from his waist as he tumbled down the hill to near Missy Ann's side.

Causally the shooter rode to his trophy. "Beckwourth here," he gibed. "Ah, two for the price of one."

On the spot he cut and tore Missy Ann's scalp from her head. Kicking her body down toward the trees...tumbling, rolling, skirt flipping up he noticed the whiteness of her legs. Curious he frowned but continued with his grizzly task.

Tuck's skin was tougher. Beckwourth rolled the body on its back and cut deeper into the blood-covered forehead...he tugged.

Lying in wait, stumbling the old wolf charged. One carefully placed shot and Beckwourth's pistol ended Nip's life.

With Beckwourth yanking on his scalp Tuck's lifeless eyes were forced wide-open. Beckwourth saw, he gasped, "Blue...silver blue." He stood up, blood tripping from his knife and hands. He stepped back and looked carefully at the man and the old wolf he had just murdered.

An impact of recognition jolted him to the marrow of his bones. "Oh damn...OH, my God."

POSTSCRIPT

November 29, 1864: Date of Sand Creek Massacre

Three weeks later, trotting triumphantly through Denver, Colonel Chivington's bloodless Third Volunteers had now earned the reputation, bloodiest of all the Indian Killers. They waved and displayed scalps and other most personal parts of their butchered victims. The ruthless ex-preacher had his day. Some years later however, a military tribunal condemned him and the massacre.

Two years after the massacre a disturbed and incoherent James Beckwourth died. Scorned by his own he retreated into the mountains of Montana. Once accepted as a son by Chief Big Bowl of the Crow, he still had enemies there as well. It is believed he met his end writhing on the ground, poisoned by those who believe he brought small pox to their village.

A fairly accurate count of those Indians killed at Sand Creek was three hundred, though Chivington's estimate was a thousand. Black Kettle, Little Robe, Makhpiya and Tuck Gray Owl lived to fight another day.

The Sand Creek Massacre did not subdue. In fact, it had the opposite effect. It became the driving force that united the Plains Indians. For the next twelve years, Cheyenne, Sioux, Arapaho and others fought side by side3, like never before. The bloodiest battle was yet to be seen.

June 23, 1875: Two days before Battle of the Little Big Horn

Last day of largest Sioux and Cheyenne Sun Dance Ceremony—all Sioux, Cheyenne, and other allies joined together for the first time.

In the central lodge Sitting Bull, Crazy Horse, Gall and Two Moons discussed the Sand Creek Massacre. Sitting Bull asked Crazy Horse, "Was that twelve winters ago?"

Crazy Horse said, "Yes, that was twelve winters ago."

Shaking his head in disbelief Sitting Bull said, "Twelve winters. That is hard to believe." A sudden silence followed.

Then Sitting Bull leaped to his feet and began rummaging through his things, a startled expression on his face. He cried, "Aahh," and pulled out what he was looking for—the hide on which Tuck Wichasa Tonga had drawn his Sun Dance Vision, twelve years before. Rolling it open, "Yes, yes," he whispered. "Twelve years, now I see."

June 25, 1875: Battle of Little Big Horn

Sitting Bull, Crazy Horse, Gall and Two Moons led the largest Indian assault ever against the impatient, impetuous General George A. Custer and the three hundred and eighty-eight doomed men of the Seventh Cavalry.

Finale death tally: At least 388 U.S. Cavalry died that day. Only 32 Sioux and Cheyenne killed in battle. Plus, the 300 massacred at Sand Creek twelve years before. It appears—an eye for an eye.

For years after, many rumors persisted. An interesting one, a mysterious Indian, named Bison who supposedly had attended West Point and learned the brilliant battle tactics used to defeat the Seventh Cavalry. Rumors spoken around campfires by whites and Indian alike, was that Bison only masqueraded as Indian.

Though no one admitted they actually saw him do it, nor could they even declare his name. Those same gossipers swore it was a young, gray-eyed, white Indian on a giant black horse, a silver wolf at his side, who actually killed Pahsuska—yellow hair Custer.

www.ingramcontent.com/pod-product-compliance
Lightning Source LLC
Chambersburg PA
CBHW031951010726
47493CB00007B/2162